FROZEN

FROZEN

Lindsay Jayne Ashford

THOMAS DUNNE BOOKS

St. Martin's Minotaur

New York

THOMAS DUNNE BOOKS.
An imprint of St. Martin's Press.

www.thomasdunnebooks.com
www.minotaurbooks.com

Library of Congress Cataloging-in-Publication Data

Ashford, Lindsay Jayne.
    Frozen / Lindsay Jayne Ashford—1st U.S. ed.
        p. cm.
    ISBN-13: 978-0-312-35581-4
    ISBN-10: 0-312-35581-5
    1. Psychologists—Fiction. 2. Murder—Investigation—Fiction.
    I. Title.

PR6101.S545 F76 2006
823'.92—dc22

                                                        2006047525

First published in Wales by Honno

First U.S. Edition: August 2006

10 9 8 7 6 5 4 3 2 1

To my family, for their love and patience.

*This book is also dedicated to the
prostitutes of Wolverhampton and Birmingham
who told me their stories.*

Acknowledgements

I would like to thank the officers of West Midlands Police whose help and advice contributed to the writing of this book – they know who they are. Outreach workers in the red light districts of Wolverhampton and Birmingham also provided invaluable information, as did pathologist Dr Chris Simpson of Aberystwyth's Bronglais Hospital and his assistant S G Lea (Leo). Thanks also to my editor at Honno, Janet Thomas, whose wisdom belies her years.

FROZEN

Chapter 1

He knew exactly where to find her. Like all of them she was territorial, but unlike most she always stood alone, jealously guarding her patch. His car nosed alongside and she climbed in without a word.

He pulled up in one of the quiet streets that wound past sleeping factories. His long, bony fingers crept along her leg like a spider, disappearing up the shiny lycra skirt to the warm darkness within.

'I'm off, Maria.'

Her soft hair wobbled like candyfloss as she turned her head sharply, meeting his eyes for the first time.

'They're moving me off Vice – end of this month.' He tried to hold her gaze as her face tightened into a bitter smile.

'Have to pay for it like everyone else then, won't you – sad bastard!'

He laughed, unzipping his jeans with his free hand. 'I said end of the month. Have to get plenty of freebies in before New Year, eh?'

She ignored him, groping in the money belt slung around her hips and winkling out a black and yellow wrapper. She waved it under his nose. 'Pina Colada flavour,' she said, in the voice she used to coax her child.

'I don't want oral – not tonight.' In one swift movement he reached across and lowered the back of the passenger seat, pressing himself on top of her. 'You know what I want, don't you?' His breath stank and she turned her face away.

1

'I'm not doing it without. You know I never do punters without.'

'Come on love.' He pushed the skirt up around her waist. 'Fifty quid I'm saving you – that's got to be worth the full treatment. Anyway, you know I'm clean.'

The smell of Birmingham Magistrates' Court – that strange unmistakeable stink of sweat and polish – filled her head as he invaded her body. Fifty quid. She'd only taken thirty so far tonight. She lay there doing mental arithmetic, knowing it was pointless.

'You do it for him, don't you? That piece of shite you call your boyfriend.' The words were punctuated with grunts of exertion.

'That's none of your fucking business, is it?'

He answered with a volley of grunts and then flopped. Great dead pig, she thought. The only part of her body she could move was her right leg and she jabbed the heel of her black leather boot into the centre panel of the steering wheel.

The scream of the horn sent him leaping back to his seat and she jumped out of the car, rolling her skirt back down her thighs as she strode away.

Out of sight, she pulled baby wipes from the money belt. It pleased her to discover that the passenger seat must have taken most of his mess. She set off down the street, wondering which one of his squad would sit in it. She hoped it would be a uniformed officer – the stain would show up more on dark fabric.

Her heels clacked along the quiet, empty streets that led back to her beat. Turning a corner she stopped dead. Her way was blocked by a sea of blue flashing lights. As she slunk into the shadow of a wall her eyes flicked upwards. She thought she had glimpsed the crouching silhouette of a man on a rooftop. A man with a gun.

Next morning Ceri Richardson listened to news of the killings on the radio as she ironed her husband's shirt.

'The body of 40-year-old Tina Jackson was found in a bedroom after officers from the Tactical Firearms Unit broke down the door of the house.' The reporter sounded young. Barely able to keep that note of excitement from his voice. She knew exactly how he felt. It had been the same for her the first time she got to cover a murder. What was it? Eleven, no, *twelve* years ago. She sighed. Seemed like a lifetime.

'The dead man was lying a few feet away,' the reporter went on. 'He has not yet been formally identified, but is believed to be Mrs Jackson's estranged husband. Police found a double-barrelled shotgun beside his body.'

The iron steamed as she picked it up again. She pressed it down hard on the crisp white fabric, tempted to hold it there just a few seconds too long.

What would he do in this shirt tomorrow, she wondered? He'd go to work in it, of course, but then to him work was elastic. He could stretch it into times and places that she could never question.

It occurred to her – not for the first time – that he might very well have sex with another woman in this shirt, that she was ironing with such care.

'Bastard!' The iron hissed and she whipped it away, just in time.

Dr Megan Rhys caught the tail end of the headline on Radio 4 as she turned the key in the ignition.

'. . . and a woman shot dead in Birmingham.'

She flicked the car radio onto the local station and turned up the volume. As she coasted down the hill to the university she pieced it together. The armed men perched on rooftops, neighbours half-thrilled, half-horrified by the drama of being evacuated from their homes. The door smashed open as the police stormed Tina Jackson's house. Images drifted unbidden from the library of corpses in her head. The waxen-featured woman, probably naked, spreadeagled on the bed. The man's head burst like a rotten fruit.

She couldn't help it. The urge to analyse, to categorize, was instinctive. This one had domestic stamped all over it.

Her estranged husband, the report had said. It made her think of Tony. *Estranged*. Odd word. But it *was* an odd thing – to be still married but living apart.

Megan reached into the glove compartment, her fingers closing round a packet of Maltesers. There were only two left. She stuffed both of them into her mouth. What she really felt like was a cigarette. It had been an exhausting weekend. Saturday spent lecturing at a forensic pathology conference in Manchester, followed by a night of maybe two hours sleep. And on Sunday, caffeine-stoked, she had marked thirty-five undergraduate exam papers.

She swung into the car park of Heartland University's Department of Investigative Psychology, glancing in the mirror as she nosed into her space. She didn't see Patrick van Zeller, who had paused by his car to wait for her.

'Good morning!'

Startled by his voice, Megan tried to suck the chocolates from her bulging cheek, but they were stuck to her teeth. She made an odd gurgling noise as she tried to speak. Patrick laughed and his breath made smoky trails in the frosty air. Finally she managed to swallow.

'Hah! Caught in the act!' she groaned. 'I'd offer you one but I've just finished the packet – I've given up smoking and it's making me eat like a pig!'

'Oh, don't apologise,' he said, 'I know what it's like. This time last year I was on forty a day.'

'Really?'

'Yes. I still get cravings – especially at parties. He gave her a sympathetic grin, his eyes crinkling at the edges. She hadn't known him long but she was getting to like him. She'd never had to supervise anyone so close to her own age and he felt more like a colleague than a graduate student. 'By the way,' he said as they trudged towards the building, 'where were you on Saturday? You missed a great night – you didn't forget, did you?'

'No,' Megan groaned again. 'I really wanted to go. I'd bought the wine and got myself all ready and then Ceri – my sister – phoned, crying her eyes out. Said the kids had kept her awake for two nights on the trot and she and her husband were nearly going out of their minds. So I ended up babysitting.' It had been more than that, but she wasn't going to tell Patrick how worried she was about her sister. About the hours she had spent listening to Ceri's fears that Neil was having an affair. It had all sounded so horribly familiar.

'Hasn't she got anyone else who can help?'

'No. My mother used to live just round the corner but she died last year. My brother-in-law's parents live in Cornwall – so I'm all they've got, God help them!'

'Poor you.' His tone sounded as if he knew what hard work small children could be. Megan wondered if he had any of his own. She had always assumed he was single.

In the lobby they passed by the Christmas tree with its sparse decorations. Only a week to go, Megan thought, and she hadn't even started the present shopping. The prospect of waking up alone on Christmas morning filled her with dread. Still, she thought, as she glanced at the pile of envelopes in her pigeonhole, it couldn't be much worse than waking up with someone you no longer loved.

'Doctor Rhys!' The porter's voice barked from the glass-fronted lodge in the corner of the lobby. 'Call for you – shall I put it through to your office?'

'Yes, thanks Eric.' Megan grabbed her mail, wedging it under her arm as she made for the lift.

'Here, let me.' Patrick darted in front of her and pressed the button. 'Go on. I'll get you a coffee – you look as if you need one.' He cast her a sidelong grin as the doors slid shut between them.

Megan's office was on the second floor. As head of department, hers was more spacious than the rabbit hutches the rest of the staff occupied. A large seascape filled the space above her desk and the other walls were lined with black and white photographs of faces. Twenty-seven men and six women – all lifers. She had interviewed each of them over the past ten years, gaining the dubious distinction of being the first woman to have been inside every maximum-security prison in the UK. And on the shelves beneath this rogues' gallery were the books she had written about them.

She picked up the phone, unbuttoning her coat with her free hand. 'Megan Rhys.'

'Hello, it's Detective Superintendent Leverton.'

She bristled at the sound of his voice. At the other end of the phone she heard muffled noises.

'I'm so sorry, Dr Rhys but someone's walked in I've got to deal with – can I call you back?'

'What's it about?'

'Will you be there for the morning?'

She said yes and he hung up. She was still holding the telephone when Patrick squeezed through the door with a mug in each hand. She watched him as he placed hers on the desk. Everyone in the building was intrigued by the Dutchman who spoke English with an Irish accent. The students were always talking about him – especially the women.

Megan replaced the receiver. 'Thanks.' She frowned as she lifted the mug to her lips. 'That was West Midlands Police.'

'What did they want?

'I don't know.' It was part of her job to work with the police. And she loved the work. It was the police themselves she had problems with. She glanced at Patrick. He's one of them, she reminded herself. She gulped down her coffee and switched on her PC. He was watching her. She pointedly turned to her work. 'I'll be out of the office this afternoon – can we catch up tomorrow morning? About eleven?'

Patrick took the hint. 'See you tomorrow, then.' He paused in the doorway. 'By the way, I like the stud – is it a sapphire?'

'No . . .' Megan touched her nose involuntarily. 'It's, er, lapis lazuli. It was my mother's.'

'Hmmm,' Patrick smiled, 'Cool or what? I've never met anyone over the age of twenty-five whose mum had a pierced nose!'

Megan ripped open a letter, suddenly self-conscious about the way he was studying her face. 'It's pretty common in India, actually,' she said in a matter-of-fact voice.

'India?'

'Yes.' She scanned the letter but wasn't reading what was on the page. 'My mother came from India. I was born there.'

'Really?' Patrick sounded embarrassed. 'Sorry . . . I mean, I didn't realise . . .'

'It's okay – not many people do.' Megan turned to look at him. 'Mum was only half-Indian; her mother was Italian. And my Dad was Welsh.' She was proud of the odd mixture of blood that flowed through her veins, but explaining it always made her feel awkward.

'Oh, right.' Patrick was looking at her through half-closed eyes as if she were some baffling piece of modern art. 'And I thought *I* confused people,' he laughed as he disappeared behind the door.

She was on her third cup of coffee when the phone rang again.

'Megan –' Martin Leverton's voice was friendly. 'Sorry about earlier. I need your help.' He was not the kind of man who bothered with social chit-chat.

'What's happened?' Megan wondered if she'd missed something in the news.

'Do you remember that young girl dumped in a lay-by off the M6 near Stafford about a month ago?'

'Yes.' Megan put her mug down. 'Have they found out who she was?'

'Name was Natalie Bailey. Staffs police say she was a runaway from a children's home in Birmingham. They've asked us if we think the killer could have been one of the local pimps. Remember Donna Fieldhouse?'

The image of a child-woman with blonde, permed hair flashed into Megan's mind. 'There's a connection?'

'Yes. We've got a forensic link with semen samples from the two bodies. But I need to see you to explain it all properly. I want you to meet Sergeant Donalsen from the Vice Squad – he's been getting information from around the red light area. How soon could we get together?'

'Now?'

'What about your lectures?'

'I haven't got any – the students broke up for the holidays on Friday.'

'Right – great!'

'I'll come to you.'

Megan pulled a newspaper cutting from a file marked 'Murder Victims – Juvenile'. Donna Fieldhouse's face grinned from the yellowing paper. Frizzy, bleached hair, a face still chubby with puppy fat, the photograph looked as if it had been taken hurriedly in one of those automatic booths.

Megan scanned the text. One word jumped out at her. Rubbish. Now she remembered. Donna's body had been found in a rubbish bin behind a factory in the red light area of Birmingham.

She slipped the cutting into her bag and made for the lift, wondering why Martin Leverton seemed so keen for her help. She had always felt he was deeply suspicious of psychologists and he was notoriously critical of profiling.

That the two victims were prostitutes puzzled her even more. Only the most enlightened police officers got worked up about violence towards women who sold sex. The usual attitude was that they were pretty much asking for it by working the streets in the first place.

'As if they had a choice,' Megan muttered, thinking of the age of the dead girls and the fact that both had been in care.

Leverton had said he wanted to explain it all to her properly. That'll be a first, she thought grimly.

Chapter 2

There was a Confederate battle flag draped across one wall and a framed photograph of Robert E. Lee on the desk. Amongst the police manuals filling the bookshelf were glossy chronicles of the American Civil War. The first time Megan had seen this office she thought the desk sergeant had made a mistake and shown her into the wrong room.

She had met Detective Superintendent Leverton on the Metro rapes inquiry two years earlier and his sensitive questioning of the victims had impressed her. She noticed the way detectives treated rape victims. She remembered telling her mother that he was almost too nice to be a policeman.

But that was before she had seen his office. Its civil war decor had given her the first hint of its occupant's chameleon nature.

'Megan! Sorry to keep you waiting – blame it on him!' Martin Leverton strode into the room, jerking his thumb at one of two men who followed him through the door. 'PC Costello – he's that keen we couldn't drag him away from the beat!' Leverton pulled two extra chairs up to his desk. 'And this is Sergeant Rob Donalsen.'

Megan shook hands, first with the younger, uniformed man. She returned his wide grin with a neutral smile, glancing briefly into eyes that were the same deep brown as her own. His close-shaved head had the elegant shape of an Egyptian pharoah and Megan was suddenly reminded of the boy king Tutankhamen.

Sergeant Donalsen was closer to her own age. He had a broken nose and the whites of his eyes were the pinkish-red of an habitual cannabis user. He couldn't be – could he? His clammy hand seemed to grip Megan's for a fraction too long.

They all sat down and PC Costello stifled a yawn.

'Sorry, sir!' he mumbled through long brown fingers.

'You'll have to excuse these two. They've just finished a shift,' said Leverton. 'I wanted to fill you in on what they've found out about Natalie Bailey.'

He laid a photograph on the desk. 'As I said to you on the phone, Megan, we've only just had the I.D. on this one. A social worker contacted us at the end of last week – turns out she'd absconded from the children's home five times before, but because she was sixteen the day she finally ran off there was nothing they could do. From a legal point of view social services aren't responsible for these kids once they reach their sixteenth birthday.'

He handed the photograph to Megan, who had taken the newspaper cutting from her bag. The two girls looked so alike they could have been sisters. Both had dyed blonde hair, Donna's permed and Natalie's short and spiky.

Megan had been in America when Donna's body was found. The date above the newspaper article was September 21st – exactly three months ago. She stared at the two pictures in her hand. They were babies once, she thought. Had anyone in their short lives ever really loved them? The pictures blurred as she gazed at them. She was thinking about the child she might have had. It would have been a teenager now. Not as old as these girls, but almost.

'We got the DNA results on Natalie Bailey yesterday.' Leverton's voice cut through her thoughts. 'There were semen traces on both the vaginal and rectal swabs. We got the blood grouping of the semen early on in the inquiry, which told us that the semen in the vagina came from one man and the semen in the rectum from another. The rectal swab revealed the relatively rare AB blood group but the vaginal semen was blood group O.

'The semen we got from Donna was also blood group O, but because it's so common, we weren't going leap to any conclusions about the two murders being linked. We had to wait for the DNA results, which are pretty conclusive. The chances of the samples coming from two different men are virtually nil.'

'The semen you got from Donna Fieldhouse's body – was it vaginal or anal?' Megan asked.

'Vaginal. The pathologist said there was no evidence of anal intercourse. I'll show you the forensic reports in a minute but I'd just like you to hear what PC Costello and Sergeant Donalsen have been finding out. Rob, can you tell Doctor Rhys what you've come up with so far?'

Sergeant Donalsen shifted in his chair. Leaning back with his arms folded, he addressed what he had to say to Leverton rather than Megan.

'We know a lot more about Donna Fieldhouse than Natalie Bailey. Donna was sixteen and her last known address was a children's home in Wolverhampton, but they say she absconded last Christmas and they never saw her again.

'Donna was a crackhead – couldn't see any further than the next rock. She'd do anything a punter wanted for the price of a fix. The other girls hate the crackheads because they drive the prices down and they'll do sex without a condom – so Donna didn't really have any friends. The only thing the girls did notice was that she always arrived at the beat on foot, which suggests that she lived somewhere nearby.'

'Had you ever arrested her?' Megan asked.

'Yes, a couple of times.' Donalsen looked at his notes. 'The first time we found out she was underage and we sent her straight back to the children's home. The second time she was covered in bruises and we offered her a medical examination.' He sniffed. 'Doctor found out she was three months' pregnant, which she claimed not to know, and when we asked if she wanted to press charges against the person who'd beaten her up she said no.' He flicked over a page of his notebook. 'She was charged for soliciting but she never turned up in court. There was a warrant out on her when they found her body.'

Megan looked at the chubby face of Donna Fieldhouse in the photo-booth snap. Pregnant. So whoever killed her had killed her baby too. 'Did the post-mortem show any evidence of crack addiction?' she asked Leverton.

'Yes – they did a hair strand test,' he replied. 'It showed she'd been taking it for around six months.'

'What about Natalie Bailey? Was she on it too?'

'If she was, she'd only just started. There was a trace of it in her blood but the hair test was negative.'

'That's strange,' Megan said, thinking aloud. 'Donna was the crack addict – the one you would expect to be selling kinky sex without a condom – but it was Natalie who had unprotected anal intercourse.'

'I know – doesn't add up, does it?' said Leverton. 'The other confusing thing is that Natalie seems to have been operating out of Wolverhampton rather than Birmingham.'

'Wolverhampton? Why Wolverhampton?' Megan asked. 'Didn't she run away from a Birmingham children's home?'

'Yes, she did,' said Leverton. 'We think the connection between the girls could be a Birmingham-based pimp, but one that ferries his girls to different beats around the Midlands to evade suspicion.'

He nodded at PC Costello, who took up the story, fixing her with his mesmerising eyes as he described what he'd found out in Wolverhampton's red light district.

'None of the women on our patch had seen Natalie soliciting and we'd never arrested her. But then we spoke to a couple of girls who'd come over to Birmingham because things were getting a bit hot in Wolverhampton – there'd been a big splash in the local paper about the prostitution problem, and when that happens the local Vice usually have a crackdown to get the media off their backs – anyway, these two girls said they'd seen Natalie on the Wolverhampton patch a couple of times.

'I went over there the night before last and the two girls showed me the spot where they'd last seen her. They said she'd been dropped off by a man in an old, dark-coloured Ford Sierra, but they couldn't describe him or remember the car registration number because it was dark both times they saw him. They reckoned he was a boyfriend rather than a punter, but they didn't think they'd ever seen him before. He definitely wasn't one of the Wolverhampton pimps, anyway.'

'What about the local Vice Squad over there? Had they ever arrested her?'

'No – which suggests she hadn't been on the game very long,' said Costello. He shot a sideways look at Donalsen as if uncertain whether to continue.

'That's right,' Martin Leverton cut in. 'The Vice Squad in Wolverhampton has something of a reputation for its vigilance.' He looked pointedly at Donalsen. 'Even before the recent blitz the girls over there could expect to get arrested at least once a week. Some were getting done as many as three times a night.'

Megan sensed tension in the room and tried to change the subject, not wanting to be drawn into any private vendetta of Leverton's.

'So apart from the two Wolverhampton prostitutes and the social worker who identified the body, no one knows anything about Natalie Bailey?' She addressed the question to PC Costello.

'No, Dr Rhys. I've tried tracking down relatives – someone she might have run to when she left the home – but there's no one. Her mother was a junkie who died of a heroin overdose five years ago and according to her birth certificate the father's unknown.'

'What about brothers and sisters, a grandmother or an aunt or something?'

'No one. According to the staff at the children's home the mother was the only relative.'

'Have you spoken to any of the other children at the home? Anyone who might have been her friend?'

'She'd only been there six weeks, so she never really got to know the other kids. She'd been transferred to Birmingham from a home in Shropshire because of her wild behaviour. She was too busy running away to make many friends.'

When Costello and Donalsen had gone, Leverton took the forensic reports on Donna Fieldhouse and Natalie Bailey from his desk drawer.

'I wanted you to meet those two before they move on,' he said, sorting through a parcel of photographs.

'They're both due to leave Vice in the New Year – Donalsen's going to be a beat sergeant in Sparkhill and PC Costello's being promoted onto the Fraud Squad.'

'Isn't that going to hamper your inquiry into these murders?' Megan asked.

'I'm telling you this in confidence, Megan, and I know you won't repeat it – the fact is Donalsen's more of a hindrance than a help these days. I can't say any more than that, but I'm sure you can imagine the temptations officers face in a job like this.'

'What about PC Costello? He seems to have covered quite a lot of ground since Natalie's body was identified. I mean, considering he's so young.'

'Oh yes – the Boy Wonder!' Leverton laughed. 'He's not as young as he looks. He's in his mid-twenties and he's got a kid – little boy, I think. Anyway, I admit I'll be sorry to see him off this case – he's very keen and the girls seem to open up to him.'

Megan could understand why. She took the photographs Leverton passed across the desk and studied them while he went through the forensic report on Donna Fieldhouse.

Her body had been discovered within hours of her death, but the body dump site was not the scene of the murder. She must have been killed elsewhere, probably in a house, because of the carpet fibres found on her heels and the backs of her legs. The cause of death was heavy blood loss – Donna had had her throat cut, the deep wound clearly visible in the scene-of-crime photograph Megan held in her hand.

It was a chilling picture. Donna's killer had stuffed her naked body into a black wheelie bin, feet first.

Either he'd been in a terrific hurry or he wasn't concerned about concealing his crime, because he hadn't troubled to push the body down. Her bare, blood-streaked shoulders were exposed, her head lolling back against a wooden fence that ran the length of the car park he had chosen for a graveyard.

The next photograph showed Donna lying face up in the mortuary. The pathologist had yet to make the 'Y' incision that would further violate her young body. Apart from the appalling crimson slash across her neck, some smaller, shallower cuts were just visible on her lower arms and shoulders.

'The pathologist thinks there was a struggle,' said Leverton. 'The smaller cuts were made by a knife, he reckons, so it looks as if Donna tried to fend off her attacker before he finally cut her throat. There were no fibres in the wounds, so she was naked or partially clothed when the attack began.

The fibres on the heels and the backs of the legs suggest that she was dragged across a carpet before being transported to the dump site.'

'What about her fingernails?' Megan asked. 'If there was a struggle she might have scratched him – was there any blood there?'

'No, there was nothing under the nails at all – they were as clean as if she'd just stepped out of the bath.'

Megan tried to imagine how it had happened. Maybe Donna *had* been in the bath or shower. She pictured the naked girl, her wet curls clinging to her head as she reached for a towel. Was it someone she knew, then? Someone with whom she'd willingly had sex before he turned on her?

Leverton picked up the post mortem file on Natalie Bailey and handed Megan a second batch of photographs. The first picture simply showed a black bundle lying beside a grass verge.

'As you know, Natalie was found in a layby off the M6. It was about five miles south of Stafford and roughly fifteen miles north of Wolverhampton. She was wrapped in a couple of black binliners, but again, no real effort to conceal the body. She'd been dead for approximately twelve hours when she was discovered.'

Megan stared at the photograph. What sort of person had done this? Two girls, hardly more than children, dumped like so much rubbish. 'What about the cause of death?' she asked. 'It was different to Donna, wasn't it?'

'Yes. Strangulation this time – manual, not with a ligature. The pattern of the bruises on the throat suggests that she was strangled from behind.'

Megan studied the second photograph. Natalie looked like a naked white angel, her spiky blonde hair a halo around the lifeless head. The photograph had been taken before the bruising had come out. The third photo, taken the following day, showed purple marks like lovebites on her throat.

A fourth photo showed a close-up of Natalie's wrists, both of which bore red weals. 'What are these marks on her wrists?' Megan looked up at Leverton, who was leaning across the desk, peering at the upside-down image.

'Handcuffs or wire, the pathologist says. The marks are very recent, so he reckons Natalie was restrained shortly before she died or while she was being killed.'

Megan shuffled through the photographs. 'Donna didn't have marks like this, did she?'

'No – just the cuts on the shoulders and arms, which were made by a knife.'

'You know, if you hadn't told me about the DNA match between those two semen samples I would have sworn these girls were killed by two different men.' She tried to think through the possibilities, resisting jumping to conclusions. She laid the photos down on the desk and stared at Leverton for a few moments before continuing, but he stayed quiet, eager to hear what she had to say.

'To me, the motivation for Donna's murder is very different from Natalie's.' She pursed her lips. 'The way Donna died suggests a straightforward fight. Maybe with a pimp. We know she was a crack addict, so the chances are he was too, and we both know how aggressive crack-addicted males can get. Perhaps they had a row that went to far.' Megan frowned. 'She was pregnant. Maybe he'd just found out and didn't like it.'

Leverton nodded slowly. 'And Natalie?'

'Natalie's death is much more sinister. She was penetrated anally and handcuffed or tied up. She was strangled from behind, so perhaps the killer was the man who had anal sex with her? It sounds very much like rape.' Megan swallowed. There was a time when she had been unable to say that word without her stomach churning. 'After all,' she went on, 'Natalie was no crackhead. She'd only just started on the game and she was young and pretty enough to be choosy about what she did for punters.'

Leverton frowned. 'But the DNA evidence?'

'I know. It just doesn't fit. Unless, of course, the man who had vaginal sex with both Donna and Natalie on the day they died was not involved with their deaths – and that's pushing the limits of credibility a bit far, isn't it?'

Leverton sighed and sat back in his chair. 'The problem for us is this guy's DNA doesn't match anything on our database. We picked up one good fingerprint from Natalie's body but it doesn't tally with anything we've got on file. We've got literally nothing to go on.'

Megan felt uneasy. She wasn't sure he was being straight with her. She decided to face him. 'You're asking me to come up with a profile?'

Leverton nodded.

'Why? I mean dead prostitutes aren't going to get Joe Public howling for retribution.' She watched him. His eyes immediately flicked down to the desk. 'Martin, I hope you wouldn't think of using me in some private battle with one of your colleagues . . .'

The sound of him drawing in his breath was almost imperceptible. He looked back at her, eyes unwavering this time.

'Of course not.' He paused just long enough to make Megan feel uncomfortable. 'Will you trust me on this one? I can't say exactly why I've asked for your help. All I can say is that I need a completely independent, unbiased view of what sort of man committed these murders. Will you help me?'

Megan's eyes narrowed as he held her gaze. So, she thought, this is all about police corruption. Who's he after? A cop who murders prostitutes? A cop in a pimp's pocket?

She felt a nudge of guilt. Was she completely independent

and unbiased? 'Okay,' she said slowly. She had no desire to do Leverton favours but the case intrigued her. 'I'll see what I can come up with. I'll give you a call, say, lunchtime tomorrow. Will you be here?'

'Yes – barring any major incidents.' He grinned and rolled his eyes. 'If I'm not in the office, you can get me on the mobile.' He scribbled a number on the back of a card and handed it to Megan. 'Thanks – I really appreciate this,' he said as he led her to the door.

Ceri Richardson was wrapping a Christmas present for her husband.

It was a silk tie. Not very romantic, she thought, as she cut out a rectangle of green and gold paper. It was the sort of present a daughter might give to her father or a mother to her son.

She thought of the gifts she had given Neil when they had first met. That first Christmas together in a rented flat. She had tried to make it so exciting; a chocolate-box couple young and in love. Except that they weren't – at least, she wasn't. She could see that now, although at the time she had managed to fool herself.

She tore pieces of sellotape with her teeth, sealing the gift in its festive shroud. What should she write on the label? 'All my love'? What a joke! Perhaps 'Lots of love' would do?

Of course, what she would really like to write was, 'Hope it throttles you, darling.'

Chapter 3

When she left the police station Megan took a deliberate detour through Birmingham's red light district. She knew Donna's body had been found somewhere in this maze of run-down streets.

Even in daylight it was depressing. She crawled past dough-faced women standing at a bus stop, cheap coats pulled close around their hunched bodies. Despite the bitter wind the younger ones wore no tights or socks, their mottled legs stuffed into ill-fitting shoes.

Megan looked away, scanning side roads for the street name. She pulled up at a set of temporary traffic lights. Suddenly she caught sight of it. A graffiti-covered sign on a factory wall: Inkerman Place. It was a short blind alley with the rusting metal gates of an abandoned printworks at its far end.

The lights changed and Megan swung the car into the alley. Now she could see the high wooden fence of the factory car park where Donna's body had been dumped. She got out of the car, walking past the padlocked gates along the length of the fence. Although many of its spars were missing there was no gap large enough to get a body through. Above the fence was a length of barbed wire, so it was unlikely that the killer had climbed over. If he had thrown Donna's body over the fence the forensic examination would have revealed post-mortem bruises and fractures.

She peered through one of the gaps. The car park was

littered with broken bottles and used condoms. Megan wondered how long ago the factory had closed. She suspected that prostitutes had been working the nightshift long before those rusting gates had been locked for the last time. So there could be another way in – a back or side entrance known to the women who worked in the red light area. Whoever killed Donna knew about it too.

The theory that he was a local pimp was certainly plausible. So was the idea that he was a policeman. But other men would know of that second entrance: anyone who had worked at the factory or visited it regularly. And then there were the punters, led there with assurances that no one would be watching . . .

Megan got into the car and drove back down Inkerman Place, turning right and right again to follow the perimeter of the factory site. There was no other entrance that could be seen from the road.

She parked and got out of the car again, pulling her collar up against the wind. A row of straggling laurel bushes rustled against the fence where it joined the high wall of the building next door. Megan wondered if it was possible to get behind them. She stepped onto the rubbish-strewn patch of earth and peered into the foliage.

Yes! She felt a stab of triumph. The bushes were concealing a big gap in the bottom of the fence. There was just enough space behind them to get through without being scratched to pieces.

She ducked behind the leaves and met a wall of black plastic. The wheelie bins. Something crunched beneath her feet and she looked down to see half a dozen syringes lying on the ground. Megan stepped over them as she edged round the bins. She glanced up at the backs of a row of houses whose first floor windows overlooked the car park on one side. They looked derelict. Filthy windows, uncurtained or with scraps of tatty fabric hanging askew.

She caught a sudden movement out of the corner of her eye and whipped her head round. A face. She was certain she had seen a face pressed against one of the gaps in the fence, looking at her. She scrambled back out and jumped into the car, driving round the block again. But she saw no one.

On the car radio a news bulletin was just coming to an end. She glanced at her watch, tutting under her breath. She was due at a meeting in the city centre in twenty minutes. As she picked up speed, she glimpsed a woman in thigh-length boots, mini skirt and a short fur jacket standing on a corner. God, she thought, it's a bit early. She wondered what sort of man would go looking for a prostitute at ten past two on a Monday afternoon.

The BTV building soared above the newly-developed canal basin in the centre of Birmingham. Megan almost ran to the revolving doors of the main entrance. It was freezing cold and the towering concrete buildings created a wind tunnel that took her breath away.

Despite the bitter cold, the city was heaving with Christmas shoppers. The traffic had made her late and she hated being late. Now the security man on reception was wasting more time checking her in. She sank into one of the low sofas. It was lime green and brand new. So was the decor. How long had it been since she was in this building? Must be getting on for two years, she thought.

Yes, two years exactly; that awful Christmas party with Tony's other woman in the same room . . .

'Doctor Rhys!' Perhaps it was his accent, but Megan thought the security man emphasised her title with the hint of a sneer in his voice. 'Miss Lobelo will see you now. Do you know your way up?'

He must be new too. She didn't think she had seen him before. Did he know that her husband used to work in the building and that she had hung around the corridors of BTV waiting for him more times than she cared to remember? Don't be ridiculous. How could he? she asked herself.

Without acknowledging the man she swept up the open staircase. Thank goodness she was wearing trousers. The architect who had designed this building just had to be male, she thought grimly. That security guard probably spent most of his time looking up the skirts of unsuspecting female visitors.

Delva Lobelo was standing by the window when Megan walked in. Her African profile contrasted oddly with the icy grey backdrop of the canal. The wind was whipping up the water into white-capped ridges and people walking along the towpath were muffled in scarves, hats and heavy over-coats. In the warmth of the office Delva looked like an exotic bloom, long legs wrapped in a sarong skirt with a matching jacket of orange silk.

Megan suddenly felt drab. In her own office she had felt overdressed – not difficult amongst male academics – but here the black linen suit and cream wool sweater seemed dowdy. And her hair! Windblown wisps were trailing from the tortoiseshell clasp that was supposed to hold it in place. It was the same colour as Delva's, but there the resemblance ended. Delva's was braided into scores of tiny plaits drawn together in a dramatic swathe.

'Megan! Great to see you.' Delva was her usual, welcoming self. She had a knack of putting people instantly at ease. 'Let me get you a drink – I bet you're freezing, aren't you?'

'Thanks, Delva – can I have a cup of tea? I've drunk about a gallon of coffee already today.'

Delva fetched the tea herself and led Megan through to a windowless room, one wall of which was lined with TV monitors.

'We only finished editing it this morning. There's a gap

at the very beginning where it's just shots of you in the office and at police headquarters – I'll be doing a voiceover to go with it, but I haven't had a chance to record it yet. You can see a transcript if you want to. It's a potted history of you: your meteoric rise to fame, that sort of thing.'

Delva smiled as Megan winced. 'Come on, don't be modest – it's all true! How many other women in this country have made it to head of a university department at the age of 36, not to mention being a.k.a. Britain's Sexiest Sleuth!'

'God, Delva, you're not quoting the gutter press in this documentary, I hope!'

Delva had a very loud laugh – the kind that made people smile when they were trying to be serious.

'Don't worry, I wouldn't stoop to their level. Apart from the intro the fact that you're a woman is hardly mentioned. Mind you, I had a bit of a tough time convincing the producer. A real old dinosaur – came into TV from being a reporter on one of the tabloids in the seventies – he wanted shots of you "relaxing at home", as he puts it – by which he means you wearing as little as possible, in the bathroom brushing your teeth, that sort of thing.'

'You're joking. What on earth for?'

'Oh, "the human face of the female super-sleuth".' Delva shook her head. 'I reminded him that if you were a man he'd ask for no such thing. He wasn't very happy but he's already been leaned on by the ITC for sexist innuendo in programmes, so he backed down without too much of a fight. Anyway, would you like to see the programme now?'

Megan spent the next hour uncomfortably watching images of herself on one of the monitors. For the past three months unknown editors and production assistants had been glued to every move she had made during the filming sessions last summer, deciding where to cut and which shot of her face or body to use. They must have grown sick of the sight of her, she thought, cringing inwardly.

She wondered how the dinosaur producer would feel if he found out she was involved in the prostitutes' case. Would he be cutting pictures of Donna and Natalie with hers? The victims and the professional expert, as if they were worlds apart. She wished she'd never agreed to this. Neil had talked her into it. He had a way of persuading her to do things she didn't want to do. Neil Richardson. The new male face of BTV news. Delva's co-presenter. No wonder poor Ceri was feeling insecure.

'Don't worry – you look great!' Delva patted her arm, misreading her expression.

As the credits began to roll Delva stopped the tape and asked Megan what she thought.

'It's fine,' Megan faltered.

'You don't sound too convinced.'

'No – it's really flattering. It's just that it makes me out to be someone whose job is catching criminals and it isn't. Occasionally I help the police narrow down the list of suspects, but I'm a researcher, not a detective.'

'You're too modest, Megan.' Delva smiled as she opened the door and led the way back along the corridor to her office. 'If it hadn't been for you West Midlands Police would never have caught the Metro rapist!'

Megan shrugged and shook her head. Yes, she had pointed the police to a man they had already interviewed but dismissed as an unlikely suspect. But it was only because she had been carrying out research at the Domestic Violence Unit at the time. Going through the records she had come across a man of the same name who had been reported for assaulting his wife. When she had questioned the officer who dealt with the case he had revealed that an earlier charge of rape had been dropped when the wife decided not to press charges. After that, everything had fallen into place. It had been a lucky break.

And there had been other cases. A series of armed robberies in Scotland; a paedophile ring in the south-east. The theories she had evolved from all those prison interviews had certainly helped. But that was what she was. A theorist. She lectured police officers, probation officers, social workers. Only rarely did she get the chance to apply her theories herself. And now, for the first time, she had been called in on a murder case.

'When's it going out?' she asked.

'Ten-thirty on the night after Boxing Day. Should be a big audience.'

'Hmmm. I might be in Wales then. Don't think BTV reaches much beyond the border.'

'Nice try, Megan, but you can't escape – it's being networked!'

'I shouldn't have done this,' Megan said before she could stop herself. 'God knows who'll see it, what nutters it'll stir up.' She picked up her coat. She turned to say goodbye and was shocked to see Delva's face. The lively brown eyes had lost their sparkle and a line had appeared between her eyebrows.

'Delva?'

'I'm sorry. Can I ask you something? I mean, I shouldn't be using this meeting to ask you for a favour.'

Megan had never seen Delva upset before. The confident, cheerful persona had fallen away.

'I've been getting these awful letters'. Delva was staring out of the window at the narrowboats, their lights piercing the twilight. Megan thought she could see tears in the corners of her eyes.

'I didn't take much notice at first. Newsreaders always attract nutters. It goes with the territory and most of them are harmless. But this guy is sick – really sick.' She turned to Megan, biting her lip. 'I've told the police but they don't seem very interested. It's driving me crazy.'

'Have you got them here?'

Delva pulled a briefcase from underneath her desk. She turned it upside down, spilling out a sheaf of letters in a rainbow of different coloured envelopes. The only colour missing was white.

'I don't want you to have to read all these,' Delva said, 'but it gives you an idea of how many I've been getting.'

'Have they been fingerprinted?'

'Yes – I mean the police dusted the first couple I got but there was nothing.'

'So, either he's known to them and is smart enough to keep his paws off the paper or he's one of these rubber fetishists who likes to wear a pair of Marigolds while he's jacking off.'

Delva looked at Megan in astonishment. 'How did you know – about the masturbating, I mean?'

'Oh, it's very common with these sicko letter writers. I remember reading about a woman who did the same job as you at an American cable station. She got letters from a bloke who said he used to spray the TV set whenever she read the news.'

'Ugh!' Delva smiled in spite of herself.

'I know. When you read about it happening to someone else it seems laughable. But when it's happening to you, it's all horribly threatening.'

Megan opened a pink envelope on the top of the pile. 'Is this the most recent one?' She peered at the smudged postmark.

'Yes – it came this morning.'

Megan unfolded the large white sheet of paper. It was almost completely covered by a photograph which had been cut from a glossy magazine and glued down.

The woman was naked apart from a bodice made of black leather thongs. She squatted above the prone figure of a man, aiming a jet of urine over his face. Underneath the photograph was a scribbled message. It described the act of masturbation which had apparently gone on as the words were being written and urged Delva to urinate in the centre cubicle of the ladies' toilets on the first floor of the BTV building immediately after that evening's news bulletin.

'Do any of these others specify locations at BTV?' Megan asked.

'Er . . . yes – two or three. There's one in particular where he was asking me to rub myself against one of the machines in an editing suite. He actually wrote "Suite A".'

'So you don't need me to tell you that this guy is someone who's been in the building. Could even be someone who works here.' Megan looked at Delva, wondering if she already had an idea of who it might be.

If Delva did suspect someone, there was no hint of it in her face.

'Is there anyone at work you might have offended?' Megan went on. 'Or maybe someone who tried to flirt with you and got a put-down?'

'The only person I've ever consciously offended was a security guard who told me off for parking in a loading bay – but he left a few months ago. BTV put things like security and catering out to tender and when the new firm took over they didn't re-appoint him.'

'Hmmm, a security guard.' Megan instantly thought of the leering, impertinent man on reception. 'The spelling and the punctuation suggest someone who hasn't been very well educated. I would have said it was someone in a blue collar job. But then again, we could be dealing with someone really smart who wants to make you think he's some semi-literate nutcase.'

'But why would he do that?'

'Well . . .' Megan hesitated, thinking aloud. 'What if it was a colleague? Someone you work with in the newsroom. Possibly someone who's asked you out and been rejected?'

Megan caught her breath. A horrible idea had occurred to her. Please God, she thought, don't let it be Neil.

Delva had turned her face away and was staring at the lamplit canal basin beyond the window. It occurred to Megan that if Neil was the man Delva suspected, she was unlikely to say so. Delva knew perfectly well that Neil was Megan's brother-in-law. If she had suspected him would she have sought Megan's help in the first place?

'I'm not sure . . .' Delva sounded like someone coming out of a trance.

'Would you like me to talk to the police? I'm seeing Detective Superintendent Leverton tomorrow and he owes me a favour.' Megan sounded more optimistic than she felt.

Delva frowned. 'I hate to put you to this trouble – I'm sure you've got enough on your plate.'

'It's no trouble.' Megan wondered if Delva suspected her involvement in the prostitute cases. There must have been speculation in the newsroom over the deaths being linked. She picked up a handful of the letters. 'Can I take these?'

'Of course.' Delva gave her a grateful smile. 'I'll walk you down to reception.'

They walked in silence along the maze of corridors. As they neared the stairs Megan stopped in her tracks.

'What is it?' Delva caught her arm. 'You look as if you've seen a ghost!'

'It's okay.' Megan swayed slightly. Her insides had turned to ice. 'It's her. Clare.'

Delva followed Megan's eyes. Standing on a landing below them was a young woman in a red dress. The fabric was stretched tight over her enormous belly. 'Oh Megan, I'm so sorry – you didn't know?'

Megan shook her head, her lips white.

'Come back to my office. I'll make you some more tea.'

'No.' Megan swallowed hard. 'No, thank you – I'm fine, really. Just a bit of a shock.' She didn't want to talk about it. Had made a point of not talking about it. Not even Ceri knew why things had gone so badly wrong between her and Tony.

Megan knew all about his office fling. Had hardly been surprised when she'd discovered he'd been taking his pleasures elsewhere. Tony had left BTV soon after she'd rumbled him. He'd taken a job at the BBC. Said he needed a fresh start. Now she knew why it hadn't worked. Why he'd moved out within weeks of begging for her forgiveness. Clare was about to do what she could never do. Tony was going to be a father.

Megan made herself walk to the reception desk. Past Clare. She didn't see whether the woman recognised her or not because she kept her eyes firmly fixed on the stairs. Delva followed silently behind her. 'I'll be fine, now, honestly.' Megan forced a smile as the security guard took back her visitor's pass.

Delva looked at her, concerned. 'Take care, you hear?'

Megan braced herself for the blast of cold air that buffeted her as she stepped through the doors. Glancing back she caught the guard leering up at Delva as she climbed the stairs.

Megan sat in the car for a few minutes before driving off. Why hadn't Neil told her about Clare being pregnant? She wondered if he'd said anything to Ceri. It was more than likely. She put herself in Ceri's shoes, realising what a burden that knowledge would be to her sister.

It was through Ceri and Neil that she had met Tony. Tony and that other bastard. Back in Birmingham after four years' absence, she'd been happy to be drawn into Ceri's hectic social life. In those days Ceri, Neil and Tony had all been reporters at Radio Heartbeat. She felt her stomach tighten as she remembered the party at Neil's house. What happened that night would stay in her mind until the day she died.

Biting her lip, she started up the engine. Work. She had work to do. A careful analysis of the files Leverton had given her. Donna and Natalie. The faces of the dead girls filled her mind's eye, pushing out the image of the girl on the stairs. And the memory of that other face.

Chapter 4

Megan was sitting in her office, pen in hand, staring at the wall in front of her. She had come in early, before the porter and the cleaners, but the profile she was working on had progressed no further than a few scribbled notes.

On a white-board next to the desk were two columns listing everything she knew about Donna and Natalie. Red and green lines criss-crossed the columns, linking similarities, highlighting differences.

She scanned the list of behavioural characteristics gleaned from the murders. _Two different killers_. She had underlined the words. Underneath she had written: _O and AB – but O has sex with AB's victim. How? Why?_

She looked at the date Natalie's body had been found. November 29. Not quite four weeks ago. If she was right, if Natalie's killer was the type of man she suspected, he was almost certain to strike again. She bit the end of her pen. How long before Delva was reading out more headlines about murder?

Delva. The identity of her perverted admirer nagged at Megan. Delva hadn't mentioned Neil by name but the seeds of suspicion had taken root in Megan's mind. To the outside world Neil came across as the archetypal New Man, but Megan knew that he picked up the role only when it suited him.

How would Ceri react if she told her Delva Lobelo was getting sexually explicit letters from someone who worked at BTV? Megan tried to convince herself that if Neil was really having an affair he was unlikely to be the author of those letters. But what if it wasn't an affair? What if Ceri had sensed something was wrong but misinterpreted it?

Megan had tried hard over the years to bury the antipathy she felt for Neil. She'd had to, for Ceri's sake. She had never told Ceri how he'd let her down. How he'd defended his friend against Megan's allegations, refusing to believe him capable of something as shocking as rape.

Her thoughts were interrupted by a knock on the door. Patrick walked in with a sheaf of notes in his hand.

'You did say eleven o'clock, didn't you?'

Megan looked at her watch. 'Oh, I'm sorry Patrick – I lost all track of the time.'

'Dreaming of summer?' Patrick pointed to the blown-up photograph of the sea on the wall in front of her desk. It must have looked as if she was staring intently at it.

'Where is it?' he asked, 'Somewhere you've been on holiday?'

'It's a place called Borth on the Welsh coast – you've probably never heard of it. It's near Aberystwyth.'

He looked blank. 'My father's family come from round there,' she went on. 'When my grandmother died she left us her house. You can just about see it in the photo.'

Megan pointed to a small, whitewashed cottage on the seafront. 'It's opposite the baker's – bad news when you've got a weakness for cream cakes!'

'Do you go there in summer?'

'When I can. Actually I like it better in winter. No tourists. Sometimes I have the whole beach to myself. And if it rains I just sit by the window watching the sea. It sounds really boring, I know, but I love it.'

'No – it doesn't sound boring at all.' Patrick smiled, putting his papers on her desk while he pulled up a chair.

'Perhaps I can come and visit you there one day. Wales is one of the places I want to explore while I'm over here.'

'Er, yes, of course.' Megan didn't quite know what to make of this. 'It only takes a couple of hours to get there.' She was going to add that he could come for a daytrip if he wanted to, but realised that would sound rude when she could easily offer him the spare room for a weekend. She decided it was better to keep things vague, and changed the subject. 'How's the PhD coming along then? Anything in particular you want me to look at?'

Megan was supervising Patrick's thesis on serial sex offenders. The fact that a detective from Holland had taken a sabbatical to study at Heartland was a tribute to her growing academic reputation.

'I finished compiling the list of behaviour types from the paedophile group this morning and I've just started feeding them into the computer so I can't really say much about those until I get the printout. I've got the list, though, if you want to see it. I took it from these victim statements and crime scene photographs.'

Megan glanced at the file that lay on top of Patrick's bundle of papers. The case notes were in Dutch. The face of a girl of about nine smiled from the page. Her name and date of birth were printed underneath. 'You're not just using Dutch cases, are you?' Megan took the list from Patrick's outstretched hand.

'No. That one just happened to be on the top. I'm using the cases from the Belgian paedophile ring and the Robert Black murders as well.'

As Megan read through the depressing list of behavioural characteristics of men who had raped, tortured and killed young children, Patrick stared at the photograph of Natalie Bailey lying on the desk.

'Can I be very nosey and ask what you're working on?' he said as she put the paper down.

Megan felt a stab of possessiveness, as if she wanted to protect Natalie from curious onlookers. Then she remembered Patrick was as much an expert as she was. If he was an onlooker, what was she?

'Yes, of course,' she said. 'As a matter of fact I'm having a lot of difficulty with this one – you might be able to help.'

'She looks very young.' It was the head and shoulders photograph from the post-mortem report; the one taken before the bruises came up on the neck.

'I know – she's sixteen. Take a look at this, though.' Megan pulled the second photograph of Natalie from the folder on her desk.

'Ah! It's that runaway they found by the motorway a few weeks ago, isn't it?'

'How did you know she was a runaway?'

'It was on the news at lunchtime; they said the police had finally identified the body as a kid who'd run away from a children's home here in Birmingham.'

'Was this TV or radio news?'

'Why do you ask?'

'I was wondering how you recognised her. I mean, even if it had been on the TV news there shouldn't have been any photographs; as far as I know the only photos the police have are the post-mortem ones and they'd never let the press have those. What was it, an artist's impression or something?'

'No. I mean, I don't know – I heard it on the radio in my office. I don't know whether it's been on TV or not.'

'So how did you recognise her?'

'I didn't recognise *her*, I recognised the way she was killed. The case reminded me of one of Robert Black's victims. The newspaper report said the police had found the body of a young girl wrapped in black dustbin bags by the side of the M6. It said she'd been strangled and that the police were having difficulty identifying her.'

'Oh.' Megan reached into the file again. 'Yes – Black did dump one of his victims very near there.' Was that significant? She handed him the photograph of Donna Fieldhouse taken at the crime scene in Inkerman Place. While he studied it Megan watched his face as he frowned in concentration. For no reason at all she found herself thinking of Tony; picturing him walking into a hospital ward full of new mothers and Clare, young and radiant, holding out his newborn child.

'She was pregnant?' Patrick's question crashed in on her thoughts and for a split second she wondered if he had somehow read her mind. Glancing at the desk, she saw that he had taken the notes on Donna Fieldhouse from the folder.

'Yes – and I think it could be significant.' Megan began telling him about the forensic evidence linking the murders. Would he come to the same conclusion she had?

'So both were in care, but at different children's homes?' Patrick rubbed his chin.

'Yes. It's a bit confusing because Donna ran away from a home in Wolverhampton, but ended up as a prostitute in Birmingham. Natalie was in a home in Birmingham, but she was only ever seen soliciting in the Wolverhampton area.'

'What about the manner of death? This one – Donna – had her throat cut, but the other one was manually strangled.' Patrick retrieved the first photograph of Donna from the desk, studying the gaping wound and lolling head of the body in the dustbin.

'I know. That's one of several things about these murders that doesn't add up. I mean, to me, Donna's murder looks like a straightforward domestic between a prostitute and a pimp – maybe a row over her pregnancy that got out of hand because one or both of them had been taking crack. He dumps her body in the car park of a disused factory where prostitutes take their clients for sex. There's a concealed entrance not many people would know about. If he's a pimp he'll know it's the kind of place he can get rid of the body without being seen.

'But Natalie's death is totally different. The manual strangulation from behind, the wrists handcuffed or tied with wire, the anal intercourse; to me that's the signature of a woman-hating sex-killer who deliberately lures his victim to her death.' She felt on edge, ready to argue if he told her she must be wrong.

'What do the police think?'

'I get the distinct impression that the only reason I've been called in is to help Detective Superintendent Leverton nail a bent officer within his own force.'

She found it hard to conceal her dislike of policemen. Strange that she'd never felt that hostility towards Patrick. Perhaps it was because they'd only ever met in an academic setting.

'He wants me to come up with a profile for the man responsible for both murders,' she went on. 'The fact that the DNA in the vaginal semen samples is an exact match tells him that the man who had sex with both girls also killed them both. He hasn't really taken the other forensic evidence into account, but the more I look at it, the stronger the indication that these murders were committed by two different men.'

'So what are you going to do?'

'Play along with Leverton. I mean, there could well be a corrupt policeman involved.'

Before Patrick could respond, the phone rang.

'Hello Eric. Yes, put him through.'

It was a brief conversation; no more than thirty seconds. Megan put the phone down, her face hot, her breath tight. 'That was Martin Leverton. He wants me to meet him at the mortuary in half an hour.'

'Another prostitute?'

'No – not this time.' Megan slid the forensic reports back into the folder. 'Did you hear about the siege at that house in Moseley at the weekend? Man and woman, both shot dead – looked like a domestic?'

Patrick nodded.

'Well it wasn't. Apparently she was strangled first by a third party, who also shot the husband and made it look like suicide. There's also evidence of anal intercourse and restraint.'

'Sounds like it's a good job you didn't waste too much time on that profile. How come it's taken them two days to work out she was strangled?'

'Bruise marks on the neck took a while to come out, although there should have been other signs.' Megan stood up, walking to the door to grab her coat from the hook.

'Perhaps they were so convinced it was a domestic shooting they didn't bother being too thorough.' She paused before opening the door. 'I'm sorry to cut things short, Patrick . . .'

'No problem. I wish I was coming with you!'

She returned his wide smile with a look of mock horror. 'Don't worry,' she said, 'I'll fill you in on all the gory details later. Just concentrate on your paedophiles until I get back!'

'Here – catch!' Patrick fished in his pocket and tossed something across the room. 'You might need a few later!'

Megan managed to catch the red missile before it reached the floor. 'Maltesers! How did you know?'

Patrick pointed at the telltale wrapper protruding from her wastepaper bin. 'What are you on now?' He smiled. 'Packet a day, is it?'

'Huh! Can't a girl have any secret vices?' She pulled a face at him, grinning to herself as she walked off down the corridor.

The man went into a room where he knew he would not be disturbed.

Locking the door behind him he slid a photograph from his trouser pocket, placing it carefully on the table. The secrecy of his actions was enough to give him an erection. Unzipping his flies, he leaned forward, moving his hand up and down.

His eyes were fixed on the photograph until the moment he ejaculated. With a gasp his head fell back against the chair.

He sat for a few seconds, panting, before pulling tissues from his pocket to wipe his hands. Then, with a pair of tweezers, he picked up the photograph, sliding it into a pale pink envelope.

Chapter 5

Martin Leverton was waiting by the door of the mortuary when Megan arrived.

'Megan – what a wonderful outfit! You look as if you've stepped out of one of those pre-Raphaelite paintings at the art gallery!'

'Thanks. I – er – bought it in the States.' Megan felt embarrassed by the compliment. Leverton had never made any sort of comment about her appearance before.

It was the first time she had actually had the nerve to wear the coat. It had looked great when she tried it on in Bloomingdale's, but somehow it had seemed a bit over-the-top for the streets of Birmingham. However, after seeing Clare yesterday at BTV, she'd needed to brighten herself up, grabbing the coat from the wardrobe and putting it on without looking in the mirror.

Now the wind was tugging at the crimson wool, making it billow out like a medieval cloak behind her. As they went inside she pulled back the cowled hood, her long black hair spilling over her shoulders.

'Thanks for coming at such short notice, Megan. I wouldn't normally ask you to do this, but it's vital that we establish exactly what's happened to this pair. I didn't want to have to wait for photographs and anyway, I think it's important that we both see these bodies.'

'Have you seen them yet?'

'No. I only got the call from the pathologist an hour ago.

By the way, he's a new chap – haven't come across him
before.'

'Well, the first thing we need to know is the blood group
of the anal semen sample.'

'I know. The results hadn't come back from the lab when
I spoke to him but he's promised to chase it up. They should
have done the tests by now, so hopefully they'll phone us
here with the results.'

He knocked on the opaque glass panel of the door,
shuffling his feet impatiently as they waited. It was opened
by a young woman with bad acne, who let them in without
a word. Her overalls were spattered with an assortment of
stains in varying shades of brown. As they followed her
along the rows of dead bodies, Megan found herself wondering what this girl's friends and relatives had said when
she announced that she wanted to be a mortuary technician.

Megan's mother had been a forensic scientist and her
children used to tell their friends she was a medical version
of Sherlock Holmes. Sometimes, after school, Megan would
wait for her outside the big white doors of the laboratory,
trying to imagine what was going on in the forbidden zone
inside.

When she was finally allowed a guided tour of the place
she had discovered it was nowhere near as gruesome as the
pictures in her mind. Her mother spent most of her time
peering down a microscope, quite detached from the bodies
her samples came from.

But to choose to spend one's life surrounded by corpses –
that was something Megan had never really been able to
understand. She glanced again at the girl leading them
through the mortuary. Perhaps for her it was a refuge. If she
was embarrassed about her skin, this was one place she
could work in peace, free from the risk of cruel stares or
pitying looks.

'Detective Superintendent Leverton!' A man's voice boomed from behind a screen and the girl scurried off like a beetle to a dark corner of the room.

The pathologist emerged, having apparently changed into a clean set of green overalls. He adjusted the cap on his head before shaking hands with Martin.

'Ed Horrobin. And this is . . .?' He turned to Megan and she noticed how young he was. All the pathologists she had ever met had been at least fifty, and knowing how long it took to qualify for the job she was surprised to see someone who could easily have been mistaken for an undergraduate.

'This is Doctor Megan Rhys,' Leverton cut in before she could answer for herself. 'She's helping us build up a profile for the Natalie Bailey and Donna Fieldhouse murders – if this case proves to be linked she needs to see the forensic evidence as quickly as possible.'

'Yes, I've been on to the lab and they've promised to call back with that blood group result before two o'clock.' He pulled back the elasticated cuff of his overalls, glancing at his watch. 'So – that gives us twenty minutes to show you the bodies and get you back out on the trail!'

For one so new, he was remarkably cocky, Megan thought. He led them over to the corpse of a small, thin man. It was virtually impossible to estimate his age because most of the head was missing.

'Right!' the pathologist went on in the same, almost theatrical tone he had used earlier. 'This is Mr Dudley Jackson, aged 38 years. Cause of death is arrest of brain function due to a gunshot wound. The weapon was a double-barrelled shotgun fired into the mouth. Tests carried out since we took delivery of the body reveal that Mr Jackson could not have blown his own brains out because his arms weren't long enough.'

Horrobin perched on a nearby stool, legs apart, holding

an imaginary shotgun between his knees. 'You see, he was only five foot four, very slight build. We measured the barrel of the gun and the only way he could have done it was if he'd held the gun between his feet and pulled the trigger with one of his toes. As he had his boots on when your lot found him, I'd say that's pretty unlikely.'

He bounded from the stool across the room to the corpse of a woman, not waiting for any kind of answer from his audience.

'Of course there's no way that *she* could have killed *him*. She was found lying face down on the bed and some of the shot from the gun had passed right through her body into the mattress. The entry wound confirmed that she'd been shot through the back while lying on the bed. Of course, we now know that the actual cause of death was asphyxiation and that she was already dead when the gun was fired.'

'Why did it take you two days to work that out?' Megan could have made the question sound less like an accusation, but in the circumstances she was inclined not to.

'Blame it on the ballistics boys, not me,' he replied, immediately on the defensive. 'I had no reason to believe this was anything other than a domestic murder followed by a suicide. I was as surprised as everyone else when they told me he couldn't have fired that gun.'

'What about the bruising on the neck?'

'Didn't come up until this morning – people bruise at different rates depending on their skin type. This one was slower than most.'

'But surely you checked for damage to the cartilage inside the throat?'

'Not possible.' He pulled away the plastic sheet that covered the woman from the neck down, revealing an incision which ran from her chin to the exit wound in her stomach. 'We only make a 'V'-shaped incision in the trunk if strangulation is suspected from the start. That allows us to take the throat right out for a thorough examination. But this seemed such a clear-cut death by shooting that we went ahead with a straightforward longitudinal cut.'

Megan couldn't believe this. 'So any evidence of pressure to the throat was destroyed by your scalpel.'

From the corner of her eye she saw Martin Leverton's eyebrows arch. Horrobin flushed, apparently lost for words for once.

He was spared further embarrassment by the loud ring of a telephone. Although the girl was on her way to answer it, he darted across the room, grabbing the receiver from her hand.

Megan took a closer look at the body of Tina Jackson. The marks on her wrists were almost identical to the ones in the photographs of Natalie Bailey. But although the manner of death was identical in both cases, this woman could not have been more different from tiny, fair-haired Natalie. Tina Jackson had long, dark hair that looked as if it might have been dyed. Much of her skin was mottled purplish-red from where the blood had settled after death, but from the unaffected portions of the body Megan could see that Tina was an olive-skinned woman.

She turned to Leverton, who was peering at the bruise marks on the neck. 'How old was Tina Jackson?'

'Forty.'

'Any kids?'

'No. The body was identified by her sister. I'm going to see her as soon as we've finished here – would you mind coming with me?'

Before Megan could reply the pathologist bustled over to Leverton, waving a piece of paper in his hand. 'The results!' he boomed triumphantly. 'First of all, let me tell you about the Jacksons: Dudley Jackson was blood group 'O', as was his wife Tina. The semen sample on the swab came from a man with blood group AB, of a type present in only 2% of the population.'

Leverton took the paper from him with a gleam in his eye. Studying it, he muttered something under his breath. Then he turned to Horrobin, fixing him with a look that warned him not to botch anything else. 'Right – let's get this clear. This AB blood group result came from an anal swab and there was no semen in this woman's vagina?'

'Correct.' Horrobin cocked his head to one side, staring Leverton out.

'Right. I think we've got what we came for, Megan.' With a curt word of thanks, Leverton turned his back on the man, his arm brushing Megan's shoulder as he ushered her out of the room.

'What a balls-up!' Leverton shook his head as he paused in the lobby, putting on his coat and gloves.

'I know. I've never come across a pathologist who was so – well –'

'Cocky?'

'Yes. To be so self-assured even when he knew he was in the wrong.'

'Evidently this is his first week in the job. I suppose we should sympathise, really. I mean, it's got to be pretty tough luck to land a case like that on day one.'

'Anyway, at least we've got pretty positive evidence of a link with the Natalie Bailey murder. How long before we get the DNA result on that semen swab?'

'Tomorrow afternoon.'

'Right, but until then we're working on the assumption that the same man had anal sex with both Natalie and Tina?'

'Yes. Looks like your theory about two different killers was spot on. But I still can't work out why Natalie had semen from Donna's killer in her vagina if she was killed by the man who had anal sex with her.'

'Could be two men working together.'

Leverton gave her an odd look. A mixture of surprise and confusion.

'Remember the case of the Hillside Stranglers?' Megan didn't let him answer. 'Killed ten women in the Los Angeles area in the late 'seventies?'

'Vaguely, yes. They went for prostitutes.'

'At first, yes. Later it was any young girl they thought they could abduct without getting caught. Anyway, the point is that they did several murders together, but then one of them started killing alone.'

'Go on.'

'Well, imagine Donna Fieldhouse was killed by her pimp in a straightforward fight, like we said before. What if this pimp has a friend – some regular punter who likes kinky sex behind closed doors? What if Natalie Bailey was persuaded to participate in some sort of three-in-a-bed session which escalated into rape and murder? That would explain the presence of the two types of semen in her body.'

'But what about Tina Jackson? She only had sex with one of them.'

'That's the point. Imagine this punter gets a taste for murder and decides to do it alone next time. Maybe the sort of girls the pimp goes for are not really the punter's type. So he goes out searching for the right kind of victim.'

'Which would explain why Tina Jackson looks nothing like Donna and Natalie.'

'Exactly.'

Leverton was staring at Megan curiously.

'What is it?' she asked, uncomfortable under his gaze.

'Long, black hair, olive skin, age between thirty and forty . . .'

'Yes – and?' she said, a note of impatience creeping into her voice.

'Well, that's you, isn't it?' he said, a half-smile on his face. 'You'd better be careful, Megan.'

Megan froze. Could it be? No – God, he was joking!

Before she could respond to this fatuous remark, his face snapped back into its customary expression of measured concern. 'What do you think are the chances of either or both of them killing again?'

She looked at him, her pulse still racing. 'We're dealing with two very different killers here. It looks as if the first one – let's call him O – killed Donna almost by accident. He might have played no part in the death of Natalie Bailey; he might have had sex with her before the other man arrived and then left him to it. Were there any fibres on Natalie's body like the ones you said were on the backs of Donna's legs?'

'Yes, I was going to phone you to tell you just before I got the call about the Jackson case: there were tiny amounts of fibre on one of her heels. They've just done a comparison and it's identical to the stuff they found on Donna's body. They're trying to trace the manufacturer at the moment.'

Megan had a momentary vision of a small lifeless body being dragged across a faded carpet. Perhaps she'd driven past the very house where it happened. She remembered the dismal windows overlooking the car park where Donna Fieldhouse's body had been found. If someone was murdered in one of those derelict buildings, would anyone hear the screams?

'As I was saying –' she forced her mind back to Leverton's question – 'O might never kill again – at least not deliberately. But the other guy: well, he's a very different type. What he did bears all the hallmarks of an organised sex killer who uses women as vehicles to get even with society. This is a man whose violence has been triggered by some traumatic event in his life; probably something quite recent. He won't stop killing until he gets the nerve to confront the cause of his anger.'

Leverton nodded. 'Let's go and see the sister,' he said, opening the passenger door of his sleek BMW. Megan climbed in. The scent of new leather filled her nostrils as he slammed the door. The car was immaculate, like its owner. So unlike her own car, with its dashboard littered with empty Malteser packets and discarded car park tickets, an orange-scented air-freshener masking the lingering smell of sick which she'd tried without success to scrub out of the upholstery after Emily, her two-year-old niece, had been ill on their last trip to Wales.

She wondered who cleaned Martin Leverton's car. She could hardly imagine him doing it himself. But neither could she imagine him entrusting this precious beast to his wife. Perhaps he paid one of those professional car valet firms to do it.

'Take a look at these.' Leverton pulled a folder from the back seat and passed it to her before starting up the engine. Inside was a set of photographs showing the carnage in what had once been the Jacksons' bedroom. The first one was a shot of Tina Jackson lying face down on the bed. 'This is how we found her after the lads broke the door down.'

Megan bit her lip. The dead woman might have been a slab of meat on a butcher's block for all the dignity the photograph afforded her. She was spread-eagled, naked except for a white lacy bra. Near its straps, the flesh was speckled black where casing from the shotgun pellets had scorched it. Her hands were stuck through the gaps in the iron bedstead.

'No handcuffs, then?'

'No.' Leverton pushed in the cigarette lighter and reached into his jacket pocket. 'The killer took whatever he used to restrain her away with him. Nothing we found in that room matches up with the marks on the wrists. Want one?' He waved a packet of Marlboro under her nose.

'No thanks, I'm trying to give up.' Megan wrinkled her nose as he lit his cigarette. The craving was almost unbearable. She concentrated on the photograph. There was a black high-heeled shoe near the bed and a small pile of dark-coloured, shiny material that looked like a dress and underskirt twisted together.

'Are these her clothes?'

'Yes.' Leverton blew out a plume of smoke. 'It was her birthday, poor cow. According to the sister she was getting ready for a night out.'

'But not with the husband, presumably,' Megan said, opening her window and taking a gulp of fresh air. 'They were separated?'

'Yes. He'd gone back to live with his parents. They own a farm near Wolverhampton. The shotgun was theirs, evidently.' He glanced at her. 'Are you all right? Do you want me to put this out?'

'No, it's okay,' she lied, wishing she hadn't left Patrick's Maltesers in her car. 'So, Tina Jackson was dressed up for a night out with someone else. Dudley came to the house with a shotgun. She was restrained and strangled then shot through the back.' She frowned. 'We know Dudley Jackson wasn't responsible for the anal penetration, but do we know for sure that he didn't either strangle or shoot her? Any prints on the body?'

'Nothing. He must have been wearing gloves – the killer, I mean. There are prints of Dudley Jackson's all over the house and on the gun, but nothing on Tina's body.'

'Do we know how long after she was strangled the shots were fired?'

'Not long. The pathologist said that the spread of bloodstains on the bedclothes showed that she'd been shot almost immediately after death. Otherwise the blood would have congealed and there wouldn't have been so much loss.'

'Do you think Dudley Jackson caught her in bed with someone else?'

'Certainly looks that way.'

'You said on the phone that she wasn't a prostitute – how can you be sure?'

'I can't, really. All I can say is that she appears to have been fairly respectable. She worked in a building society in West Bromwich.'

They drove on in silence, Megan sifting through the horrific photographs in her lap. The light was beginning to fade and Christmas decorations winked incongruously from every lamp-post. Megan thought of the sister they were going to see. Every Christmas was going to be hell for her now.

When Leverton finally pulled up she noticed a patrol car parked a few yards further down the street. A uniformed policewoman got out of the passenger seat and walked towards Leverton's car. Megan wondered how the sister would feel about being questioned by three people.

Charlotte McGahy lived in a rambling Victorian house that had been converted into flats. When she opened the door, Megan immediately noticed how attractive she was, despite the absence of any make-up and the blank expression on her face.

'Miss McGahy,' Leverton offered her his hand. 'You know WPC Cartwright, don't you? And this is Doctor Megan Rhys – she's a psychologist and she'd like to talk to you about your sister's death.'

The woman nodded blankly and led them into a large, cold room with an ornate marble fireplace. A single-bar electric fire stood in the hearth giving out a pathetically inadequate amount of heat.

'You're a bit late, aren't you?' Her question was addressed to Megan.

Megan blinked and turned to Leverton, who looked as

confused as she was. 'I'm sorry?' she said, anxious not to say anything that would upset the woman even more.

'I phoned your lot six weeks ago about Dudley. They knew he had a history of depression and that he'd hit Tina when they split up. I warned them he was dangerous and wanted locking up. Psychologist? What's the use of a bloody psychologist now? It's too bloody late, isn't it?'

She wept into a pink paper tissue tugged from inside her sleeve.

The policewoman put an arm around her shoulder but she shrugged it away, blowing her nose and reaching across to a coffee table for another tissue.

'I'm all right!' she whispered, looking away from them at the glowing bar of the fire.

'I'm sorry Miss McGahy, Doctor Rhys isn't here to talk about your brother-in-law. You see it wasn't Dudley that killed your sister.'

'What?' Charlotte's gaze shot from the fire to Leverton.

'Tests have been carried out on the shotgun found in your sister's bedroom. Dudley couldn't have fired it into his mouth himself. We believe someone else killed both Tina and Dudley.' Leverton paused, waiting for this new bombshell to sink in.

She stared at him, her mouth slightly open. 'Someone else? How could it have been someone else? It was Dudley's gun. I've seen it at his mum and dad's house in a case on the wall!'

'I'm sorry, I know this is going to be very hard on you but we need to know who else might have been in the house when Dudley arrived with the gun. Would you mind if Doctor Rhys asked you a few questions?'

The blank stare returned to the woman's face and she nodded dumbly, as if there was nothing else that anyone could say or do that would make the pain any worse than it already was.

The policewoman went to make cups of tea and Leverton walked over to the bay window. The curtains had not been drawn and he stood, looking out. There couldn't have been much to see in the lamp-lit street, but Megan was grateful for his tact. She leaned forward in her chair, speaking softly.

'The first thing I need to know is how long your sister had been separated from her husband.'

Charlotte looked puzzled, as if she couldn't see the relevance of the question, but answered all the same. 'Not long; Dudley only moved out a couple of weeks ago.'

'How long had they been married?'

'Ten years. God knows how she put up with him for that long.'

'You said he'd hit her when they split up . . .'

'Yes, but it wasn't the first time. She used to make excuses for him. She couldn't stand the thought of them breaking up, said she didn't want to be a failure.'

'Why did she think she was a failure?'

'I don't know. She was always doing herself down. It was his fault. He made her like that. Always criticising her.'

'What was it that finally led to the break-up?'

There was a long pause. 'I think it was when she started doing the soup run.'

Megan frowned. 'Soup run?'

'She took soup round the red light district. For the prostitutes and the down-and-outs. She was like, you know, a volunteer. She did it a couple of nights a week and Dudley didn't like it. He was so jealous – wanted her to stay in with him every night. They had a big row about it and he smacked her across the face. Next day she had the locks changed and went to see a solicitor about keeping him away from the house.'

Megan nodded slowly. The red light district. So there was a connection. From the corner of her eye she saw that

Leverton had turned his head and was listening intently. She waited for him to speak but he said nothing. 'Do you know if she'd been on the soup run the night she died?' Megan held her breath.

'Yes.' Charlotte sniffed. 'We were supposed to be going clubbing. It was her birthday. We were going to go for a meal first but she said she couldn't make it before ten because she was on the soup rota and there was no one to swap with.' She blinked. 'That's the sort of person she was. Wouldn't dream of letting anyone down – not even on her birthday.' She bent her head, her shoulders heaving as she sobbed.

Megan crossed the room, sitting on the sofa beside her. Instead of putting an arm around her, she tried to find words that would encourage her to open up again.

'I'm really sorry I'm having to ask you all these questions. I've got a sister myself. I can't pretend to understand how you're feeling now. All I can say is that if someone killed my sister I'd want to do everything in my power to get them locked up.'

Megan paused, trying to gauge the effect her words were having. 'Why do you think Tina volunteered for the soup run?'

'She said she wanted to give something back.' She mumbled the words into her tissue. 'Said she was so lucky to have a good job and a nice house.'

'Do you know if Tina was seeing anyone else?'

Charlotte turned slowly round to look at Megan, dabbing eyes that were now puffy and red. 'No I – I –' she stammered – 'I don't think so.'

Megan spoke slowly and softly, trying to keep the urgency out of her voice. 'What about the soup run? Are you sure there was no one? One of the other volunteers, maybe?'

'No. I'm sure she would have told me.' She reached for another tissue. 'We're – we were – very close.'

Megan pursed her lips, trying another tack. 'How would you describe Tina? Physically, I mean?'

'She was beautiful,' she replied, a faraway look in her eyes. 'I mean, she was 40 but she didn't look it. I'm three years younger than her but people always think I'm the eldest. She could easily pass for early thirties.'

'This is an awful question to have to ask you, but do you think Tina could have been mistaken for a prostitute? The reason I ask is because we think her death might be linked to the murder of a young girl who worked in the red light district.'

Megan braced herself for what might follow, but the woman merely shook her head. 'Oh no. She always wore what she called her scruffs when she did the soup run. Old jeans and hoodies – that sort of thing. It was partly because of Dudley being so suspicious, I think. She made herself look as plain as possible.'

'Even after they'd split up?'

'Yes.' Charlotte sniffed. 'I spoke to her on the phone just before she went out. She was joking about how she'd have to do a quick change and put on a bit of slap to look decent for later.'

'Did she say anything else? Mention who she was doing the run with?'

'No. All she said was that she was worried about Dudley getting into the house, it being her birthday and everything. He knew Tina was planning a night out. She was scared he might try breaking in and she'd come home and find him waiting for her.'

The policewoman came in with a tray of tea, trying to be as unobtrusive as possible. Leverton left his post at the window and sat down, judging this a suitable moment to ask a few questions of his own.

'This voluntary organisation your sister worked for – what was it called?'

'I'm not sure. I think she found out about it through a friend at work.' Charlotte reached for a mug of tea and cradled it in her hands, as if seeking comfort from its warmth.

'Would that friend have been a man or a woman?' Leverton persisted.

'A woman. Her name's Gail something. Sorry, I don't know her last name.'

'We can soon check that. Do you know how many people she did the soup run with?'

'It would have been her and one other person,' Charlotte said, staring at the steam curling from the mug. 'They always went in pairs. For safety reasons, she said.' Her chin wobbled and a tear splashed into the tea.

Leverton looked at Megan before getting to his feet.

Back in his car, he punched out numbers on his mobile. 'Sweet Fanny Adams,' he grunted, slamming it down on the seat.

'No one there?' Megan glanced at her watch.

'Bloody answerphone. Probably off on a Christmas piss-up.'

'Well, unless this Gail woman saw Tina home, it's unlikely she'll be much help.'

Leverton frowned. 'What are you thinking?'

'That whoever did this saw Tina in the red light district and followed the soup van. Waited for her to finish and followed her home.'

'And then what? How did he get in?'

'Conned her with some ruse,' Megan said. 'Like Ted Bundy with his fake broken arm. Maybe he knocked at the door and pretended to be someone needing help. Sounds like Tina would be a sucker for that sort of thing.'

'So we're looking for a smooth-talking kerb-crawler who knocks about with a pimp and fancies scruffy dark-haired forty-year-olds?' There was more than a hint of sarcasm in Leverton's voice.

'Not exactly what I would have put in the profile.' Megan arched her eyebrows. 'But yes, a charming, persuasive man who is familiar with the red light district. As for Tina being scruffy, from the way her sister described her it sounds as if she'd have stood out from the crowd whatever she wore.'

Leverton gave her a sidelong glance that made her feel uncomfortable. As he drove on through the dark streets, Megan thought about Tina. She'd gone out that night, looking forward to celebrating later and no doubt happy to be free of her vicious husband. And what had happened? She'd been stalked by someone even worse.

And Natalie. It was bad enough that she went, like Donna Fieldhouse, from a children's home to the streets; bad enough what her usual punters asked of her, without being used by some monster to stand in for all his hatred of the world.

Stand in. Something flickered in her mind. He used them as a stand-in for the real object of his hatred. Who? A wife? Girlfriend? Mother? Boss?

And he used the pimp – the O man – to hide behind too. O got Natalie for him. Perhaps O dumped her body as part of the deal. A murderer hiding behind another killer. She shivered. And they had no idea who either of them were.

Chapter 6

Megan stood on a duckboard in Tina Jackson's bedroom. For the past two days scenes-of-crime officers had been carrying out a painstaking search of the entire house. Anyone who entered was required to put on protective clothing and getting from one room to another meant walking on the raised wooden boards that criss-crossed the floors like stepping stones in a stream.

The room now bore little resemblance to the crime scene photograph Megan held in her hand. The bed had been stripped, its duvet, sheets, pillows and mattress taken away for forensic examination. All that was left was the brass and cast iron frame. Megan could see how easy it would have been for the killer to handcuff Tina to its rails.

The clothes and the shoe in the photograph had been removed, and there was a large dark stain on the carpet where Dudley Jackson's body had been lying.

With some difficulty Megan stepped onto another duckboard, the bulky overalls limiting her movement. She drew level with a dressing table and carefully opened the top drawer. Inside was an assortment of neatly folded underwear. Something hard and shiny stuck out from beneath the pile and Megan pulled back the clothes to see what it was.

The smiling faces of Dudley and Tina Jackson looked up at her. It was a wedding photograph, hidden from view in the same way that Megan had hidden hers.

Charlotte McGahy had been right about her sister. She was

beautiful. She reminded Megan of Penelope Cruz. She had that same slightly vulnerable look about her.

'What have you found? Anything interesting?' Leverton appeared round the doorway, stepping across the boards with apparent ease.

'No – just a wedding photo. Any news on the friend?'

'She was with her on the soup run. Says Tina drove herself home from the place they cook it.'

'Nothing suspicious?'

'Not that she remembers. Says it was a quiet night.'

'Where are they based?'

'It's a house in Cheddar Road. Owned by the woman who set up the charity. It's a women-only thing.'

'And this Gail didn't have any other ideas? No boyfriend we don't know about?'

'No.' Leverton frowned. 'We're going to have to hold a press conference soon: someone's leaked the pathologist's report to the papers. Any chance of you coming up with something by, say, lunchtime tomorrow?'

Megan paused before answering. A press conference? Was this Leverton's idea? It couldn't be. There was no way he would go public on his suspicions if there was any suggestion of police corruption. Either he was playing some game Megan couldn't fathom or someone else had been responsible for the leak.

'I'll see what I can do.' She moved on. 'Let's go over what happened here step by step; once I've got all the crime scene evidence I can build up a more detailed description of this killer before I start working on a profile of the guy who murdered Donna.'

'Okay, this is what the SOCOs have come up with so far: No signs of a break-in – windows all closed and intact and both doors locked; a partial footprint in blood on the landing which doesn't match any footwear belonging to either Dudley or Tina Jackson; a clear footprint of the same shoe in earth next to the path leading from the back door. The toe section was facing away from the house.'

'So it sounds like he let himself out the back way?'

'Yes.'

'Okay,' Megan said. 'This is what I think might have happened. She gets back from the soup run and goes upstairs to get changed – hence the new outfit we found on the bedroom floor. He's followed her home and is watching the house. Perhaps he catches a glimpse of her through the bedroom curtains and gets even more turned on. He rings the bell and comes up with some hard luck story. Maybe he tells her his car's broken down and asks to use her phone. Anyway he gets into the house.' She peered round the door. 'Is there a downstairs loo?'

'No. Why?'

'Because he had to have some way of getting her upstairs. If he'd dragged her up kicking and screaming there'd be evidence. Scratches or scuff marks on the wallpaper, even traces of blood.'

Megan stepped out on to the landing. 'He uses the phone and then asks if he can use the loo. She shows him where it is.' Megan waved her arm towards the blue bathroom door. 'Instead of going in, he grabs her and shoves her into the bedroom, throws her down on the bed. He flips her over and grabs both her wrists. He's got the handcuffs or wire or whatever in his pocket and he restrains her by looping it round the bedrails and then round her wrists. He penetrates her anally and strangles her. When he's finished he undoes her wrists and he's about to leave when the nutty husband arrives.'

Leverton rubbed his chin. 'How would Dudley have got in? Tina had had the locks changed and it was all locked up when my lads turned up because they had to break the front door down to get in.'

'She might have left the door on the latch when she let AB in. She wouldn't have been expecting him to stay more than a couple of minutes.'

Leverton nodded.

'Let's assume Dudley drops the latch behind him because he doesn't want Tina running out of the door. He prowls round the house trying to find out which room she's in. AB hears someone coming. Whoever it is, he's got to get rid of them. He hides behind the door and waits.'

Megan stepped back into the bedroom. 'There's a mirror on the opposite wall so he can see Dudley before he gets into the room. He grabs him from behind and knocks the gun out of his hand. Then he gets him on the floor and shoots him in the mouth. He blasts Tina in the back to make it look like Dudley did it.

'He gets out as quickly as he can because he realises people will have heard the shots. He goes out the back door, which locks automatically unless it's been left on the latch. He goes through the back yard into the alley behind the houses and he's away without any of the neighbours seeing him.'

'Why did he bother to shoot Tina?' said Leverton.

'It's all part of the game,' Megan said, her voice even.

'What do you mean?'

Oh come on, Martin, she thought, you're taking this independent, unbiased viewpoint thing a bit far, aren't you? If you think I'm going to come straight out and say it's a copper, you can think again.

'What I mean,' she said, 'is that he's deliberately led you all up the garden path because he enjoys it. When the media reported it as a domestic murder followed by a suicide he'd have been revelling in the fact that he'd misled the press, the police – everyone.'

'What makes you think that?'

'Well, as I said before, the way Natalie and Tina were

killed suggests a man who wants revenge for some traumatic event in his life. Often killers like this feel that the world in general has let them down. Any women they attack are vehicles for the rage they feel inside, but fooling the police and the public would give this kind of killer even greater satisfaction.'

'Like sticking two fingers up at society, you mean?'

'Exactly. Oh, and there's something else you should ask Tina's sister.'

'What's that?'

'Trophies – you know how some serial killers like to take mementoes of their victims?'

'Like clothing or body parts, you mean?'

'Yes; we know Tina's body wasn't mutilated in any way but do we know if the killer took anything she was wearing?'

'We found pants, tights, underskirt, dress and shoes on the floor, so I'm pretty sure he didn't take any of her clothes.'

'What about jewellery?'

Leverton fished a piece of paper out of the file in his hand. 'According to the SOCOs she was wearing two rings on her right hand and a pair of gold stud earrings.'

'So no necklace or bracelets?'

'No – nothing else.'

'I think that if she was dressed up for a special night out there's a good chance she'd be wearing more jewellery than that.'

'You're right. And I suppose Charlotte would know if anything was missing from Tina's jewellery box – they seemed pretty close.'

Megan nodded. Like everything else it was a long shot, but if the killer had taken something distinctive and it was described at the press conference there was a chance someone who recognised it might come forward.

It wasn't unknown for serial murderers to give trinkets taken from their victims to their wives or children as presents.

It gave them the same sort of kick as revisiting the scene of the crime or seeing the murder reported on TV.

She wondered what Leverton would do with this piece of information. She realised now that he was unsure about the identity of Tina Jackson's killer. Yesterday in his office Megan had got the impression that he suspected someone in his own force – someone in particular – of being involved in the prostitute murders. But the Jackson case seemed to have shaken his confidence. What was going on in his mind? Had it suddenly occurred to him that he might have got it all wrong?

She opened her bag, looking for her car keys, and caught sight of the bundle of pastel envelopes she had taken from Delva.

'Martin,' she began, 'it's my turn to ask you a favour.' As soon as the words were out she regretted them. She hated the thought of being beholden to him.

Leverton raised his eyebrows.

'It's about Delva Lobelo – the newsreader at BTV. She's been getting some very unpleasant mail.' Her teeth clenched, she handed him one of the letters.

He took it out of the envelope, looked at the picture of the squatting woman and grunted. Megan saw the hint of a smile on his face.

'This is serious. She's had dozens of these.'

He shrugged. 'There's a lot of strange people out there and a lot of them watch television.'

Megan felt heat rising from her neck to her face.

'From what's in the letters I think it's probably someone she works with.' She looked him in the eye. 'I've come across too many cases like this before, Martin. You might think it's harmless, but I know what it can lead to.'

He gave a heavy sigh. 'All right, all right. I'll send a uniform round there tomorrow.'

'She's already been to your lot and they weren't interested.'

'Well, the sight of a boy in blue in the building might do the trick if it's a work colleague.'

She frowned. He was being condescending.

'Happy now?'

She bit her tongue, realising there wasn't much else she could do.

When Megan got home she flicked on the hall light and hung up her coat. As she did so something caught her eye. On the shelf above the hall radiator was a display of shells brought back from Borth. She had arranged them in three groups, each with a piece of driftwood behind it. But someone had re-arranged them: the shells were all together at one end of the shelf and the three pieces of driftwood at the other.

Had Emily done it? Megan frowned. It was more than a week since her niece's last visit. Surely she would have noticed before now? She hastily re-arranged the shells and the wood, feeling slightly uneasy. Tony was the only other person with a key. Had he been sneaking around while she was at work? She couldn't imagine why. He'd cleared out his stuff months ago. Perhaps it was time to get the locks changed. The image of Tina Jackson on the mortuary slab leapt into her mind and she shuddered.

Delva Lobelo hadn't enjoyed her supper very much. Whenever she was on a late shift she had to decide between venturing into the city centre to eat in a restaurant or going to the BTV canteen.

Either way she usually ended up eating alone, so it was a straight choice between good food eaten in public or lousy food eaten in private. She usually went to the canteen because it was less hassle. Being stared at by curious members of the public made her feel like an animal in a zoo.

Tonight the canteen menu had plumbed new depths. The

top layer of the vegetable lasagna would not have looked out of place wrapped around the wheel of a mountain bike and the cheesecake tasted like toothpaste.

Delva took the lift back up to the newsroom. Her stomach felt heavy and her waistband was uncomfortably tight. It had been a nightmare of a day and she found herself wishing away the next three hours, longing for home and bed.

Before she reached her desk she saw something on it that made her feel sick. It was another pastel-coloured envelope. Someone must have put it there while she was in the canteen. She spun round, her eyes scanning the rows of empty desks. The only other person in the room was the night sub. Delva strode across to the other woman's desk.

'Jane – did you put this on my desk?'

'No – what is it? Not another pervy letter?'

'Looks like it.' Delva's eyes were blazing as she ripped it open. 'Oh my God . . . look at this!'

'Bloody hell, Delva, that's appalling. I mean, this is something else, isn't it? That's a Polaroid photograph – not something he's cut out of a magazine.'

'Did you see anyone come in here while I was in the canteen?'

'No. I nipped out for a sandwich but I was only gone ten minutes or so.'

Delva marched down the stairs to the front desk.

'Have you let anyone other than staff into the building over the past hour?'

The security guard was a scrawny, elderly man and Delva towered over him. Her abrupt manner took him by surprise and he stared blankly at her for a moment before glancing at the visitors book in front of him.

'Er, no. Not since twenty-five to seven.'

'Who came in then?'

'A guest for the programme: Stuart Booth. You know – you interviewed him about the turkey rustlers.'

Delva sighed impatiently. 'I know who he is. Look, is your boss still in the building?'

'Er, I shouldn't think so, no. Shall I check for you?'

Delva took a deep breath, trying not to lose her temper. 'Yes, if it's not too much trouble.' She barked out the words and the man fumbled with his walkie-talkie, turning his face from her withering gaze.

'Hello, Frank? Has Dave Simon gone home?' The walkie-talkie squawked a reply and the guard turned to Delva apologetically. 'I'm sorry, he's gone. But you can phone him if it's something urgent. His number's on the wall in back security – okay?'

'Thanks.' Delva spat out the word between clenched teeth, covering the distance between the front desk and the back entrance to the building in a matter of seconds. This so-called head of security was going to get a roasting.

As she approached the security booth she could see that the door was slightly ajar. Two men were sitting inside, leering and sniggering at something in a newspaper. She slowed down, creeping softly as a cat along the corridor. The newspaper's masthead had given them away. From the doorway Delva saw what they were looking at before they saw her.

She marched into the booth and snatched the phone off the wall, the two men jumping from their seats in bewilderment.

'What's the matter, Miss Lobelo?' The older one put a hand on her arm but she shrugged it off.

Ten minutes later the head of security arrived.

'What's the problem, Miss Lobelo?' David Simon looked from Delva to the guards with a look of concern.

'I'll tell you what the problem is,' Delva blazed. 'I came down here to tell these prats I've had another sick letter and what were they doing?' She snatched the newspaper from the table and thrust it in his face. 'See? Just the sort of filth that sets off the bloody perverts in the first place!'

'Yes, I see.' David Simon glowered at the guards. He screwed the newspaper into a tight ball and tossed it into the bin. 'I can only apologise and promise you that it won't happen again. Will it, lads?' He gave them a stern look.

The men looked at him sheepishly. 'No, Mr Simon.'

'Now, what about this letter?' He looked at Delva. 'Where did you find it?'

She explained what had happened.

'What did it say?'

Delva hesitated, unwilling to go into a detailed description of the contents in front of the two guards.

'It was a very disturbing photograph,' she said. 'Of a woman.'

Simon nodded. 'Similar to the sort of thing he's sent before?'

'Well, similar, yes – but much worse.'

'I think one of your colleagues is playing a practical joke, Miss Lobelo. A very sick joke, granted, but I don't think you should let it get to you.'

'Is that all you can say?' Delva turned on him. 'How would you like it if your wife or girlfriend or whatever was getting stuff like this in the post'

'I understand how you must be feeling, believe me.'

'I doubt that!'

'Look, I'll see if we can get a CCTV camera set up in the newsroom. That should put a stop to it.'

'And how long will that take?'

'If we get the okay we could get it installed by the New Year.'

Bloody great, Delva thought. She was going to have to call Megan.

Chapter 7

Megan poured herself a large whisky and took it up to the bathroom. All evening she had been feeling jumpy. It wasn't just the bodies and the photographs she'd seen. It was those shells. Ridiculous, she thought. It had to have been Emily. It was just the kind of thing she would do. But the feeling of unease refused to go away.

While she waited for the bath to fill up, she lit the candles in the wrought-iron candelabra on the mantelpiece. Then she started picking at the wallpaper by the window. The room needed redecorating and she was planning to get it done after Christmas. But there was a loose bit of border paper sticking out and it had been annoying her for ages. She had tried pasting it down but the condensation kept making it come loose again. As she pulled it a whole strip of wallpaper came away with it. The wall underneath was a mottled terracotta colour: a mixture of old, painted plaster and dried-up wallpaper paste. In the candlelight the bare wall had a certain charm.

She tugged at another piece, thinking about the profiles she'd been working on. AB just had to have a police connection. Whoever killed Tina had known too much about forensics. A con with that much knowledge would be on file, for sure. So who, then? She thought about Rob Donalsen. Leverton already had him down as bent. Could it be him? He certainly didn't fit the profile.

She had ripped off nearly all the paper on one wall when

she realised the bath was on the verge of overflowing. She put her hand in to pull out the plug. The water was luke-warm because the hot had run out.

'Damn!' she said, pulling her bathrobe back on.

There was no point waiting for the water to heat up again. She might as well go straight to bed.

She snapped on the light. Turning to reach a bottle of cleanser from the cupboard, she caught sight of the stripped wall. It looked a complete mess. The romantic ambience of a faded Tuscan farmhouse had given way to something reminiscent of a vandalised council flat. Thank goodness there was no-one but family visiting her for Christmas.

She was in the middle of brushing her teeth when the phone rang. She spat hurriedly and wiped her mouth on the back of her hand as she grabbed it from the floor.

'Megan, it's Neil.' He sounded out of breath.

'What's the matter?'

'We've had to take Joe to hospital.'

'Oh my God! What's happened?'

'Don't worry, he's okay. He started throwing up every-where. It's called projectile vomiting or something. They're going to have to operate but it's not serious.'

'Are you sure?'

'Yes. The doctor says that's why he's been screaming all the time. The operation should put it right.'

'Where's Emily?'

'At the hospital with Ceri – I'm going up there now to fetch her back. Ceri's going to stay the night with Joe. They're doing the operation first thing in the morning.'

'Do you want me to come over?'

'No, it's okay. There's nothing you can do at the hospital – they only allow parents to stay – and I can cope with Emily. I've got tomorrow and Thursday off.'

'Are you sure? I mean if you wanted to stay at the hospital as well I could have Emily.'

'No. Thanks for the offer, but they wouldn't let both of us stay. Listen, I'll phone you in the morning as soon as I hear from Ceri, okay?'

He put the phone down, obviously in a rush to get to the hospital. Megan stood for a moment staring at the bath as the last of the water gurgled into the plughole. She shivered and ran to jump into bed.

Sitting hunched under the covers she felt frustrated and useless. Her nephew's tiny body, only two months old, was about to go under the knife. She wished she could be with Ceri to help her through it. As if she hadn't got enough on her plate already.

Megan was just drifting off to sleep when the phone rang again.

'Megan?' It was almost a whisper.

'Delva, what is it? What's happened?'

'I'm really sorry to phone you so late but I've had this awful photograph . . .' Delva paused and Megan heard her take a breath, as if she was trying to stop herself from crying.

'What photograph? Has he sent you another of those magazine cuttings?'

'No. This is a real photograph: one he's taken himself, I mean, and it was delivered by hand. There's this poor girl lying on a bed and she looks drugged or unconscious or something. I think the police ought to see it but I wanted you to look at it first.'

'Of course I will.' A host of possibilities ran through Megan's mind. Delva's voice sounded so different: like someone on the verge of a breakdown. There was a note of paranoia in that barely audible whispering. Megan wondered if this photograph could really be any more disturbing than the cuttings she had seen in Delva's office.

'Where are you now?'

'I'm at home.'

'I'll come over.'

Megan had never seen Delva without make-up. Usually her brown, almond-shaped eyes were expertly outlined with black kohl pencil, the lids and brows highlighted with shimmering ochre or terracotta shadow.

But now her face was bare. There were dark hollows under her eyes and although she was several inches taller than Megan she seemed to have shrunk. All the buoyancy and sparkle that made her such a natural on TV had disappeared. She stood shivering in the doorway, fragile as the leaf skeletons frozen to the path beneath Megan's feet.

'Come in.'

Megan went ahead of her into the living room, glad to see a fire blazing in the marble-framed hearth. Two vast honey-coloured sofas stood either side of the fireplace. On the coffee table between them was a bowl of fruit, a pink envelope propped against it.

'Have you shown this to anyone else?' Megan picked up the envelope with her gloved hand, prising out the flap as carefully as she could.

'Er, yes – does it matter?' Delva looked worried and confused as she sank down onto one of the sofas.

'Only if it's been touched. There may be fingerprints, you see: just because he hasn't left any up to now doesn't mean we can rule it out.'

'Oh . . . I never thought of that.' Delva looked as if she might burst into tears. 'I, er, I showed it to Jane. She was the late night sub in the newsroom. She didn't actually touch it, though, I don't think. I can't really remember . . .'

'Anyone else?' Megan sat down next to Delva on the sofa, sliding the photograph gently out of the envelope.

Before Delva could reply, Megan gasped.

'It's shocking, isn't it?' Delva glanced at the photograph and quickly looked away. But she was unaware of exactly what about the photograph had made Megan catch her breath.

It showed a woman, slim and of mixed race, lying on a bed. The naked top half of her body and her head almost filled the frame. There was a tattoo in the shape of a butterfly above her left breast and her head was slumped to one side, wisps of long, black hair concealing most of her face. But it was the arms that had startled Megan. They were stretched out above the woman's head, the forearms crossed, and there was something grey and shiny in the top left-hand corner of the photograph at the point where the woman's wrists would have been. The camera had been too close to its subject to get the wrists in, but Megan's instant impression was of a woman handcuffed to a bed.

'You – you don't think she could be dead, do you?' Delva's voice trembled.

'I don't know. I think the police need to see this as soon as possible.' Megan had no intention of upsetting Delva even more by telling her what was going through her mind. 'Apart from the woman you were working with last night, does anyone else know about this?'

'Yes.' Delva's face tensed as she spoke. 'I was furious when I found it on my desk. I'd just come up from the canteen and I couldn't bear to think that this pervert could actually get right into the newsroom without being seen. I had a go at the security people about it.'

'What did they say?'

'It was a complete farce. I caught a couple of them drooling over a Page Three girl. They didn't hear me coming and they tried to cover it up, but it was too late – I'd already seen it. I was so angry I called their boss. He was a bit more human. Gave them a bollocking and promised it wouldn't happen again. But I don't think he took the letter seriously.' She pursed her lips. 'He said it must be one of my colleagues playing a practical joke. All he could offer was the possibility of putting a CCTV camera in the newsroom – but not until New Year.'

'Big deal. What did you say?'

'Not a lot. I had to read the 10.30 bulletin so I tried to calm myself down and finish my shift.'

Megan slid the photograph back into the envelope. 'These security men – did they actually handle the photograph?'

'No. I didn't even show it to them. I was going to; I mean I had the envelope in my hand, but when I saw them leering at that newspaper it put me right off. When the boss arrived I just told him I'd had another sick letter and then I started off on this rant about pornography.'

'So the only prints on it are likely to be yours and possibly your female colleague's?'

'Yes. I can check with Jane whether she actually touched it. She's on with me again tomorrow.'

'Are you sure you're up to working at the moment? This must have really shaken you up.'

'Yes, I'll be fine, honestly. I'm better off going to work – it takes my mind off things.'

'But what if you get another one?'

'I'll phone you straight away – if that's okay?'

'Of course it's okay. This is much more serious than some sick fan telling you what he'd like you to do to him. Whoever took this photograph has probably committed a serious offence.'

Megan paused, hoping that Delva would fail to put two and two together. She wasn't sure what she was going to say if Delva raised the possibility of a connection between the woman in the photograph and the murders of Donna, Natalie and Tina.

Whatever Delva was thinking she remained silent as Megan rose to leave.

'I'll take this to Detective Superintendent Leverton,' Megan said. 'I mentioned the letters to him. I'll ask him to get it analysed for prints.'

Yes, she thought grimly, he wasn't the slightest bit interested, but I think he will be now. She wondered if Delva realised just how much she was playing the whole thing down. Anyone who worked in a newsroom was bound to know enough about the murders by now to make a connection with a photograph like that. Perhaps she was just too shaken to put her suspicions into words.

Megan slipped the envelope into a clear plastic wallet she had bought with her and put the package into her bag.

Past experience indicated that the search for fingerprints would be a waste of time, but when she had been looking at the photograph on the sofa the flickering firelight had drawn her attention to something else that marred its shiny surface. Closer inspection had revealed a tiny, white, crystalline blob in the bottom right hand corner. Unless Megan was very much mistaken, that blob was going to be Martin Leverton's most important piece of evidence to date.

'Morning Doctor Rhys!'

Eric's booming voice was all Megan needed. She nodded at him and hurried past the porter's lodge, stifling a yawn. She'd only had four hours' sleep. Leverton wasn't answering his mobile. No one at the station seemed to know where he was.

She got coffee before she even looked at her post. There were three Christmas cards on the top of the pile of internal mail in her pigeonhole. As she tucked them under her arm she couldn't help noticing Patrick's mailbox. It was next to hers in the row and was stuffed to capacity with envelopes of all sizes and colours.

Megan found herself wondering who they could be from. Most of the students had sent their Christmas cards to the staff last week when they broke up for the holiday. Perhaps they were from people in Holland – but why would they send them here rather than his home address?

She resisted the temptation to delve into the pile to look at stamps and postmarks. Why on earth should it matter who Patrick was getting cards from?

The minute she had sat down at her desk there was a knock on the door.

'Can I come in for a minute? I'm here for my gory details. Fair exchange for that packet of Maltesers, wouldn't you say?' Patrick's eyes twinkled and the frown disappeared from Megan's face.

'Sorry, I've got to go out in a minute.' She hesitated, glad to see him.

He smiled. 'I was hoping you'd help me celebrate?'

Megan stared at his downcast eyes, a puzzled smile on her face. 'What do you mean?'

'It's my birthday. Would you like to come out for a meal with me tonight?' Megan was amazed to see that he was actually blushing. 'Don't worry if you can't. I know it's short notice. You're probably going somewhere already. Christmas party or something . . .'

'Oh. I, er . . .'

'It's okay,' he cut in. 'I thought the answer would probably be no.'

'No! I mean, I wasn't planning anything apart from writing a few dozen overdue Christmas cards. I'm just amazed that you're asking me.'

'Why?'

'Well, I would have thought you'd be out partying with the students.'

'You're joking! I haven't got the stamina for all-night raves any more!'

'Taking one of them out for dinner, then.'

'What on earth would I talk to a student about for a whole evening?' He grinned and put his mug on the desk. 'All they're interested in is sex and drugs.'

Megan nearly choked on her coffee. 'What?'

'They keep asking me about what sort of things you can buy in the sex shops in Amsterdam and whether policemen smoke cannabis in cafés – that sort of thing.'

'Whereas I, by contrast, am only interested in sex and violence.' Megan's smile widened. 'Are you sure you want me for a dinner companion?'

'As long as you promise not to mention 3-speed vibrators or Lebanese Gold.'

Megan laughed, shaking her head. 'Where were you thinking of eating?'

'One of the balti places in Sparkhill – is that okay?'

'Great. I'll pick you up if you like. Then you don't have to worry about driving.'

'Are you sure?'

'Yes. It's a bit sad if you can't have a few drinks on your birthday.'

'We could always get a taxi.'

'No, it's okay. I don't drink much these days anyway.' It wasn't a lie: more of a convenient excuse. Offering to drive was her way of being in control, but she didn't want Patrick to know that. Changing the subject before he could pursue the idea of a taxi she asked him what he thought of the Jackson case.

'Well, I'm intrigued by this faked suicide,' he replied. 'If you hadn't already mentioned this business of corruption I'd have guessed at it being an ex-policeman.'

'Why?'

'Well anyone who plays games with the police has to know a certain amount about the way they operate. You say this guy has never been fingerprinted or had a blood or saliva sample taken?'

'That's right.'

'So he probably didn't gain his knowledge simply from

being arrested a few times, which means he must have come in contact with the police in some other context. Whatever it was, it's left him with a grudge against them.'

'That's exactly what I thought. I mean, it all points to either a bent copper or an ex-copper. I got the distinct impression last night that Martin Leverton had been knocked off balance by this latest case. It's turned into something very different from a couple of dead prostitutes and I think he's far less confident than he was yesterday morning.'

'What's he like, this Leverton?' Patrick asked, leaning back in his chair. 'Has he had much to do with our department in the past?'

'Not really, no. I first met him a couple of years ago on a local rape inquiry. He seemed very nice – you know, enlightened approach to rape victims and all that.' She paused, her good mood fading. 'But since then I've only really had dealings with him when I've been requesting access to police records, or bringing him here as a guest lecturer. We haven't worked on any actual cases together.'

'What made you think he was trying to use you to get someone in his force?'

'Well, it was several things, really. First of all, I couldn't work out why they'd call in a profiler for two dead hookers. Secondly, I know Martin Leverton doesn't rate profiling. He thinks psychology is just common sense and that any detective worth his salt shouldn't need an academic to tell him where to start looking.'

'Did he say that?'

'Oh no, not in so many words. I can just tell by the things he's said at conferences. He's always been incredibly polite to my face, but I'm sure he doesn't rate me for anything other than the academic research this department produces.'

Megan sipped her coffee and gazed out of the window. Tiny flakes of snow had dusted the cars like icing sugar. Grey, pot-bellied clouds hung in the sky like sieves poised to shake. 'There's another thing he said yesterday that made me suspicious of his motives.'

'What?' Patrick put his empty mug on the desk and glanced across at Megan. She was still staring out of the window.

'He made a point of bringing two Vice Squad officers in to speak to me about the murdered prostitutes. They didn't really tell me anything he couldn't have told me himself, and after they'd gone he said they were both being moved to other jobs in the New Year. He as good as told me that one of them – the sergeant – was getting the push because he'd been messing about with some of the women on his beat.'

'Sounds a bit heavy-handed,' Patrick said. 'If that's the bloke he suspects, why would he want to make it so obvious?'

'Just what I thought,' Megan replied, swinging her chair round to face Patrick. 'It almost makes me think it's some kind of double bluff. My best guess is that Leverton thought a pimp had murdered Donna Fieldhouse and Natalie Bailey, and someone in the Vice Squad – probably this Rob Donalsen – knew but was being blackmailed by the pimp to keep quiet.'

'And he called you in to put the frighteners on the guy?'

'Something like that, yes. The stupid thing is that on the evidence of the prostitute murders alone I wouldn't necessarily have pinpointed a police officer as a suspect; it was the Jackson case that suggested a police connection, which makes Leverton's attitude even more strange.'

'Is he still after a profile?'

'Yes. They're holding a press conference.' She looked at her watch. 'In about half an hour.'

Patrick looked at her incredulously. 'A press conference? Whose idea was that?'

'Good question. According to Leverton, someone leaked

the pathologist's report on the Jackson case to the papers. They've got to say something, so muggins here has been asked to come up with the goods.'

'So what are you going to give him?'

'Well, I've got three profiles – one for the press and two others for Leverton's own private consumption.' She handed him a sheaf of papers and he read them as she finished her coffee.

'You think the one who killed Donna Fieldhouse could be a local pimp. So what's the connection between him and the other guy?'

'I think the AB guy is dominating the O character in some way. He has some sort of hold on him because I don't think O is a true serial killer. Donna Fieldhouse looked like the victim of a domestic argument that went too far. I don't think O would necessarily have killed again if it hadn't been for the involvement of this other guy.'

'You think he's blackmailing the O man?'

'Could be, if he knew about Donna's death before Natalie was killed.'

'But that policeman – the Vice Squad sergeant you mentioned – he couldn't blackmail a pimp if the pimp knew he was bent, could he?'

'No, probably not.' Megan put her empty mug down on the desk, her eyes narrowing as she stared at a patch of sea in the photo on her wall. 'But I never said I agreed with Leverton, did I? I do think the AB killer has some sort of police connection, but he could just be a regular punter who knows O well and happened to be around when Donna was murdered. On the other hand he could be a drug dealer who supplies the O man. We know Donna was a crack addict and Natalie had traces of it in her blood. Suppose O is on it too and he owes the supplier money?'

Patrick frowned, weighing up the odds of each of these possibilities being likely.

'What I do know,' Megan looked at the bundle of papers in Patrick's hand, 'is that I've left nearly as much out of those profiles as I've put in.'

'What do you mean?'

She shrugged. 'I can't get anywhere near the truth while Leverton's being so cagey, so I'm about to play him at his own game.' She looked at him, wondering if she could trust him. God, she thought, you've just agreed to go for dinner with the guy – you're getting paranoid. 'Something happened last night.' She told him about Delva's photograph. 'I might be wrong, but it looked so like what happened to Natalie and Tina.'

'You think the AB man has been sending Delva these sick letters?'

'No. Not AB. O.'

'O? The pimp?'

'Sounds crazy, doesn't it? That's why I'm not telling Leverton what I really think. It can't be AB because he's into domination – not *being* dominated, as all Delva's other letters suggest. I'm sure there's a connection but I haven't worked it out yet. I need to know if that stain on the photo is semen, and if so, what the blood group is.'

'And if it's O?'

'Get a DNA test done. See if it matches up with the swabs from Donna Fieldhouse.'

Patrick nodded slowly.

Megan glanced at her watch. 'I'm going to have to go,' she said. 'I've got to catch Leverton when he comes out of the press conference.'

'I'll walk you to your car.' Patrick held the door as she grabbed her coat. 'This Vice Squad sergeant – what's his name again?'

'Rob Donalsen.'

'Is there any chance he could be the AB killer?'

'A chance, yes – not very probable, though.'

'Why not?'

'His behaviour. Couldn't charm his way into a paper bag, let alone a woman's house.'

Patrick laughed. 'Do you think that's what's got Leverton confused?'

'Probably, yes. What intrigues me, though, is this blood group thing.' She pushed open the plate glass doors. Powdery snow crunched under their feet as they walked towards the car park. 'Up until yesterday Leverton was focusing on the type O samples found on Donna and Natalie, but he now knows that Tina's killer has AB type blood. If he suspects Donalsen, he could easily get hold of his medical records and check out his blood group. In fact, when I think about it, he could have checked him out long before the post mortem on Tina Jackson.'

'How?'

'Well, Leverton said they'd found a fingerprint on Natalie Bailey's body, but it didn't match anything on file – he could easily have checked to see if it matched Donalsen's. The thing is, he had that forensic report on Natalie before he called me in on the case.'

'So the print couldn't have been Donalsen's, could it?' Patrick said. 'Otherwise why would he have bothered calling you in?'

'Exactly,' Megan replied. 'So what the hell's he playing at?'

Megan took out her car keys. As she opened the door her mobile rang out. 'Hello? Neil! How did it go? Oh, that's great news!'

Patrick raised his hand in a brief farewell. Megan nodded back, too distracted to notice that he had walked off with the profiles in his hand.

Chapter 8

The foyer of police headquarters was milling with photo-graphers, cameramen and journalists when Megan arrived. The press conference had just ended and they were jostling each other in their rush to file the latest news.

A television reporter was filming a piece to camera outside the main doors. He looked vaguely familiar and Megan spotted the BTV logo on the side of the camera. She pulled the soft woollen hood of her coat closer to her face, not wanting to be recognised.

Leverton had seemed anxious not to reveal her involve-ment to the press. She thought again of his remarks about her resemblance to Tina Jackson. Was this attempt to keep her out of the limelight some misguided act of chivalry on his part? She somehow doubted it, suspecting that the real reason had more to do with Leverton's self-interest.

She wondered if he had had to field any difficult questions about the murder of Donna Fieldhouse. The media had never been informed of the forensic link between her body and Natalie Bailey's. Leverton's strategy for the press conference was simply to tell them that Tina and Dudley Jackson had been murdered by a third party. If asked about a link with Natalie Bailey he would merely say that the police were not ruling it out.

She settled down to wait in Leverton's office, wondering how he would react to the photograph in her bag.

'Hello Megan. What's happened?' He breezed into the

room, looking totally unfazed by the interrogation he had no doubt received at the press conference.

'There's something here I think you should see.' Megan laid the plastic wallet on the desk. 'Don't open it yet: if it's what I think it is, it'll need to go to the forensic lab.'

'I'll get someone up here.' Leverton reached for the phone. 'Are you going to tell me what it is – the suspense is killing me!'

'Sorry!' Megan smiled. She waited while he spoke to his secretary and when he put the phone down she began describing her visit to Delva and the photograph inside the envelope.

He stared at her. 'Delva Lobelo's pervert is our AB killer?'

She hesitated, not wanting to answer directly. 'The first thing that made me link this pervert to Tina Jackson's killer was the way the woman in the photo was lying,' she said. 'The arms were twisted in a really unnatural way: as if someone had handcuffed her to the bed while she was lying on her front, then turned her over onto her back. Then I noticed this tiny stain in the corner of the picture. I didn't say anything to Delva, obviously, but I'm almost certain it's semen.'

Megan flipped the plastic wallet over, revealing the front of the envelope. 'This was hand-delivered. It's got her name and BTV's address on but there's no stamp or postmark. Like I said before, looks like it's someone who works there.'

Leverton pulled the plastic wallet towards him, peering at the writing on the envelope.

'The thing is,' Megan went on, 'no one can get in or out of that building without being logged by the guards on the front or back desks. Unless they've got an appointment with someone they won't get any further than that.'

Leverton's gaze flicked from the envelope to Megan's eyes, a look of amazement on his face. 'So you think that the guy who killed Tina Jackson works at BTV?'

She hesitated. She needed to play this very carefully. 'Well, I'd certainly say there was a connection, wouldn't you?'

Before he could reply there was a knock at the door. A uniformed officer delivered gloves, tweezers and an official scenes-of-crime evidence bag. Leverton donned the gloves and picked up the tweezers. He opened the wallet and prised out the envelope.

Megan studied his face as he drew the photograph from the envelope with the tweezers.

'My God!' Leverton shook his head as he took in the image of the naked woman on the bed. 'You're right! He's twisted her round for the photograph, hasn't he?'

'There's no other explanation for it.'

'Not that I can think of.' He moved the image closer to his face. 'That's part of the handcuffs!'

'Could be, couldn't it?'

'Where's this semen trace you spotted?' Megan stood up and walked round to Leverton's chair. Leaning over his shoulder she pointed to the small blob in the bottom right-hand corner. Leverton moved the photo slightly, catching the light.

'Oh yes! I see what you mean!' He turned it over, angling the matt white side of the photo to the light with the tweezers. 'Look at that!' Suddenly Megan could see an even larger patch of the same crystalline substance she had spotted on the image of the woman.

'Right!' Leverton slid the photograph back into the envelope. 'We need to get this DNA-tested as quickly as possible. In the meantime, though, I need to speak to Miss Lobelo. Does anyone at BTV know she's given you this photo?'

'I shouldn't think so. Why?'

'Well if the bloke who's been sending her these letters really is our AB man we need to tread very carefully. We certainly don't want him to know the police have been called in.'

Megan nodded. 'As far as I know she hasn't told anyone about my involvement. I suppose quite a few people know that we've been working together on a documentary but there's no reason why anyone should think she's talked to me about the letters.' She paused, frowning.

'What?'

'That uniformed officer you said you were going to send round – better call him off.'

'Oh, right.' Leverton shifted in his seat.

Bastard, Megan thought, he's done sod all about it.

'Could you give Miss Lobelo a bell now and ask if I can call in on her as soon as she gets home?' He pushed the phone across the desk.

Yes, sir – three bags full, sir. Megan dialed the BTV switchboard. She could hear the hubbub of the newsroom as the woman on reception put her through.

'Delva, it's Megan. Can you talk without being overheard?'

Delva paused for a moment before replying. 'No, not really. Hang on a minute . . .'

Megan waited while she transferred the call to another room. Delva sounded out of breath when she picked up the phone.

'Sorry about that. I had to put it through to one of the editing suites – it's the only place I know I won't be disturbed. What's happened?'

'Detective Superintendent Leverton wants to talk to you about the letters but it's important that nobody at BTV knows the police are involved. When will you be home?'

'I don't finish until 10.45 tonight, but I might be able to nip out for half an hour after the teatime news.'

'So what time would you get home – about 7.30?'

Megan looked across at Leverton, who nodded.

'Yes. Is that okay?' The relief in Delva's voice was obvious. Poor thing, Megan thought. It's taken something of this magnitude to get the police to take her seriously. Before she could reply, Delva spoke again. 'Megan, there's something else. I was about to phone you.'

'Not another photo?' Megan exchanged glances with Leverton.

'No, it's a letter. He wants to meet me.'

'What!'

Delva's voice was shaking again as she spoke. 'He's asking me to meet him at a wine bar in town tomorrow night.'

Leverton was looking quizzically at Megan and she scribbled the gist of what Delva had said on his notepad while continuing the conversation. 'Don't worry, Delva. Just bring the letter home with you tonight and the police will work out how to handle it, okay?'

'Well, what do you make of that?' Leverton said as Megan put down the phone.

Megan tried to think, but there were too many possibilities. 'I don't know. It's got to be some kind of trick. I mean, surely he's not stupid enough to actually turn up?'

'I should say the odds are against it. If he was an out-and-out nutter, I'd be pretty optimistic. But this guy's not your run-of-the-mill loony, is he? The kind of bloke who goes to all the trouble of keeping his paws off those letters and photos isn't going to blow it by appearing in public.'

Megan held Leverton's gaze for a split second, wondering what sort of image of the killer was forming in his mind.

'Martin,' she said slowly, 'there's something I need to ask you before we go any further.'

'What is it?' He settled back in his chair.

'In those unofficial profiles I faxed you this morning I made it fairly clear that the AB killer has some sort of connection with the police and I explained why. In the light of this new connection with BTV I'd say the most likely connection is that he's an ex-policeman, possibly someone who's left the force within the past few years. I need access to the medical records to check whether anyone fitting that description has AB type blood.'

She watched Leverton's face, wondering what his reaction would be. He sighed and fingered the corner of the plastic wallet on the desk in front of him.

'Not possible at the moment, I'm afraid, Megan. When I got your profiles this morning, the first thing I did was to access our personnel files. I was planning a search of the entire male workforce – currently-serving officers as well as any who had left within the last five years – but apparently the disc's corrupted. Absolutely zilch on the screen. We've got someone coming in this afternoon to have a look at it.'

'Oh . . .' Megan was knocked off balance. 'Do you think it's been sabotaged?'

'I hope not. I mean, I'm hoping that by this time tomorrow it'll be sorted. As soon as it's up and running again I'll be going through it myself and you're welcome to join me.'

'So in the meantime,' she asked, 'what are you going to do about Delva Lobelo?'

'I'll try to talk her into going to the meeting place just in case.' Leverton caught the look of alarm in Megan's eyes. 'Don't worry, we'll make sure the place is crawling with plain clothes people. Will you be able to come with me tonight when I go and see her?'

Megan said yes automatically. Then she remembered her promise to Patrick.

'What's the matter? Is it a problem?'

'No, I don't think so. It's just that I've arranged to pick up a friend at 8.30. We're going out for a meal. But we won't be at Delva's house long, will we?'

'No. I won't keep her talking more than half an hour. Does she live far away, your friend?'

Megan hesitated before replying. 'It's a he, actually. It's a work colleague who's come over from Holland. He doesn't know many people here . . .' Megan trailed off, wondering why she was attempting to justify her date with Patrick to Martin Leverton.

'Hah! Just my luck! I was going to take you for a drink after we'd finished.' Leverton covered his embarrassment by laughing at himself. She mumbled something about looking in her diary when she got back to the office, but he skillfully changed the subject, asking for Delva Lobelo's address and what time Megan could meet him outside.

As she drove home Megan thought about the corrupted computer disc. It seemed too much of a coincidence that the personnel files should be wiped off on the very day those medical records needed accessing. Was it sabotage, or was Leverton simply lying?

And what about this invitation to go for a drink? What was that in aid of? As far as she knew he was still married to a policewoman who worked in the Crime Prevention Unit. There were no photographs of her in his office, or of any children they might have produced, but that didn't mean they were no longer together. Why, Megan thought to herself, did she get the impression he was being over-friendly?

She tried without success to squeeze her car into the narrow gap between two others parked outside her house. Parking in a street of terraced houses was a constant nightmare, but it was the price she and Tony had been prepared to pay for living in the beautifully-restored Victorian villa with its carved staircase and lofty ceilings.

Over the past few months she had often thought about looking for somewhere smaller. But the idea of moving house was more than she could face. The memories of her life with Tony were too newly-buried to disturb.

Megan wished she could go to sleep and wake up to find

Christmas had come and gone. The only thing that made it bearable was the thought of retreating to the cottage at Borth on Boxing Day. Away from all the fake bonhomie of the festive season she would curl up in front of a log fire on New Year's Eve.

Her brother was talking about joining her but she was rather hoping he would change his mind. Gareth would probably insist on dragging her to the local pub to drink into the early hours with distant relatives of Granny Rhys. Much as she loved him she was determined to avoid his misguided attempts to cheer her up.

As she took off her coat, she glanced at the shells. 'Idiot!' she said aloud, cross with herself for even thinking about it. They were exactly as she had left them. She stood still for a moment, suddenly aware of a noise coming from upstairs. A scraping noise, like fingernails on glass. She crept up the stairs, her heart thumping. It was coming from her bedroom. She pushed open the door and snapped on the light. Nothing. Her bed, still unmade. Yesterday's clothes piled on the chair. Curtains still drawn. Everything as she had left it. She put her hand to her head. Was she going mad? Hearing things? No – there it was again. Behind the curtains. She bounded across the room and threw them open. The window was open and flapping in the wind, the leafless branches of a tree scraping the glass.

Megan pulled it shut and fastened the catch. She was certain she hadn't opened it last night. Not with it being so cold. She shivered. Had she done it in her sleep?

She went to make a hot drink. As she walked into the kitchen she noticed the pile of unwritten Christmas cards sitting accusingly on the table. She looked at the clock. Three hours to go before she was due at Delva's. She made a pact with herself to write as many cards as she could in the next hour-and-a-half and then take a long soak in the bath as a reward.

She sat down at the kitchen table and tried to concentrate on the cards. She wondered how Ceri was getting on at the hospital with Joe, wishing she was allowed to visit them. She hoped Neil would phone soon. She had forgotten to tell him she was going out this evening.

Suddenly, images of Neil flashed unbidden into her mind: Neil taking that photograph; Neil sending those letters. After all, she thought, he once counted a rapist among his friends. What might he be capable of?

'Don't be stupid!' she said aloud. Of course it was stupid. Neil might not be the perfect husband but she had never seen him do anything that could be described as violent. He didn't even believe in smacking children. And yet – a nagging voice inside her head reminded her of the facts: Neil's age: 32; his marriage under considerable strain with the suggestion of an extramarital affair; works at BTV in the same office as Delva Lobelo . . .

She told herself over and over again that it couldn't be him. But the tiny voice tormented her with a litany of names: *Ted Bundy; John Cannan; Jeremy Bamber; Denis Nilsen. . .* All charming, persuasive men, just like Neil Richardson.

Megan took the phone with her when she went upstairs for her bath. Still unable to relax, she lay in the warm, foamy water. When her mobile rang she jumped, sending water surging over the sides of the bath.

'Megan – it's Neil. I just called to tell you how Joe is.'

'Is everything all right?'

'Yes, he's doing fine. I can't talk for long – I've only just got back from the hospital and Emily's starving. I'm going to have to feed her before I do anything else.'

'Oh, yes, of course you must. Listen, I've got to go out later. Will you call me in the morning?'

'Yes, of course. Have a good night!'

Megan put the phone down with a sense of shame. How

could she have thought ill of Neil while he was rushing backwards and forwards from the hospital and doing his level best to care for his daughter single-handed?

However fickle his interest in the children had been in the past, Megan reflected, he certainly seemed to be making up for it now. After all, he could easily have taken her up on her offer to look after Emily, but he had chosen to shoulder the responsibility himself. She glanced at the clock and decided she had better start getting ready.

Rummaging through her make-up bag she picked out an eyeshadow compact she hadn't used for ages. It contained shades of bronze and smoky grey and she spent a couple of minutes longer than usual applying it, adding kohl pencil to the insides of her eyelashes.

There was a solitary bottle of perfume on her dressing table and she picked it up, spraying minute amounts onto her pulse spots. Although it triggered mixed memories, it lifted her spirits. Safari was the only perfume she ever wore. Ceri always bought her some for Christmas and a bottle usually lasted her a whole year because she rarely wore it in the daytime. This year, she noticed with a grim smile, there was still quite a lot left.

Grabbing a long, black skirt from the wardrobe, Megan scanned the hangers for a suitable top. She chose a green chenille sweater, pulling it on before peering in the mirror to change her nose stud. Then she sifted through her jumbled jewellery box for a pair of emerald dropper earrings to match.

Martin Leverton's car was already parked outside Delva's house when Megan arrived. As she walked towards it, he leaned across to open the passenger door.

'Mmm, you smell nice!' he said as she leaned in. 'Hop in – there are a couple of things I want to tell you before we go inside.'

Megan climbed into the passenger seat, trying to stop her wrapover skirt from parting over her thigh. There was a flash of black lycra as she tugged the skirt back across her knee and she knew without looking up that Leverton was staring at her legs.

'I know you've got to rush off afterwards,' he said, looking straight out of the windscreen as she turned her head towards him, 'so I need to have a quick chat with you before we go into Miss Lobelo's house.'

'What's happened?'

'Nothing unexpected, really. It's the DNA result on the semen sample from Tina Jackson: it matches the one taken from Natalie Bailey.'

'Well – surprise, surprise.'

'I know. Shame we didn't get the result before the press conference, but there you go.'

'What else were you going to say?' Megan looked at Leverton, who was still staring straight ahead. 'You said there were a couple of things you wanted to tell me.'

Leverton jerked his head round suddenly, as if emerging from a daydream. 'Oh yes, sorry. I was just thinking about that photograph. I think I'll get Vice to take a look at it. Could be a prostitute, couldn't it?'

'Yes, I suppose there's a good chance.' Megan could see from the look on Leverton's face that he wasn't listening. He was puzzling over something and she wondered what it was.

'The thing I can't work out is whether or not she's dead.' Leverton turned to look at Megan, as if she might have the answer. 'If the woman in the photograph is another of the killer's victims, why hasn't anyone reported her missing?'

'No one reported Donna Fieldhouse or Natalie Bailey missing,' Megan reminded him.

'I know, but they were kids, runaways. This one looks to be much older. I'd put her in her mid-to-late twenties.'

Megan summoned up the image of the woman with the butterfly tattoo. 'It's hard to say, really, because part of her face was covered by her hair.'

Leverton nodded. 'I'll tell you what struck me after you'd gone. She looks very much like Tina Jackson, doesn't she?'

Megan thought for a moment. 'I suppose she does a bit,' she said slowly. 'Although the woman in the photo looks to be mixed-race, doesn't she, and Tina was white.'

'Yes, but Tina was quite dark-skinned – sort of southern European-looking.'

Megan nodded. 'Which adds even more weight to the theory that the guy who took the photograph is Tina's killer. Have the forensic people had the chance to look at it yet?'

'Yes. That's the other thing I was going to tell you: the good news is that the stuff you noticed is definitely semen.'

'And the bad news . . .?'

'They're not going to be able to give us a DNA result until after Christmas.'

'What?'

'I know – it's a nightmare. Believe me, I've tried everything to speed things up. The trouble is there's a backlog of samples waiting to be tested at the moment. The current waiting time is eight weeks for non-urgent tests. We had to pay £2,000 to get the sample from Tina Jackson done quickly, but even if we pay that again we still won't get a result until the day after Boxing Day.'

Megan looked at him incredulously. 'But that's next Wednesday. How can we wait a whole week to find out whether this guy's the killer?'

'We've got no choice. When the forensic people picked up the photo this afternoon they said the DNA lab is under-staffed at the moment because of a 'flu bug and it's closed anyway on Christmas Day and Boxing Day, so the earliest we can get a result is next Wednesday morning.'

'So where does that leave the investigation?'

'Well, we should get a blood grouping on the semen within the next couple of days,' Leverton replied. 'That'll tell us if we're in the right ball park. But until then I think a lot's going to depend on Miss Lobelo.' He glanced at his watch. 'It's half-past. Shall we go in?'

'By the way,' Megan asked as they walked up the path, 'any news on that personnel disc?'

'Oh, it gets worse.' Leverton shook his head. 'Turns out the entire file's been wiped.'

'Isn't there some sort of back-up? Card files or something?'

'Nothing. We're going to have to get everyone's details from scratch. God knows how long that'll take.'

How very convenient, Megan thought.

She was about to ring the bell when Leverton's mobile rang out. She watched his eyes glint in the lamplight as he listened.

'Well, well.' He put the mobile back in his pocket. 'Tina Jackson's killer took a gold pendant in the shape of a shamrock from her body.'

Megan raised her eyebrows. 'Charlotte?'

'Yep. We got her to look through Tina's jewellery box. There was nothing missing except the pendant, which Charlotte had given her as a birthday present.' Leverton pursed his lips. 'So he's into taking trophies. What are the chances of some lucky lady finding that necklace in her Christmas stocking?'

Delva was much calmer than when she had last seen her, but Megan sensed that it was all a front. She sat, quite composed, as Leverton questioned her. He was asking exactly the things Megan had asked already. Delva repeated the answers she had given before. No, she said, there was no-one working at BTV that she suspected. No one she could think of who might bear a grudge.

When the time came for them to leave Megan saw the nervous, haunted look return to her eyes.

'Don't worry, I'll be fine,' Delva said as she showed them to the door. 'Jane's coming round in half an hour. She's staying the night.'

Megan frowned. 'You're quite sure you want to go through with this thing tomorrow night?'

'Yes. And I'll call you if that creep sends anything else between now and then.'

It had snowed again while they were inside. Leverton insisted on taking Megan's arm and walking her to her car.

'I think she needs protection,' Megan said. 'Can't you get someone to watch the place tonight?'

'Don't worry, I'm on to it. Bye, Megan. Have a nice night.'

She saw him wink. Cheeky sod, she thought.

The main roads were gritted but Megan almost skidded as she turned into the cul-de-sac where Patrick lived. She sounded her horn and saw the light snap off as he came downstairs. 'Sorry I'm a bit late,' she said as he got in beside her. 'I had to go out on an interview with Martin Leverton and it went on longer than I expected.'

'It's okay.' Patrick smiled. 'The table's booked for nine o'clock so we should be all right.'

The place Patrick had chosen was one of the more upmarket balti houses in a part of Birmingham renowned for its Indian restaurants. All the waiters were in traditional costume and framed batik prints of elephants, hippos and tigers decorated the walls.

As Megan and Patrick were shown to their table they passed a trolley of sizzling meat on a silver platter. The smell of it had an almost magical effect on Megan's mood, temporarily lifting her from the gloom that had set in while she was listening to Delva and Martin Leverton.

She glanced at Patrick over the top of the menu. He looked

happy and relaxed and she made a conscious effort to get
him to talk about himself rather than launching into the latest
developments on the work front. As they ate she asked him
about the Irish side of his family.

'I lived in Ireland until I was ten,' he explained between
mouthfuls of prawn and spinach balti. 'The company Dad
worked for was setting up a factory in Dublin. My grand-
parents ran a lodging house and he moved in and met my
Mum.'

'Sounds very romantic.'

'It wasn't really.' Patrick laughed. 'The first time he saw
her she opened the door with a towel round her head. She
was really cross because she'd had to get out of the bath to
let him in and he thought she was a dragon. I don't think it
was love at first sight!'

'Are they still alive, your parents?'

'Oh yes. Dad retired last year and they're talking about
moving back to Ireland. They fancy a little cottage on the
west coast, I think.'

'Sounds lovely. I've never been to Ireland.'

'Would you like to?'

'Yes. I've often thought of going to Dublin for a weekend:
you can get flights from Birmingham airport.'

'Well, if you decide to go while I'm over here, you've got
to promise to let me show you round.'

'Are you serious?' Megan gave him a sideways look as she
snapped a poppadom into jagged pieces.

'Of course!' he said, his eyes widening. 'I've got loads of
relatives there and I can take you to all the best pubs.'

Megan wanted to say that yes, she would love to take him
up on his offer. It would be much more fun than going to
Dublin alone. But past experience had made her cautious.
She defused the situation by turning it into a joke. 'It's not
a very fair swap, is it? You show me Dublin and I show you
Borth. It's not exactly throbbing with nightlife, you know.'

Patrick laughed and dug his fork into a bowl of curried vegetables. 'Mmmm! Taste this!' Before Megan could protest he leaned towards her, holding the fork to her lips. She hesitated for a moment before opening her mouth. There was something very sensual in the way he gently slid the food into it. He was looking into her eyes the whole time and Megan felt herself struggling to suppress a sudden gush of lust that threatened to overwhelm her.

Instinctively she started talking about work, telling him about the meeting Delva's pervert had requested.

'If this guy's the O killer – the one you think could be a pimp – what sort of age do you think he'd be?'

'Older than AB.' She spooned more lime pickle onto her plate. 'At first I thought he'd be younger because of the domination thing. But then I thought of the car Natalie Bailey was seen getting out of in the red light district in Wolver-hampton. The other prostitutes said it was an old Ford Sierra. That's not the sort of car a young, successful pimp is going to drive. They usually go for brand new black BMWs with state-of-the-art sound systems blaring out.' She broke off a piece of Peshwari nan and dipped it into her balti. 'I think this guy is a bit of a has-been. I'd put him between 35 and 45.'

'Do you think he's going to try and pull a stunt while they're watching the wine bar?'

'I wouldn't be at all surprised. Question is, what?'

They were still talking about the murders as they left the restaurant.

'How did you get on with Leverton about those medical records?' Patrick asked.

'Oh, that was really weird. I don't know what he's playing at, but he came up with some tale about the computer disc corrupting. He reckons they've lost all the records and everyone in the force is going to have to fill out their medical details all over again.'

'Sounds pretty unlikely – I mean, they'd be sure to have some kind of back-up.'

'Just what I thought. Oh, that reminds me,' she said with a smile, 'what were you doing walking off with my profiles this morning? By the time I realised they'd gone you'd swanned off somewhere and I couldn't get them back!'

'Oh – did I?' Patrick mumbled, 'I, er, didn't realise.'

'It's okay, it didn't matter!' She laughed at his embarrassed face. 'I printed out another set. You can keep them if you like – as long as you don't leave them lying around for the students or anyone else to see.'

The car drew up outside Patrick's flat. Megan kept the engine running. 'Thanks for the meal,' she said. 'It was a real treat.'

'Thank you for coming.' He leaned across, kissed her on the cheek and was out of the car before she had time to register what had happened. He turned and gave her a quick wave before disappearing through the front door.

Megan pulled away feeling vaguely disconcerted. What had she been expecting, she mused, as she drove home through the snow-muffled streets. An invitation for coffee in his flat? An attempted seduction?

Her mind switched gear, suddenly filled with disturbing images she tried to keep buried. No one was ever going to get the chance to use her like that again.

At home she put the kettle on and went to the fridge for milk. Opening the door she caught a flicker of movement.

'Ugh!' She recoiled in horror. A half-eaten chicken on the middle shelf was crawling with maggots. 'Oh God!' She staggered over to the sink, retching. She'd bought the cooked chicken on Sunday and had been picking at the remains for the past couple of nights. How could it possibly have got like that?

She pulled on rubber gloves and ripped a dustbin liner

from a roll under the sink. Walking gingerly back to the fridge she tipped the chicken, plate and all, into the bin liner and rushed out to the dustbin in the yard.

Back in the kitchen she shuddered with disgust. Maggots? In the middle of winter? As she reached for disinfectant and a scourer, the feeling of unease that had crept over her the previous night came back with a vengeance. *Someone's been in here*, the voice in her head whispered. *Someone's trying to scare you*. But who? No one, other than Tony and her sister, had keys. Why would Tony want to do that to her? Perhaps if *she* had been the one who'd had an affair . . .

What if it's him? That voice again. *What if AB knows you're involved and he's turning the tables? Putting the frighteners on you? What if he's a policeman? Donalsen? Easy enough for a cop to break into a house . . .*

'You're being stupid.' She said it aloud, trying to convince herself. She shouldn't have thrown that chicken carcass away. She should have taken it back to the supermarket and complained. Probably past its sell-by date.

With shaking hands she took another bin liner and swept everything except the milk from the shelves of the fridge. Then she set to work with the disinfectant, scrubbing with the scourer. Scrubbing and scrubbing as if the effort would drive away the panic she felt inside.

Chapter 9

The car park at BTV was deserted as David Simon cruised past the raised barrier. He pulled up outside the back security gate.

'Evening, Adrian.' He gave the man on duty a wave as he strolled past the window on his way into the building.

'Evening, Dave,' the guard called. 'Thought you'd gone home.'

'No. Another bloody drinks do. Management Christmas party.'

'And you're complaining?' Adrian laughed.

'Well, you get a bit sick of it. It was the technical staff do last night and I've got the newsroom party tomorrow. Probably have that bloody woman breathing down my neck again!' He shrugged, giving a short grunt of a laugh. 'Not what you need when you feel as if you've got a permanent hangover.'

'What you need is a glass of milk. Put a lining on your stomach. Come in here a minute.' He pulled up a chair and pressed a button on his walkie-talkie. 'Frank!' he said, raising his voice, 'Can you fetch us another carton of milk from the fridge?'

Five minutes later another security guard appeared round the door.

'Thanks mate.' Adrian took the proffered carton of milk, pouring a large glassful and handing it to his boss. 'Do you fancy a coffee, Frank?' he said, turning to the man, who was still hovering in the doorway. 'I've got something to liven it up a bit!' He bent down, taking a bottle of whisky from a cupboard near his feet. 'None for you, though, Dave,' he laughed. 'You've got to pace yourself!'

Half an hour later David Simon was still sitting in the security booth. 'Right, I'm off.' He took a swig from the whisky bottle and rose to his feet a little unsteadily. 'And remember – keep your filthy little habits to yourselves while you're on duty. Yes, Frank, I mean you!' He gave the guard a menacing look and then winked. 'I don't give a flying fuck what you get up to in the privacy of your own home, but don't let Dildo Labia catch you at it again – got it?'

As he turned to go, a car drew up alongside the booth. He peered through the window at the driver. 'Evening, Neil. Going to the Management do?'

'No chance!' Neil grinned back at him. 'Just popping in for some stuff I'm working on – I'll only be five minutes.'

Simon caught a movement in the back of the car. It was a little girl. She had been asleep in her car seat and woke with a whimper.

'That your daughter?' Simon smiled. 'Doesn't she look like her mum!'

Neil grunted a laugh. With a quick wave he drove into the car park.

'Emily? Is Daddy there?' Megan heard nothing at the other end of the phone. She waited for what felt like an eternity, wondering what to do. There was no point replacing the receiver and redialing: her two-year-old niece had developed a habit of answering it and then wandering off to play with her toys.

'Emily!' she shouted, hoping the child might be within earshot and remember that the phone was off the hook. Finally she heard a faint cry of 'Daddy!' and the sound of footsteps approaching the phone.

'Neil – it's Megan. Any news from the hospital?'

When he spoke his voice was gruff, as if he'd just woken up. 'Yes – sorry, Meg, I meant to ring you . . .' He broke off. Megan thought he sounded strange. As if he didn't really want to talk to her. Maybe it was just stress.

'Sorry,' he said after a long pause, 'I must have dozed off after Ceri phoned. I had a bit of a rough night with Emily. She kept waking up and asking for her mum.'

'How's Joe? Is he still okay?'

'Yeah, he's fine – no worries. The op was a success. Ceri's got to stay with him again tonight and tomorrow night but they're hoping to let him come home on Saturday.'

'Oh, that's brilliant! I thought they might have to keep him in over Christmas.'

'No, I shouldn't think so. Ceri sends her love and says will it be okay to have Christmas dinner at our house instead of yours? I think she's worried about Joe travelling so soon after she brings him home.'

'Of course it's okay – tell her not to worry. I'll buy all the stuff and bring it over on Sunday night. Actually, I could come on Saturday if you like – if you and Ceri need to catch up on your sleep I could sit up with Joe.'

'Thanks. Actually, I was going to ask if you could come and babysit tonight.'

Megan hesitated for a moment, remembering Delva's assignation at the wine bar and wondering if Leverton would want her to be there.

Neil continued apologetically, 'I feel really bad about asking you . . .'

'No, it's okay.' She felt torn between work and family. If she went to the wine bar she just might see the killer. But surely that was a very remote possibility? And if he *was* someone from BTV and he recognised her, wouldn't that screw up the whole operation?

'I'll have to check but I think I can do it,' she told Neil. 'Tell you what: I'll call you back within the next hour if I can't make it. What time do you want me to come?'

'Oh not till about half-eight. And I won't be late. I'll only be out for a couple of hours.'

Megan replaced the receiver, still torn. Should she leave Delva to the police? Almost immediately, the phone rang out.

'Doctor Rhys – message for you from Mr Van Zeller. He asked me to let you know that he won't be in today because he's going to interview someone at Long Lartin jail.'

'Oh, right. Thanks, Eric, for letting me know.' Megan frowned and reached under her desk for her bag. She fished out her diary, flipping through the pages to December 21. It was blank.

Patrick usually let her know of prison visits at least a fortnight in advance, and she could have sworn the inmate he wanted to interview at Long Lartin had turned him down. There must have been a last-minute change of mind. How strange, she thought, that he hadn't mentioned it at the restaurant.

She glanced at the clock. Dialling Leverton's number, she wondered if Delva would back out of going to the wine bar when the time came. Last night she had agreed to go through with it, but would she change her mind as it drew nearer?

'Martin? It's Megan.'

'Oh. I'm glad you called. I've just been on the phone to Delva Lobelo.'

'She hasn't called it off, has she?

''I was worried that she might, so I sent one of my DCs round to her house this morning to fill her in on what we're planning to do. I've just been talking to her about the route she's going to take when she leaves the wine bar.'

'Why? Do you think he might try following her?'

'Possibly, yes. As far as I'm concerned the meeting's a red

herring. I reckon he might sit in a car somewhere near and wait for her to leave; then he'll follow her and find out where she lives. That's if he doesn't already know, of course.'

'Do you think he does know? It wouldn't be hard to find out.'

'Especially if you're right about him working at BTV. Anyway we won't be taking any chances. We'll keep the house under surveillance and make sure she's tailed to and from the wine bar.'

'What if he's planning to break into the house while she's at the wine bar and lie in wait for her?'

'Don't worry – we'll be watching the place all night.'

'What will you charge him with if you get him?'

'Depends where we catch him. Technically if he follows her home that makes him a stalker, so we might be able to nail him for that. Up to now all we can really do him for is sending obscene material through the post, so it really all depends on what he does tonight.'

'What do you reckon are the odds of him turning up at the wine bar or the house?'

Leverton paused. 'Not good. If this guy's one of the killers he'd have to have a screw loose to risk a stunt like this.'

Megan considered this before making her decision. 'You don't need me to be there, do you, Martin?'

'Not if you don't want to be, no.' He sounded surprised and slightly disappointed.

Megan gave Leverton her sister's telephone number in case he couldn't raise her on the mobile. It suddenly occurred to her that he ought to be told about her connection with Neil.

'Martin, I should have told you this before. My brother-in-law works at BTV. He co-presents the early evening news with Delva Lobelo.'

There was a moment of silence at the other end of the phone as Leverton took this in.

'Neil Richardson – he's your brother-in-law?' His tone of voice was a mixture of surprise and curiosity. He paused again and said, 'Does Delva Lobelo know that?'

'Yes.'

'Forgive me for saying this, Megan, but I assume you've ruled out any possibility of him being involved in this?'

Megan could hear the embarrassment in his voice. Of course, he had to ask and she had to give him an answer. She suddenly realised that with a few carefully chosen words she could find out exactly what Neil was up to: get him tailed and find out if Ceri's fears about him having an affair were justified. It would be so easy. The merest hint that Neil's behaviour had been giving her sister cause for concern would get Leverton on his trail like a fox after a rabbit. It was so tempting.

Megan summoned up a mental image of her mother. What would she have done in a situation like this?

'Yes, of course I've ruled him out,' she heard herself saying.

Emily was sitting in her pyjamas watching Nickleodeon when Megan arrived. She leapt out of the chair and pulled at the sleeve of Megan's coat.

'Flintstones!' she lisped. 'He throwed the cat out of the window!'

Neil poked his head around the door, his shirt undone and his hair still wet from the shower.

'Bye, Meg – I won't be late. Help yourself to food and stuff.' He kissed Emily on the head and breezed out, slamming the front door behind him.

'Daddy gone to Elizabeth's,' Emily informed Megan, her eyes still glued to the television screen.

'Oh,' Megan said, taken by surprise. When she spoke again she tried to sound unconcerned. 'What does Elizabeth look like? Have you seen her?'

Emily glanced round at Megan, looking at her as if she had said something quite mad.

Megan tried again. 'Does Mummy know Elizabeth? Do you go to Elizabeth's with her?'

'Course!' Emily replied, wearing the same expression Ceri put on when asked a stupid question. 'Look! Dino bited Fred on the bottom!' She went into a fit of giggles and Megan realised that interrogating a two-year-old was a pretty pointless exercise.

Delva Lobelo sat at a table in the crowded wine bar staring at the half-empty glass in front of her. Out of the corner of her eye she could see two plain-clothes officers chatting over a bottle of red. Out of sight on the other side of the room there were at least half a dozen others all pretending to be punters out enjoying a pre-Christmas drink.

Delva had never felt so alone. She glanced at her watch. She'd arrived on the dot of eight and it was now twenty-five to nine. She was aware of the curious glances of the people at the next table. She knew she'd been recognised and that made it even worse. She felt her face burning. How much longer was she going to have to wait?

Megan managed to lure Emily away from the TV with the promise of a bedtime story. It was nearly ten o'clock by the time the child finally closed her eyes. Megan sat gazing at her for a long time. Did all children look so angelic when they were asleep? She thought of Tony's new baby and wondered when it was due. By the look of his girlfriend's bump it couldn't be long. She wondered if Ceri knew. There was so much she wanted to talk to Ceri about.

She crept downstairs and switched on the television. She wanted to see the local news bulletin. Not that there was any real chance of Delva's stalker being apprehended at the wine bar.

'The BTV headlines tonight . . .' Megan recognised the newsreader. It was the reporter she had seen at yesterday's police press conference. After the first thirty seconds she relaxed. If anything had happened it would have been mentioned in the headlines.

There was something, though, further down the bulletin and relegated to a few lines of copy. It was about the Jackson case, simply stating that the police were no nearer to finding the killer. A non-story, really.

'That's all from us for tonight. Elizabeth Dawson will bring you the next news from BTV at ten past six tomorrow morning . . .'

Megan sat bolt upright. *Elizabeth who*? She couldn't remember Neil ever having mentioned an Elizabeth working in the newsroom. But then again, she reasoned, BTV was known for its short contracts and high turnover of staff. She wouldn't have recognised the chap reading the bulletin if she hadn't seen him at the press conference.

Her mind raced. What should she do when Neil arrived home? Ask him outright if he'd spent the evening in bed with one of his colleagues?

Megan's train of thought was derailed by the sudden sight of her own face filling the television screen. She stared, open mouthed, in total bewilderment until the voice of the continuity announcer kicked in.

It was a trailer for the documentary BTV was screening next week. How cunning of them to show it straight after the news. Someone in the newsroom obviously suspected that she was involved in the Tina Jackson case.

Those sly words of Leverton's suddenly played back in her brain: '*Long, black hair, olive skin, age between thirty and forty – that's you, Megan. You'd better be careful.*'

A horrifying image was forming inside her head: the killer, sitting on a sofa watching television; savouring the news and then catching sight of her face seconds later.

'Stop it!' she said out loud. 'Stop being so bloody paranoid!' The memory of the maggot-covered chicken flashed into her mind and she began to panic at the thought of going home. She could stay here, couldn't she? No. She mustn't give in to it. She mustn't let this case get to her.

The man was struggling. His fingers were almost numb with cold. She was big, this one. Taller than the others and heavier, too. He lay her down in the snow. She was stiff as a board. The only thing that was still soft was her hair. It trailed across the ground like dirty cobwebs as he pulled her along.

The boot was open ready for its cargo. Panting with effort he shoved her in. Christ, she was too long! The legs were sticking out at least six inches.

Cursing, he dragged her back to the shed. It didn't take long to find the axe, but he hovered in the doorway, hiding it behind his back, making sure he couldn't be seen. He told himself not to be so stupid. Who on earth could be watching?

By the time he reached the dump site he was much warmer. The chopping had thawed his fingers and the car's heater had eased the stiffness in his legs. He opened the car door. On the other side of the wall he could hear Christmas revellers spilling out of a pub. He thought of the bottle of single malt whisky waiting in the kitchen cupboard at home. Get it over with, he thought. At least there wasn't any blood; not this time.

Megan jumped when she heard the door opening.

'Hi Meg! Sorry, did I wake you up?' Neil looked flushed and his eyes were brighter than usual.

'It's okay.' Megan peered at her watch. She'd been sitting with her eyes closed, thinking about Delva. She hadn't meant to doze off.

'Sorry I'm late – it went on longer than I thought.'

'Where was it you went?' She tried to make her voice sound casual.

'Oh, just an office do.' He turned away from her as he spoke, going back into the hall to hang up his jacket. 'I didn't really want to go but I had to,' he called from the cloakroom. 'Internal politics and all that – you know.'

When he returned he was carrying Megan's coat and scarf. 'I was hoping to just show my face and make a quick get-away,' he smiled, 'but I got collared by the Head of Current Affairs – what a bore! Anyway, at least the food was good.'

Megan took her coat, floored by Neil's easy, open manner. She needed time to think before making the accusations she had been storing up for his return.

'Did you manage to get Emily to bed all right?'

'Oh yes, she was fine.' *She told me you were going to Elizabeth's.* The words drummed inside Megan's head but she wouldn't allow herself to say them. 'By the way, who's looking after her tomorrow? Are you back at work?'

'No. They've given me another day off – compassionate leave – so I'll be able to look after her.'

Neil stood in the doorway waving as she drove off. The digital clock on the dashboard flicked to midnight. Where had he been? She glided along deserted roads onto the M54, skirting Wolverhampton on her way back home. Even with the snow it would only take three quarters of an hour. If he had made the same journey he could have spent nearly two hours in Birmingham before tearing himself away.

She was annoyed with herself for not confronting him. He'd charmed his way out of it the way he always did. Always so plausible, so persuasive.

She thought of Delva. If Neil was involved with someone at BTV, surely that meant he couldn't be the one sending those letters? She pulled into a lay-by and punched out Leverton's number on her mobile. She had to know what had happened.

'Martin – any news?'

'Nothing.' He sounded tired.

'Where are you?'

'Outside Miss Lobelo's house. She's gone to bed.'

'No sign of anyone?'

'Not a dicky bird. We followed her home and we'll be keeping her under surveillance for the next 24 hours. She's going to work as normal tomorrow and we'll keep an eye on things there.'

Megan sat thinking about what he'd said. If the pervert hadn't shown, what was the point of it? Just a stupid hoax or something more sinister? What was he doing while all those police officers were watching Delva?'

She started the engine. Huge flakes of snow were falling on the windscreen and she flicked on the wipers. As she pulled out of the layby a car's headlights flashed in the mirror. She frowned. It must have been parked behind her. It was hard to make out anything in the snow. She couldn't even tell if there was anyone in the passenger seat.

She turned off the Hagley Road and headed towards Harborne. The car followed. What was it? A BMW? She strained her eyes in the darkness but it was impossible to make it out. Get a grip, she thought, it's probably some couple who pulled over for a quickie.

Her fingers tightened on the steering wheel. AB was a stalker. Someone who had been cruising the red light district the night Tina was on the soup run. He had followed her home. He followed women. My God, she thought, what if he's following me?

She swerved left without indicating, turning into the street before her own. Her car skidded slightly. She glanced in the mirror and breathed a sigh of relief as the other car drove on down Harborne High Street.

As soon as she'd let herself in she went round the house

checking. The shells, the fridge, the bedroom window. Everything was as she had left it. She made herself a mug of hot chocolate and poured a slug of brandy into it. What she needed was a good night's sleep.

She was in bed when the car came back. She didn't hear the sound of the engine as it pulled up a few yards from her house.

The driver sat for a while, staring up at her bedroom window. Then he got out and walked through the dirty snow to her front door. Taking something from his coat pocket he reached forward. He paused. Changing his mind, he replaced the object and went back to the car.

Chapter 10

Sergeant Donalsen was eating his breakfast when the phone rang. He laid the half-eaten bacon sandwich on his desk and grabbed the receiver.

'Rob?'

It was Martin Leverton. Donalsen's greasy hand tightened and the phone jumped like a slippery fish, somersaulting to the floor with a crash.

'Sorry, sir,' he mumbled, grasping the receiver with both hands this time. 'Phone slipped.'

'I'm coming down for that list. Is it ready?'

'Er, yes, sir. I've just got to run it through the photocopier.'

'Right. I'll be down in two minutes.'

Donalsen swore as he rummaged through his in-tray. He pulled out the list of names, smearing it with greasy thumb prints.

By the time Leverton walked through the door Donalsen was stuffing the remains of his breakfast into his mouth. The photocopied list was lying on the desk but Leverton didn't look at it. Instead he shoved something under Donalsen's nose. Donalsen took one look and almost choked.

Leverton let the photograph drop onto the desk. The image of the naked woman with the butterfly tattoo on her breast swam accusingly before Donalsen's eyes. Leverton was studying his reaction.

'One of yours, is she?'

Donalsen swallowed hard and looked down at the desk,

desperate to avoid Leverton's eyes. It was as if he knew. The way he phrased that question – had it been deliberate?

He began fumbling in his desk to cover his confusion. 'She might be, sir,' he said, trying to make his voice sound casual. 'If you can give me half an hour I'll look through the files and check it out. What's she been done for – drugs, is it?'

'Oh no,' Leverton sneered. 'It's something much more serious than that – and if we don't get an ID on her by this afternoon I'll have to cancel your Christmas leave!'

He snatched the list of names from under Donalsen's elbow. 'These the pimps?'

'Yes, sir,' Donalsen replied through clenched teeth.

'Convicted or suspected?'

'The ones above the black line are convicted; the ones below are cases where the tom dropped the charges before it got to court.' Donalsen addressed this information to the fluorescent light on the ceiling, still refusing to meet Leverton's accusing glare.

'Don't get insolent with me, Rob.' Leverton's voice dropped to a barely audible growl. 'You may be leaving this office in the New Year but for the next ten days you're still head of Vice. So bugger the bloody files. Get your fat arse out onto the beat and find out who this poor cow is, will you?'

'Yes sir.' Donalsen stared at the desk, stony-faced. Then he remembered something. 'PC Costello's back on duty this afternoon, sir. He'll know straight off if she's one of ours.' His eyes darted up at Leverton, hoping to win him over, but the look he met was withering.

'Don't be lazy, Rob, or I might start getting *really* angry.' Leverton swept out of the room, slamming the door behind him.

David Simon groaned and buried his face in the pillow. It was still dark outside.

'Mother, it's only seven o'clock,' he said, hearing the clunk as she placed a teacup on his bedside table.

'I know that.' She snapped on the light. 'We need to make an early start. The traffic will be awful if we leave any later than seven-thirty.'

'But I wasn't planning to go into Birmingham today.' He sat up, rubbing his eyes. 'Most of the staff at BTV finished for Christmas yesterday. The place can run itself. Anyway –' he reached across for his tea – 'I thought you'd done your Christmas shopping.'

'I have. Most of it.' She glanced in the mirror, patting her hair. 'But I want something nice to wear on Christmas Day.' She opened his wardrobe, pulling out clothes and tossing them onto the bed. 'And I've still got to get something for Franco. We can't have him to dinner and not give him a present.'

'Don't suppose he'd notice either way,' he grumbled, pulling on the silk shirt, trousers and sweater his mother had selected.

'Of course he would notice. Anyway, I want you to take me to lunch at that nice place off Corporation Street.'

'Not the one that charges ten quid for a cucumber sandwich and a glass of fizzy water?'

His mother glared at him. 'How dare you moan about taking me out for lunch when you're rubbing shoulders with those television people all day long. Don't you think I want a bit of glamour in my life too?'

By the time they reached the centre of Birmingham, it was snowing again. The Mercedes turned off Broad Street down to the canal basin, past the bobbing narrow boats in their blankets of white.

The BTV car park was deserted. His mother frowned as they drove past rows of empty spaces.

'Where are you going?'

'Round the back. There's a covered loading bay. Don't want to come back to find the car under a foot of snow, do I?'

She took a lipstick and a compact from her handbag, examining her make-up as they drew to a halt. 'Can we cut through the building to the shops? I'll ruin my shoes if I have to traipse back through this snow.'

'Yes, mother. Now can you get out and guide me in? Don't worry, you won't get your feet wet!'

Gingerly she opened the car door, stepping onto the tarmac of the loading bay. A sudden gust of wind sent snowflakes swirling under the canopy into her face. Turning her head away, she caught sight of something that stopped her in her tracks. She screamed.

David Simon leapt from the car as his mother staggered towards it.

She pointed to a skip wedged between the outside edge of the loading bay and the car park wall. The first thing he saw was the legs, or what was left of them. From the butchered stumps of the calves, his eye travelled along the naked body. Lying on her back among broken slabs of concrete, the woman's head hung over the edge of the skip. Long black hair moved limply in the breeze and the snow fell like confetti on her upturned face and breasts.

Unable to stop himself, he moved closer. The crunch of his shoes in the snow seemed deafeningly loud. Now he could see her face.

'David!'

He spun round. His mother, ashen-faced, was slumped against the boot of the car.

Megan was wedging a large frozen turkey into a shopping trolley when her mobile rang. She steered into a relatively private spot behind a display of Christmas crackers before answering.

'Hello?' She had to shout above the noise of the hordes of other shoppers crowding the aisles on either side.

'Megan? It's Martin. Where are you?'

'Safeway! Sorry, can you hear me?'

'Just about. There's another body – it was found first thing this morning in the car park at BTV. Bastard had chopped her feet off!'

'What?' Megan gasped. 'Who is she?'

'No idea yet. Head of security found her lying in a skip almost covered in snow. Look, can you meet me at the mortuary? I'm on my way there now.'

'Yes, of course.' Megan looked at her watch. 'It'll take me about half an hour, though.'

'No hurry. They won't be able to start the post mortem until they've thawed her out.'

God, Megan thought, inching out of her space in the packed car park, is that what was going on during the wine-bar stake-out?

She was ushered into the mortuary by the same acne-scarred girl she had seen last time, but the figure standing next to Leverton was definitely not the objectionable Ed Horrobin. Taller, plumper and with almost white hair, it was the pathologist she had met on the Metro rapes inquiry.

Leverton stepped forward when he saw her enter the room. 'Megan, you know Dr Jefferson, don't you?'

'Yes.' She shook hands in lieu of any further pleasantries: to say 'nice to meet you again' seemed wholly inappropriate in the circumstances.

'You were quick,' Leverton said. 'I got caught up in the traffic in the city centre. Christmas shoppers! You'd think the snow would put them off.'

'Martin,' Megan said when the pathologist had disappeared to change into his overalls. 'Did Delva see the body?'

'No. It wasn't until after she'd gone into the building that my lot found out about it. The boss of the security firm must have driven in literally minutes before the guys following Delva pulled up. They heard screaming and when they got round the back they found the security chap's mother next to the skip where the body was found. Evidently he'd brought her in with him so she could go and do her Christmas shopping. She was in a terrible state.'

'Where's Delva now?'

'Don't worry – she's okay. She was pretty shaken up when she found out about it, but she's being looked after by one of the other women who works in the newsroom. We had to play things pretty carefully because we didn't want anyone at BTV to twig why we were on the scene so soon after the body was discovered. Anyway, her colleague took her home and she's going to arrange for her to catch a train to her mother's place in London. She was going there for Christmas anyway.'

'You don't think there's any danger of her being followed down to London, do you?'

'Yes. That's why I'm sending a couple of plain clothes people on the train as well.'

'I've been thinking. We need a list of exactly who was in the BTV building the night Delva found that photo on her desk. Do you remember when we went to her house, she said whoever put it there could only have done it during a ten-minute period when the night sub popped out for a sandwich?'

'Yes, I know. We're working on that at the moment. Unfortunately the place was crawling with people that night. There was a Christmas party for all the technical staff, so at the time the envelope was left there were about sixty people on the premises.'

'Oh, right,' Megan sighed. 'One more thing. Have you got the blood grouping from the semen sample on the photo yet?'

'No. They're having trouble collecting enough to do the test. Sod's law, isn't it?'

Megan looked at him. He'd probably been up half the night but she wouldn't have guessed it from his appearance. 'Is there any chance of whoever dumped this body being caught on a security video?'

'You'd think so, wouldn't you? The first thing we asked for when we got inside the building was last night's tapes. But surprise, surprise, there's one missing: it would have covered the period from nine o'clock until midnight.'

'So whoever dumped the body stole the tape?'

'Exactly. Everyone who was in the building last night's going to have to be questioned.'

A trolley was wheeled through the doors and in its wake came the pathologist. The dead woman was still zipped up in the body bag used to transport her corpse from the BTV car park.

Martin and Megan watched as the opaque outer layer of the bag was unzipped, revealing a clear plastic layer over the woman's face. Normally her features would have been clearly visible but the inside of the plastic was clouded with melting snow. As the inner zipper was pulled down and the plastic parted, Megan gasped.

Leverton had noticed it too. 'My God! It's her, isn't it?'

They were both staring at the woman's left breast. The snow that had covered the upper torso at the crime scene had melted to reveal a butterfly tattoo. A glance at the face confirmed it – although the hair was matted and the skin frosted over, it was definitely the woman in the photograph.

The pathologist looked up in surprise. 'You know her?'

'We don't know her name,' Leverton said, 'but we have a photo of her. She could be a local prostitute. One of my men was checking it out.'

He told the pathologist about the origin of the photograph. 'Doctor Rhys thinks the man who sent it was probably involved in the murders of the two other prostitutes and the Jacksons. The woman in the photo looked as if she'd been restrained in the same way Natalie Bailey and Tina Jackson were; her arms were twisted above her head and she was lying on a bed. If this is the same woman – and I'm pretty sure it is – she should have marks on her wrists.'

'Well, I won't be able to do a post-mortem for a few hours yet – the body's still partly frozen – but we might be able to see something on her wrists . . .' He drew back the flaps of the body bag and the technician eased the body onto the table. Megan shuddered at the sight of the legs with their rough white stumps of bone.

'I can see something here,' the pathologist said, cradling the woman's right hand in his own. 'There's an abrasion on the skin inside the wrist consistent with something thin and rigid like handcuffs.'

'What about cause of death?' Leverton asked. 'Was she strangled?'

'I can't say yet. Her hair's frozen to her neck in places so there could be bruises concealed underneath.'

'How long has she been dead?'

'Hard to say until we open her up. The extremities are frozen solid. She could have been killed several days ago and left outside.'

He examined the hair, pulling some of the matted strands apart. 'There are fragments of dead leaves in her hair: I didn't see any organic waste in that skip, so as a preliminary guess I'd say she'd been dragged across a garden or a park. When did it turn cold? Sunday night, wasn't it?'

Megan glanced at Leverton and they both nodded.

'So she could have been killed as long ago as last weekend.' Jefferson straightened up and turned to face Megan and Leverton. 'The state of the internal organs will give us a better idea: they're unlikely to be frozen – she'd have to have been put into a deep freeze for the cold to penetrate there. The amount of decomposition will give us a reasonable idea of how long ago she died.'

Megan had been waiting for Leverton to finish quizzing the pathologist before asking any questions of her own. 'What do you make of the legs? We haven't seen mutilation in any of the other victims.'

'The feet were severed after death. Obviously I can't say what was used to do it until I carry out a proper examination, but the absence of any blood loss from the wound suggests that the woman had been dead for some time when it happened.'

'Why cut off the feet?' Leverton mused, 'Are we looking at some bizarre fetish or what?'

'It could be something much more mundane.' Jefferson perched on a stool next to the body. 'In my experience the likeliest explanation for severed limbs is ease of disposal.'

Megan frowned. 'So you think he did this because she wouldn't fit into his car or van or whatever?'

'I'd say it was a distinct possibility, yes. We'll get a clearer picture if there are any fibres attached to the body. If she was transported in a car boot she's likely to have picked something up off the floor. The lab can usually distinguish between domestic carpeting and the stuff you get in cars.'

'What about semen traces? Will they have been preserved?' Leverton asked. 'I mean, is there any chance of picking up enough to do a DNA test?'

Jefferson rubbed his chin, thinking for a moment before replying. 'If she was sexually assaulted, the presence of semen will depend on how long after the attack the body froze. If it happened within a couple of hours there's a good chance of semen remaining in the body. You'll have to give me time to allow the body to thaw before I can take any swabs, though.'

Leverton asked Megan if she would follow him back to police headquarters. It was frustrating having to wait for the post-mortem to be carried out, but there was little else the pathologist could tell them until it was done. Megan felt faintly sick, wondering how long a woman took to thaw.

David Simon sat in a waiting room at the police station. There were two empty coffee cups beside him. He got up, pacing the floor impatiently. They'd taken his mother to hospital. Suffering from shock, they said. Not bloody surprising, he thought. He was angry. Angry at what she'd seen and angry at having to wait so long to be questioned.

'Mr Simon?' A uniformed officer appeared round the door. 'Shouldn't be long now.'

He didn't like the look on the policeman's face. It was condescending, typical of the way cops acted when dealing with security guards. In his experience they always distrusted the likes of him, never sure if they were ex-cons or ex-cops.

He wondered who would be coming to interview him. Perhaps it'd be the one he'd seen on telly yesterday. What was his name? Leverton. Three dead bodies in a week. Things must really be hotting up in this place, he thought. They might even wheel in that Dr Megan Rhys.

'The first thing I want to do is get hold of Rob Donalsen,' Leverton said as he showed her into his office. 'Remember what I said about him being a liability?'

Megan nodded, watching Leverton's face. The mention of the Vice Squad sergeant's name made her go cold. Ever since the horrible discovery in her fridge she'd been telling herself it couldn't be him. That he didn't fit the profile for AB. But he'd been in on this right from the start. Knew she was involved. And he was screwing prostitutes. *What if she was wrong?*

'I showed him that photo this morning just to see his expression,' Leverton went on. 'He went as white as a sheet. I'm sure it's a girl he's knocked off in the past, but he made out he didn't recognise her. Anyway, I told him I wanted a name by this afternoon.' He looked at his watch and smiled grimly. 'It's ten past twelve already – shall we?' Leverton stood up and opened the door.

As they descended the staircase to the ground floor Megan caught sight of PC Costello in a doorway. He wore a hooded jacket and his mouth was muffled by a thick woollen scarf so that the only part of his face that could be seen were his hypnotic brown eyes. There was snow on the hood of his jacket and it was beginning to drip onto his forehead. He wiped it with a gloved hand and grinned as he saw Megan and Leverton coming past.

'Afternoon, sir. Ma'am,' he said.

'Oh, Costello – you just starting a shift?' Leverton asked.

'Yes, sir. I've been off since Tuesday but I'm on over the weekend.'

'Hmmm,' Leverton said. 'Could have done with you this morning, really. Never mind.'

Costello followed wordlessly as Leverton carried on down the corridor, ushering Megan through a fire door. As they reached the Vice Squad office, Megan nearly collided with Donalsen, who hurtled through the door in front of her. He looked terrible: puffy-eyed and red-faced. She backed away.

'Going somewhere, Rob?' Leverton asked in a tone of voice Megan had never heard him use before.

'Er . . . No, sir. Just a call of nature, sir.'

'Well, it'll have to wait! I want that name!'

Donalsen looked sheepishly back at him. 'I've tried, guv, really. I mean, there's hardly anyone out on the beat in the mornings. I couldn't find anyone to ask. I've been all through the files and none of the mug-shots look anything like her!' There was a note of desperation in the way he said it, as if pleading with Leverton to believe him.

Leverton fixed the sergeant with a piercing glance before walking past him into the office. 'Well, perhaps PC Costello can throw a bit of light on the subject.' He handed Costello a copy of the photo. He studied it for a moment, his hood and scarf concealing the expression on his face. Then he looked at Donalsen, but the sergeant looked away.

'It's, er, hard to tell because of the hair over the face,' Costello said. 'But it might be one of ours,' he faltered. 'The tattoo, though . . . that looks familiar – although butterflies are quite popular tattoos to have. If she was on our files that tattoo wouldn't show 'cos it's too low down. They come in wearing these low-cut tops but we only get head and shoulders photos.'

Costello took off his coat and scarf and walked across to the filing cabinet, pulling out a photo after a search that took a matter of seconds. 'There's this girl, sir,' he said, showing it to Leverton. 'What do you think?'

Leverton turned so that Megan could see it too. To her, there was absolutely no doubt that it was the same woman. The grim expression she wore for the police photographer couldn't conceal her high cheekbones and full lips. Her skin was a tawny colour – a shade darker than in the other photograph – and her hair stood out around her face, glistening like black candyfloss.

Leverton read out the name at the top of the card. 'Maria Fellowes. Aged 27. Hmmm, last arrested six months ago.' He turned to Costello. 'Are you sure this one's still on the game?'

The constable scratched his head, glancing again at Donalsen before replying. Donalsen sat slumped in a chair, his head down.

'Perhaps I should be asking *you* that question, Rob,' Leverton said.

'I've told you, I haven't got a clue who she is. Sir.' The words were spoken in a monotone and he added Leverton's title almost as an afterthought.

'Is that right?' Leverton went on with the same biting sarcasm. 'In that case it probably won't interest you to know that we've just found her lying in a skip with her feet hacked off.'

With three pairs of eyes fixed on him, Donalsen rose from

his seat. His face was puce. He mumbled an excuse to leave the room and made for the door without waiting for a reply.

Leverton looked at Megan. His face said it all. She raised her eyebrows, but her expression was noncommittal. Apart from his weakness for the women he was supposed to be arresting, everything about Donalsen was wrong. His reactions were so predictable, his feelings so transparent.

'Right!' Leverton turned to Costello. 'I want to speak to Maria Fellowes's relatives – if she's got any, that is. Can you get on to it? I don't think we'll get much mileage out of him . . .' He gesticulated in the direction Donalsen had taken when he left the room.

Megan watched Leverton as he barked instructions at Costello. She felt angry, frustrated. He should be concentrating his resources on interviewing people at BTV. Tracking down the people who were in the building the night Delva got that photograph. She frowned. If he really suspected Donalsen he should be questioning him, doing a DNA test. Surely that was more crucial than interviewing members of the dead woman's family?

Once again she got the feeling she was being used as a pawn in some game she couldn't fathom. Donna, Natalie, Tina and now Maria. How many more women were going to die before Leverton started taking her seriously?

It was beginning to get dark when Megan returned to the mortuary. As she walked up the steps she saw a police patrol car pull into the car park. A woman with blonde permed hair climbed out. She looked about fifty and she was carrying a small black child in her arms.

Megan carried on through the lobby. Leverton was waiting and he beckoned Megan through another door. At the end of a corridor she could see an office where the pathologist sat writing at his desk.

'Doctor Jefferson's got a progress report for us before the mother arrives,' he said.

'She's already here, I think,' Megan replied. 'Did you know she had a child with her?'

Leverton groaned. 'Poor little sod! I suppose it's Maria's. How old is it?'

'Only a toddler, I think. It was in her arms, fast asleep.'

'Let's hope it stays that way. This is no place for a kid.'

Doctor Jefferson looked up when he heard them approaching the office.

'Right, let me fill you in on what we've been up to since this morning.' He pulled a sheet of paper from the file in front of him. 'The deceased is of mixed African and Caucasian race, aged between 25 and 30 years. Cause of death appears to be manual strangulation, and she was attacked from behind. The abrasions on the wrist you know about. Er . . . time of death . . . all we can say at this stage is that she's been dead for more than 48 hours. We need to carry out tests on the internal organs to get a more accurate assessment.'

'Have you been able to take any swabs yet?' Leverton asked.

'Yes. We've taken samples from all the orifices and we can get them tested for blood group tomorrow. I suppose you know about the log-jam at the DNA lab?'

Leverton nodded.

'I think you'll have to wait until the end of next week for anything conclusive on that front.'

The sound of footsteps in the corridor made Leverton and Megan turn their heads. A uniformed policewoman was approaching and Leverton motioned her to come in.

'Sorry to interrupt, sir, but Mrs Fellowes is here to identify the body.'

'Yes, I'd heard she'd arrived,' Leverton replied. 'There's a child with her?'

'Yes sir. It's her grandson. He's asleep at the moment. I suggested to her that I could take him while she goes in to look at the body.'

'Right. We'd better get it over with, then.'

The little boy was wrapped up against the cold in a quilted snowsuit with fake fur around the hood. Tight black curls framed his face and long black eyelashes swept his cheeks. Megan couldn't help thinking of Emily. The last time she had seen her she was in exactly the same state as this child: oblivious to any impending disaster life might have in store.

'Mrs Fellowes?' Leverton walked up to the woman and put a hand on her shoulder. At close quarters Megan could see the dark roots of her hair beneath the perm. The deep lines etched around her mouth suggested a lifetime of cigarettes and there was a faraway look in her faded blue eyes. She rose to her feet, handing the sleeping child to the policewoman. Without a word she allowed herself to be guided to the door beyond which her dead daughter lay.

When it was over Leverton sat her down with tea and a cigarette.

'Mrs Fellowes, I need to ask you a few questions. I can do it here if you feel up to it, or if you prefer I can get you back home and we can do it there.'

'You're all right, love,' she whispered, blowing out a veil of smoke. 'I'd sooner get it over while the babby's asleep.' Tears welled in her eyes at the mention of the boy. Mingling with mascara, they ran in two black rivers down her cheeks.

'Can you remember the last time you saw your daughter?'

The woman took another drag on her cigarette. 'It was last Monday afternoon. I took Wesley up town to see Father Christmas. Maria was working, you see.' She paused, glancing down at the floor. When she looked up again her expression had changed to one of resignation. 'You know what I mean.'

Leverton nodded. 'Maria lived at your house, didn't she?'

'Yes.'

'So weren't you worried when she failed to come home that night?'

'No, not really. She sometimes had to, you know, disappear.'

'What do you mean?'

'Well, if there was a crackdown on the beat, she might get arrested a couple of times in the same week, and that would have meant a hundred quid in fines, so if that happened she used to get the train to Bristol. She could work in a massage parlour down there for a few days at a stretch and earn enough money to cover the fine plus a bit extra. There was no danger of her getting arrested because the police down there turn a blind eye to the massage parlours.'

'Wouldn't she have left a note when she did something like that?'

'Not always, no. One time she had to walk straight to the railway station with nothing but the clothes she stood up in. That time her fella was after her and she was doing it to get away from him.'

Leverton's eyebrows arched. 'She had a boyfriend?'

'If you want to call him that, yes, she did. Bastard used to come round and take all her money off her.'

'What do you mean, *used to*?'

The woman stubbed out her cigarette and immediately lit another. 'We haven't seen him for a couple of weeks. I was hoping he was inside.'

'Why? Had Maria reported him?'

'You must be joking! He'd have kicked the shit out of her if she had! Anyway, she said she loved him. He's Wesley's dad, see.'

Leverton paused for a moment before changing tack. 'So, last Sunday when you saw her – what time would you normally have expected her to get back?'

'Depends on how much she took. The weather affects it a lot. If it's cold, you don't get so many punters.'

'Well, let me put it this way: what was the latest she would normally come back?'

'It varied. Never before midnight. Her fella used to come round about two o'clock in the morning to get the money off her. He used to knock her about if she hadn't earned enough. I heard them shouting some nights. Next morning she'd have a black eye or summat.'

'Didn't you ever try phoning us – to stop him, I mean?'

The woman turned her head sideways, blowing out a plume of smoke. 'You don't know what he's like. He's got mates everywhere. He once told our Maria that if she ever tried taking Wesley away from him, he'd track her down.'

'Had they argued recently?'

'Not that I know of. Like I said, he hasn't been to the house for a couple of weeks.'

'Did Maria say why she thought he'd stopped coming?'

'No. He was always on the move. I reckon he was involved in drugs. I gave up asking about him in the end.'

'What was his name?' Leverton asked. The woman looked at him with frightened eyes. 'Don't worry, Mrs Fellowes, we'll make sure he doesn't get anywhere near you and Wesley.'

She wasn't convinced. 'How can you be so sure? Like I said, he's got all these mates . . .'

'We can move you and the boy into a safe house until he's been arrested. We can move you to another part of the country if you want. Start a new life. There are organisations that help women in your position to escape from violent men.'

'You said you were going to arrest him? You think it was him did that to Maria?'

'We don't know yet, Mrs Fellowes, but on the evidence

you've just given me we can arrest him for living off immoral earnings. Once we've got him behind bars, we can find out what else he might have done.'

The woman blinked, tears threatening in the corners of her eyes. Still she said nothing.

Leverton tried again. 'Mrs Fellowes, is there anyone else you can think of who might have wanted to harm your daughter?'

'No.'

'Then for Maria's sake, please tell us her boyfriend's name.'

There was a moment of silence in the smoke-filled room before the woman finally spoke.

'Tyrone.'

'Tyrone,' Leverton repeated, sounding relieved. 'Now is that his first name or his second name?'

'His first name. I don't know his second name. Wesley's got Fellowes on his birth certificate like his mum.'

'Have you got a photograph of him?'

'Maria's got one in her bedroom.' Yellow-stained fingers flew up to the woman's eyes and her whole body began to shake. Her sobs echoed along the corridor, waking the baby who screamed when he saw the unfamiliar face of the police-woman inches from his own.

He was still sobbing when his grandmother carried him out to the patrol car. Leverton stood on the steps outside the mortuary watching the red tail lights disappear into the darkness.

'What did you make of all that, then?'

Megan shivered in the cold draught that followed him through the door. 'It could be the pimp we're looking for, but I don't think he killed Maria.'

'Because she was strangled and handcuffed?'

'Yes.'

Leverton looked at her intently. When he spoke it was as if he was thinking aloud. 'But Maria could have been one of a stable of women he had working for him: including Donna Fieldhouse and Natalie Bailey . . .'

Megan was sitting in Leverton's office when PC Costello arrived with the photograph.

'Come in – sit down.' Leverton sounded tired. They had been scanning the list of pimps provided by Sergeant Donalsen, but there was no one by the name of Tyrone.

'Any joy, sir?' Costello handed Leverton the photograph.

'No. Do you recognise him?'

'No, sir.

'Right, I'd like you to go and show this to the lads in the Drug Squad.'

'Yes, sir.'

'Do you mind if I have a look before he goes?'

Megan took the photograph from Leverton's outstretched hand, frowning as she studied the smiling faces of Maria Fellowes and her lover. She handed it to Costello, who disappeared through the door.

Leverton noticed her puzzled expression. 'What is it?'

'He's too young.'

'What do you mean, too young?'

'I think Donna and Natalie's pimp was between 35 and 45. Maria Fellowes' boyfriend doesn't look as if he's long out of his teens.'

'Could be an old photograph,' Leverton replied. He stood up. 'Come on, Megan, I'll buy you a coffee and we'll take one down for Costello. I can't wait to find out who this bastard is!'

Chapter 11

Leverton caught the pensive look on Megan's face as they walked up the stairs to the police canteen.

'I can almost hear the cogs whirring,' he laughed. 'What are you thinking about now?'

'Well,' Megan paused as they reached a set of double doors, 'let's assume for now that this Tyrone is the O man. He would have to be operating with someone who works at BTV . . .' Megan glanced at Leverton. She couldn't tell him what she was really thinking. Not until that blood group result on the photo of Maria came through.

Leverton nodded. 'And –?'

'And they have the audacity to dump their latest victim right outside the building. They must have known the effect that would have. I mean, the one that works there must realise that eventually he's going to end up being questioned.' *Eventually* being the operative word, she thought grimly.

'So you're wondering why they did it?'

'It just doesn't add up,' Megan said, 'unless they've fallen out.'

Leverton looked at her. 'You mean one's decided to drop the other in it?'

She nodded. Leverton pushed open the doors to the canteen. It was deserted apart from the woman behind the servery. He fetched three coffees on a tray and Megan held the door open for him.

'There's something else that doesn't add up,' she said. 'Why would Tyrone allow AB to do that to Maria? I'm not suggesting there was any sort of affection on his part, but she was bringing him a regular income and she was the mother of his child.'

Leverton frowned. 'Maybe he didn't have a choice. If he was being blackmailed or something.'

Before Megan could reply she spotted PC Costello emerging from a doorway halfway down the corridor. He walked up to them, waving a sheet of paper.

'Got him, sir!' he said eagerly.

'That was quick. We were just bringing you a coffee,' Leverton said. 'What's his name?'

'Tyrone Campbell, sir. He was arrested two weeks ago on a charge of supplying crack-cocaine.'

'Right! Where is he now?'

'That's the bad news, I'm afraid, sir. He was refused bail and he's on remand in Winson Green.'

'Damn!' Leverton peered at the charge sheet Costello was holding out. 'So there's no way he could have killed Maria Fellowes and he couldn't have had anything to do with the deaths of Tina Jackson and her husband either. But presumably he was out when both Donna Fieldhouse and Natalie Bailey were murdered.' He turned to Costello. 'Check that out, will you, and get on to Winson Green: I want to interview this character as soon as possible.'

'Yes, sir.' Costello took his coffee and disappeared down the corridor.

Leverton turned to Megan. 'What do you reckon?'

'It's possible,' Megan agreed. 'He could have killed Donna Fieldhouse himself and then murdered Natalie along with the other guy. Maria's death could even have been some sort of revenge killing on the part of the accomplice.'

'What, you mean if Campbell had let him down in some way?'

'Like I said, it's possible.'

'But you're not convinced?'

Megan took her coffee from the tray in Leverton's hand and took a sip. 'It's just that I can't see a pimp like Campbell allowing himself to be dominated in that way. I mean, the way Maria's mother described him, he sounds like a big-time drug-dealer with women all over the shop, a flash car and a bunch of cronies who all look out for one another. I just can't see someone like that being held to ransom by a punter – unless, of course, the punter has very strong links with the police.'

She looked at Leverton, who was frowning. Whatever his thoughts were, he obviously wasn't going to voice them. Touché, she thought.

'Apart from anything else,' she went on, 'there's the description of the car those two prostitutes in Wolverhampton saw Natalie Bailey getting out of. An old Ford Sierra, they said it was. Now to me, that doesn't fit in with what we know about Tyrone Campbell.'

'Hmmm. That could have been a punter's car, of course: those women were only guessing when they said they thought it was her boyfriend.' He turned and started walking back towards the stairs. 'Come on, let's get back to my office. I'll get on to the detectives looking after Mrs Fellowes and ask them to find out what sort of car Tyrone Campbell drives. If it's a Ford Sierra, you owe me a beer!'

They climbed the stairs in silence. As they passed a window, Megan glimpsed the pavement far below. In the glare of the streetlamps, its icy surface shone like an orange river. Megan glanced at her watch. It was nearly six o'clock. She wondered how soon Leverton was planning to visit Winson Green jail and suddenly she remembered all the Christmas food shopping in the boot of her car. She shuddered, remembering the maggoty chicken. At least the turkey wasn't likely to have defrosted.

Leverton picked up a sheet of paper as he sat down at his

desk. 'What!' he gasped, reading the brief note from his secretary.

'What is it?' Megan asked.

Leverton pushed the piece of paper across the desk towards her. 'The forensic lab called to say they've managed to do a test on the semen from the photograph. It's blood group O!'

Megan read the message and replaced it on the desk, frowning as she did so. 'That's interesting,' she murmured to herself.

'Interesting?' Leverton gazed at her open-mouthed. 'Surely this blows your whole theory about the BTV pervert being the killer out of the water!'

'Not necessarily, no,' Megan replied, returning his gaze, excited despite herself.

'But the guy that killed Tina and Natalie – the anal rapist – we *know* he's blood group AB,' said Leverton in exasperation.

'I know,' Megan replied calmly. 'When I gave you the photograph I said that the person who took it was likely to be the killer of Tina and Natalie. I stand by what I said.'

'So how do you account for this semen sample being blood group O?' Leverton was obviously trying hard not to lose his patience.

'The person who sent the photograph may not be the person who took it.'

'What?'

'It's possible that the man who handcuffed and killed Maria Fellowes took a Polaroid photograph of his handiwork. Perhaps he took several. Perhaps he gave one to his partner-in-crime or left it lying around the accomplice's house, if that's where the murder took place. The accomplice saw it and decided to send it to Delva Lobelo.'

'Hang on a minute, let's get this straight. You're now saying that the one with the blood group O – the one we've been calling the pimp – is the perverted letter-writer who works at BTV?' He looked at her incredulously. 'I thought you were convinced it was the other guy – the one with AB blood – that was the pervert?'

'I admit it seemed likely,' Megan said, still looking him in the eye. 'But in the light of this new forensic evidence it's clearly *Donna's* killer who works at BTV.'

'Are you serious?'

'Yes, of course I am.' She tried to quell the frustration she felt inside.

'I'm sorry, Megan,' he said, shaking his head, 'but if I heard you correctly, what you're saying is that the man we've been referring to as the pimp is employed by BTV?'

Megan nodded.

Leverton shook his head again. 'What as?'

Megan took a deep breath. 'Look, Martin, I know it sounds strange, but I know for a fact that BTV employs scores of casual and part-time staff. Delva Lobelo told me only this week that several of the ancillary services have been put out to tender: catering and security, for example . . .'

'Oh, I see', Leverton cut in. 'So our man doffs his chef's cap after serving up the evening meal in the BTV canteen and goes out to do a spot of pimping, does he?' He stood up. 'I'm sorry, Megan. I just don't buy it. Now if you'll excuse me,' he said curtly, 'I'm off to Winson Green.'

Megan hadn't really intended going back to the university, but found she had driven there on automatic pilot. She sat in the car park, still fuming from her encounter with Leverton. How could he be so pig-headed, she thought? While he was pissing about with that pimp in Winson Green the real killers were still out there. He should be at BTV going through the staff records with a fine-tooth comb.

'Oh for a cigarette,' she moaned, leaning across to the glove compartment. She dialled her sister's number on the mobile, crunching her way through half a dozen Maltesers before she heard Neil's voice.

'Hi. It's Megan. How's Joe?'

'Oh, he's fine. We've just come back from visiting him.' She thought he sounded edgy again.

'Have they said any more about letting him come home?'

'Yes, tomorrow afternoon. Oh, by the way, I told Ceri what you said about staying with us on Saturday night and she said yes, if it's still okay with you. She says she's dying to see you and she sends her love.'

'Great!' Megan was instantly cheered at the prospect of seeing Ceri. 'I'll see you all tomorrow – about sixish, okay?'

She was about to start the engine up again when she noticed a light in one of the windows of the building. It was Patrick's office. What was he doing in the department at this time of night? She got out of the car.

The lobby was in semi-darkness, the thin beams of the security lights casting an eerie glow over the empty porter's lodge. She glanced at her pigeonhole as she walked past and noticed a couple of Christmas cards. She stuffed them into her bag and headed for the lift.

The first floor was even darker than the lobby. As she made her way towards Patrick's office, the door flew open.

'Megan! I'm so glad I've caught you. I thought you'd disappeared for Christmas without giving me a chance to say goodbye.'

Megan was taken aback. 'I . . . er . . . had to go straight to the mortuary from home this morning and I've been with the police all day. When did you get back from Long Lartin?'

'Not until late last night. I've got a great interview – you must hear it. I'd given up hope but they phoned me at home yesterday morning to say he'd changed his mind. They told me he was about to be transferred to Parkhurst so I thought I'd better go to Long Lartin straight away. I wasn't sure if my expenses would stretch to a trip to the Isle of Wight.'

'When are you going home – to Holland, I mean?'

'Tomorrow afternoon. I was just packing a few papers to take with me. Can I take you out for a Christmas drink?'

'What, now?'

'Yes, why not?' Patrick laughed. 'Unless you'd prefer to go at eleven o'clock tomorrow morning?'

Megan didn't know what to say. She felt worn out and she was sure she looked terrible. What she really wanted was to go home and have a long soak in the bath, preferably with a large scotch balanced on the soap rack.

'Come on,' Patrick said, 'you look as if you need a drink. Did you say you've been at the mortuary again?'

Megan's expression gave her away.

'Hey, what's the matter?' Patrick asked. 'You look as if you've seen one dead body too many. '

'No, it's not that.' She sighed. 'Detective Superintendent Leverton and I have had a disagreement about the profiles I gave him. I won't be working on the case from now on.' Patrick frowned. 'It's okay,' Megan said, 'I just don't feel much like going out, that's all.'

'Well, I'm not letting you off the hook that easily.' He went back into his office and pulled something out of a holdall. He re-emerged holding a bottle of single malt whisky in one hand and a large box of Belgian chocolates in the other.

'Your place or mine?' he grinned. 'I have to warn you though, I've only got two glasses and one of those has my toothbrush in it.'

Megan laughed in spite of herself. 'Oh come on, you poor student!' she said. 'You can come back to my house. But I might get you wrapping Christmas presents or taking the giblets out of the turkey. Do you think you can handle it?'

Martin Leverton called in at BTV on his way to Winson Green. A couple of detectives had spent the day quizzing employees but they were no nearer to locating the missing tape.

A temporary incident room had been set up on the ground floor of the building. One of the detectives was studying a list of names and a man Leverton recognised as the head of security was sitting nearby.

'Evening, sir,' the detective said, looking up. 'You haven't met Mr Simon, have you?'

Leverton offered the man his hand. 'It's an awful experience, seeing something like that. How's your mother now?'

'Oh, not too bad, thanks,' he replied. 'She's gone to a friend's house – I didn't want her to be at home on her own.'

'No, I can understand that. Thanks for coming back in – we do appreciate it. It's vital that we find out what happened to that tape.'

'I know. I can't understand it. Brian O'Malley was on duty from seven o'clock last night to seven o'clock this morning. He was still here when I arrived and, you know, found the – body. He said he finished his shift and went to the canteen for some breakfast. Two of the other lads had already arrived to take over when he left the back security office. Their names are Henry Fletcher and Gary Widdowson. They're both a hundred per cent reliable. I mean, I'd trust them with my life. I can't believe either of them could be responsible for that tape going missing.'

'And the tapes are kept in a locked cupboard in the back security office?'

'Yes.'

'Is the office ever left unattended?'

'Only when the lads nip to the toilet,' Simon replied. 'I mean, we're talking five minutes at the most.'

'And who has a key to the cupboard?'

'Well, all my lads have got one, plus the senior staff at BTV all have master keys.'

'Is this a list of the security staff?' Leverton asked, taking the piece of paper attached to the detective's clipboard.

'Yes. A few of them have booked time off for Christmas,

though, so I don't know if you'll be able to get hold of everyone on the list.'

'Which ones are those?'

'The ones with an 'L' next to their name. The only one that I know has definitely gone away is Adrian Barber. I gave him a lift to the airport yesterday lunchtime. He was off to Tenerife, lucky so-and-so.'

'Right,' Leverton said. 'So that leaves twenty-six others including the three who were in this morning. It seems an awful lot of staff for a building this size. Are any of them part-timers or casual staff?'

'None of them are completely full-time here – this is just one of my security contracts, you see. I cover another firm in Stafford and I do temporary contract work as well – guarding film equipment on location, that sort of thing. Most of my lads go from one job to another depending on their availability and the number of contracts I've got on at any one time.'

'I see,' Leverton said. 'Complicated, isn't it? Do you ask for references when you take people on? I mean, we'll obviously have to check that none of these people has a criminal record of any kind.'

'I think you'll find they're all kosher,' Simon smiled. 'I know some security firms take on ex-cons, but when you're running things on a contract basis you can't afford to take any risks.'

'Yes, I can appreciate that. Right, Mr Simon, thanks for your help. You can go home now if you want to. We'll give you a call if we need to know anything else.'

'Are you linking this girl's death with those others?'

Leverton gave him a look of annoyance. 'I'm sorry – I can't possibly comment on that.'

'I only asked,' Simon persisted, 'because my mother's scared out of her wits. She's got it into her head there's some

serial killer on the loose. Will you be calling in that profiler –
the one BTV's doing a programme about?'

'Like I said, Mr Simon, I really can't comment. Please tell
your mother not to worry. Incidents like this are really very
rare, you know.'

'Still, three in one week.' Simon picked up his coat. 'Makes
you think.'

'Are you going to tell me about it, then?' Patrick was pouring
generous measures of whisky into a couple of Megan's crystal
tumblers. He handed her one, tilting his head to one side and
fixing her with his most winning smile.

Megan winced at the memory of Leverton's words. 'It's
a mess – a real mess,' she said. 'And it's my fault for trying
to play Leverton at his own game.' She told him about Maria
Fellowes and the blood group of the semen on the photograph. 'I thought that within a couple of days we'd have a
DNA result on the semen, which I hoped would be identical
to that of one of the killers.'

'But you haven't?'

'No. When I handed the photograph over, I had no idea
there was a backlog of samples waiting to be tested. The
result won't be available until after Christmas.'

'So all the police have got is the blood group result, which
tells them the pervert is definitely not the AB man.'

Megan sighed. 'I know. Like I said, it's a mess. And to
make things worse, Leverton's headed off on a wild goose
chase to Winson Green prison to interview Maria Fellowes'
pimp.'

'Who was actually locked up when the last three victims
were killed.' Patrick frowned. 'Haven't they got any record
of this – what's his name again?'

'Campbell. Tyrone Campbell.'

'Haven't they got any record of his blood group or a DNA
sample? If he's got previous he should have been tested.'

'I don't know. He was charged with drugs possession two weeks ago, but Leverton told me there's a waiting time of eight weeks at the moment for non-urgent samples. So unless he's been charged with another offence in the past year or so, there's not going to be any record of his DNA.'

'Well, if I was Leverton, I'd have checked that out before going to Winson Green.'

'I'm sure he will have,' Megan said. 'He's very thorough. Just bloody stubborn.'

Patrick topped up her glass and refilled his own. 'If he'd accepted your theory that it's the pimp who works at BTV,' he said, looking up as he lifted his glass, 'what would have happened next?'

Megan took a sip of her whisky. 'How do you mean?'

'Well, imagine he'd taken on board your idea about the pimp being some sort of casual worker there,' said Patrick. 'I mean, I'm assuming you think the pervert and the pimp are one and the same . . .'

'Yes, I do. I think the man who sent that photograph to Delva was also responsible for dumping Maria's body. It was a stunt aimed at shocking her, but it backfired because she didn't actually see it.'

'So this pimp or pervert or whatever we're going to call him – who do you think he is?'

'He could be one of dozens of people who work at BTV on a casual or part-time basis. The spelling and grammar in the letters Delva showed me suggested a blue-collar occupation. At the time I thought it could be a deliberate ploy by an educated colleague but that seems less likely now.'

'Why?'

'Well the small-time pimps – the ones who're not involved in drug-dealing – are usually either unemployed or doing some sort of unskilled or semi-skilled job. I've come across a few pimps from what you might call the professional classes, but they tend to run high-class call-girls, not street prostitutes like Donna Fieldhouse and Natalie Bailey.'

'So the pervert has some sort of blue-collar job.'

'Yes,' said Megan, 'and it's absolutely crucial to find out who he is. Nail him and he'll lead us to the other killer. Without him, it's going to be like looking for a needle in a haystack, profile or no profile.'

'But Leverton thinks he's already got the pimp, so where's he going to start looking for the other killer?'

'Well, I think he's got it in for Donalsen,' Megan replied. 'You should have seen the guy's face when Leverton told him about Maria Fellowes' body being found. He's got to be involved in some way, but I still don't believe he's a killer.'

Patrick thought for a moment, rolling the remains of his whisky around the glass. 'If I was Leverton I'd be checking if anyone who works at BTV is an ex-cop.'

'Why would he do that if he already believes Donalsen is the killer?'

'Well, let's just imagine for a minute that Leverton is right about Tyrone Campbell being the pimp who killed Donna Fieldhouse . . .'

Megan frowned.

'But,' Patrick went on, 'he definitely can't be the pervert who sent that stuff to Delva Lobelo because he's been in jail for the past two weeks.'

'So?'

'So if Leverton really believes Donalsen is the other killer that leaves him with a major problem. There has to be *someone* involved who has regular access to BTV. Wonder how he'll get round that one?'

PC Costello was cruising slowly through the red light district when a woman stepped out of the shadows and flagged him down. He recognised her as she sauntered towards the passenger door of his car.

In the dark, she looked quite attractive. She was tall and slim and wore high black leather boots and an expensive-looking jacket. He wondered how many other men knew her secret. He doubted if any of her punters had been allowed to see what he had seen. She rapped on the window and he leaned across to let her in.

'About bloody time!' she said, shivering as she eased herself into the seat. 'You going back? I need a hot chocolate. It's cold as a penguin's bollocks out there!'

Costello laughed and started the engine. He glanced at her as they drove along. She fascinated him. The thought of men paying her for sex intrigued him.

'I've got something to tell you,' she said slyly as he pulled up.

Megan was attempting to stick down a flap of Christmas wrapping paper and Patrick was trying to help her. The double whiskies had taken their toll and she ended up sellotaping his thumb to the parcel. They both collapsed onto the rug, giggling like teenagers.

'Whose idea was this?' Patrick laughed, screwing the sellotape into a ball and tossing it into the fire.

'Yours!' Megan retorted. 'Remember? Let's not talk about work, you said.'

'Okay, okay, so I'm useless at wrapping Christmas presents.'

He was lying on his back, and as Megan leaned across to retrieve her glass he pulled her down on top of him, kissing her before she could protest.

'Mmmm . . . What was that for?' She broke away, smiling as she gazed down into his eyes.

'Christmas?' he murmured. 'I didn't get you a present, you see.'

'Very funny.' Megan ran her fingers through his hair. 'But what would your girlfriend say?'

He closed his eyes. 'Who said anything about a girlfriend?'

'Oh come on, Patrick. Don't try telling me the Heartland heart-throb hasn't got someone keeping his bed warm back home.'

'The what?' Patrick opened his eyes and laughed when he saw the knowing expression on Megan's face. In a sudden, swift movement, he rolled her onto the rug, pinioning her arms above her head while he kissed her mouth and neck.

Megan knew she should be pushing him away. He relaxed his grip on her wrists, but she found she couldn't move. The sensation of his lips on her skin was setting off fireworks deep inside. It had been such a long, long time.

'Patrick . . .' She heard herself saying his name and it sounded strange and wonderful; wonderful but dangerous. She sat up, pulling her sweater back on to her shoulder. 'We mustn't do this.'

'Why not?' He ran his finger softly along her neck. 'It's Christmas, we're together – and I've been wanting to do this to you for the past six weeks.' He slipped his hand over her shoulder, delving beneath her sweater to rub her back. Then he plunged his face into the soft wool covering her breasts. Slowly he pushed back the fabric, stroking her skin with his tongue.

'No, Patrick!' She stood up and made for the kitchen. Flicking the switch on the kettle, she grabbed the coffee jar. She reached for the mugs, but he was behind her. She could feel his arms slipping around her waist.

'Why not?' he whispered in her ear.

'Because I'm your supervisor, for a start!' Her hand shook as she spooned out the coffee. 'How can I carry on working with you if we start getting involved?'

Instead of answering, he whispered in her ear, 'Can't you take me with you to that little cottage in Wales? I could fly back from Amsterdam on Boxing Day . . .' He began to nibble the back of her neck. She stood staring at the kettle, wanting him to carry on, wishing she hadn't allowed things to go this far. Steam rushed from the spout and she freed herself, concentrating hard as she poured the boiling water into the mugs. She told herself that when they had both sobered up everything would be all right. They would part for Christmas and when they met again it would all seem like a dream.

Costello watched the woman walk away. Her words were a dangerous weapon. What was he going to do?

She was climbing the steps at the end of alley. He could see her buttocks swaying from side to side, bulging out of her tight satin shorts. And that wig – was it a trick of the light or was it lopsided?

She had told him many times that she was old enough to be his mother. Not that he needed telling. In the harsh fluorescent lights of the lock-up she looked more like a grandmother. He would never forget the first time he had seen her without the wig. It had been his first week on the Vice Squad. No one had warned him about her, apart from telling him she was the oldest tart on the beat.

After it happened, she swore him to secrecy, saying none of the punters knew and if word got round it would ruin her business. She had been a pathetic sight standing there in the charge room, her painted face like a mask on a mannequin's naked head.

'What are you gawping at?' she'd said, bending down to retrieve the wig from the floor. 'Wouldn't stare at me if I was a fella, would you?'

She was right, of course. And he was sure she would be equally convincing if she stood up in court to say who she had seen picking up Maria Fellowes. There was really only one thing he could do.

Chapter 12

Megan opened her eyes and screamed. There was someone sitting on the bed beside her. He reached out for her in the darkness and for a split second she was plunged into a recurring nightmare.

'Hey, calm down. It's only me!' Patrick held her close, muffling her cries with his shoulder. 'I'm sorry I scared you – I thought you were still awake.'

'Oh God!' Megan gasped, 'You must think I'm stark raving mad, screaming like that. It's just that I couldn't work out who you were; I must have dozed off and then when I saw you sitting there I thought it was . . .' She trailed off, too embarrassed to go on.

'Who?' Patrick drew back but took one of her hands in his. In the light that filtered through the curtains from the street-lamps she could just make out his features. He was looking at her with a mixture of curiosity and concern. 'Who, Megan?'

She raised her free hand to her forehead. There was a pounding inside her skull and she rubbed the skin in a vain attempt to ease the pain. 'It's okay. It was just a bad dream.'

'Where do you keep the aspirin?' he asked, releasing her hand and standing up.

'In the kitchen, the cupboard above the kettle – thanks, Patrick.' She lay back on the pillow and closed her eyes, listening to his footsteps as he padded down the stairs. She hoped he wouldn't ask any more questions. How could she explain that she had mistaken him for a rapist?

She had never even told her sister about that night. Ceri's twenty-first birthday party. The tall, dark, pushy friend of Neil's who wouldn't leave her alone. The taxi home, unaware that she was being followed. The banging on the door that had woken her up. His face. So plausible. Saying Neil had no room and had sent him to ask her for a bed. She blinked, trying to shut out what had happened next. Neil was the only one who knew. And he had never believed her.

Patrick came back with a glass of water and two tablets. As he sat down on the edge of the bed she noticed that he was only wearing boxer shorts and a T-shirt. The sight of his bare legs made the pounding in her head feel worse. He held out the tablets and she took them, thankful that he hadn't switched on the light.

'Are you going to tell me what all that was about?' he asked gently.

'I . . . I can't. It's something that happened years ago; I'd rather not talk about it.' As she said the words she realised why she had felt such blind panic. It wasn't just the memory of the rape. All those inexplicable incidents – the maggots, the shells, the open window. She'd tried to rationalise them away, but they'd been festering in her subconscious.

'I'm sorry,' Patrick said. 'I shouldn't have come creeping up here like that, but I couldn't sleep and there was something I wanted to tell you.'

'What?'

'Well, I feel really bad about what happened. I put you in a really awkward situation and I want to say sorry.'

Megan opened her mouth to speak but he shook his head. 'No. There's something else I have to tell you.' He paused and took a breath. 'There is someone – in Holland, I mean. Before I came here I was engaged. We were supposed to be getting married next summer.'

'Married!' Megan gasped. 'My God, Patrick, I've heard of being economical with the truth but . . .'

'No, wait,' he cut in, 'I'm not engaged any more. I realised soon after I arrived here that it was a mistake. The trouble is she won't accept that it's over. She thinks that when we see each other again I'll change my mind.'

'Do you really expect me to believe that?'

'Why not? It's true.'

'So why *are* you going to see her again?'

'I can't really avoid it. She's still living in my apartment.'

'What are you going to do?'

Patrick shrugged and shook his head. 'I don't know. Move my stuff out, I suppose. It's only a rented place, so she can stay there if she likes. I'm not looking forward to it, though.'

'Do you think you'll have second thoughts – when you see her again, I mean?'

'Who knows. I expect she'll be really nice to me, which will make things even worse.'

'Do you think she'll try persuading you not to come back here after the holidays?'

'Probably. I feel really bad about letting her down. At the end of the day I'm just being selfish. When I started my doctorate it was like a whole new horizon suddenly opened up. I'm not even sure I want to go back to police work when I finish here. I suppose I just want to keep my options open.'

'But she wants you to settle down?'

Patrick nodded. 'How's your head?' he asked.

'Oh, still throbbing a bit.' She wondered if he had deliberately changed the subject. 'I think it's partly a hangover. Serves me right for drinking all your whisky.' She smiled in spite of herself. 'I think I'll try and get some sleep now.' She lay her head on the pillow. 'Goodnight, Patrick.'

'Goodnight.' He bent over and stroked her head. She froze. What had she done? Letting this man she hardly knew into her house. Into her bedroom.

'It's all right, I'm going.' She listened to his footsteps going down the stairs. Listened for the sound of the living room door closing. She slid out of bed, her head pounding with the effort of standing up. Tiptoeing across the carpet, she closed the door and turned the key in the lock.

In the grey winter dawn, the woman's skin reminded Costello of the wafer-thin smoked chicken his wife bought at Safeway. Blue veins criss-crossed the temples and her features had the gaunt look of a corpse, flesh pulled tight across the bones by the wig.

'We going in or have I got to stay out here freezing my arse off?' she squawked.

He led her through the heavy doors of the police station, grateful for the warmth and the reassuring smell of disinfectant. A couple of drunks were leaning against the desk and a woman with a black eye was sobbing silently in a corner.

'Is the boss in yet?' he asked the woman behind the desk. 'I need to take Miss Bunce to an interview room.'

When they got there Leverton was already waiting. 'Ah, Eileen! How lovely to see you,' he said, eyebrows raised at the sight of her silk shorts and thigh-length boots.

'You can shut up, you sarky bastard.' She settled into a chair. Costello noticed the flesh at the top of her legs was puckered into purple-tipped goosepimples.

'PC Costello tells me you have some interesting information for us.' Leverton seated himself opposite the woman.

'I can't talk on an empty stomach,' she replied, folding her arms on the table and leaning towards Leverton. 'I'll have a bacon butty and a cup of tea, I think.' Leverton nodded to Costello.

'Two sugars!' she shouted as Costello disappeared behind the door.

The sound of the telephone invaded Megan's dreams. She fumbled for the receiver, her eyes still closed as she mumbled her name.

'Megan? Are you there?' The voice at the other end of the phone was Martin Leverton's.

'Martin?'

'Yes. What can I say? You were right, and all I can do is offer you my humblest apologies and ask you to forgive me.'

'Martin, what are you talking about?' Megan sat up in bed, rubbing her eyes and peering at the clock. It was half-past nine.

'Tyrone Campbell – Maria Fellowes' pimp; you were right about him having nothing to do with the murders.'

'Oh, really?'

'Yes – I've just received some information that rules him out completely. But there's been another development. Listen, are you still in this? Because I've got a real crisis on my hands.'

Twenty minutes later Megan was driving past the university on her way to the police station. She wondered what Patrick would think when he woke up. He had seemed to be in such a deep sleep that she hadn't wanted to disturb him.

She had left a note propped up on the coffee table wishing him a happy Christmas and explaining why she'd had to go. In retrospect, it was probably the best thing. She hoped that by the time she saw him again the embarrassment of last night would have worn off.

She tried to concentrate on what Leverton had said, but the image of Patrick sitting beside her bed kept flashing into her mind. In a few hours he would be back in Holland; his girlfriend hell-bent on luring him back.

'My God, you really know how to pick them,' she muttered to herself, simultaneously fantasizing about waking up on Christmas Day with Patrick beside her. In reality she'd be waking up in the spare room at Ceri's with Emily leaping all over her. Still, she thought, it would be better than waking up alone in her bed at home.

She pulled into the car park outside the police station, her feet crunching across the gritted snow. Leverton had a pot of coffee waiting for her in his office. Obviously anxious to make amends, he apologised again before telling her what had happened.

'I've got this prostitute in the interview room downstairs. She swears she saw Rob Donalsen having sex with Maria Fellowes in an unmarked squad car on the night she disappeared.'

Megan raised her eyebrows but said nothing.

'As you know, I've suspected for some time that he's been taking advantage of his job in Vice,' Leverton went on. 'The thing is, I've just had his medical details back.' He paused, staring straight into Megan's eyes. 'His blood group's AB.'

Megan sat in stunned silence for a moment. At last, she thought, he's decided to lay his cards on the table. Does he really expect me to swallow that bull about only just getting the medical records?

'Have you charged him with anything yet?'

'Not yet, no. He admits picking Maria up but he denies having sex with her. He says he'd seen her soliciting and asked her to get into the car while he gave her an informal warning.'

'I know you think he's a bent copper.' Megan watched Leverton's face. 'But do you really think he's capable of something like this?'

'That's what I was going to ask you,' Leverton said with a grim smile. 'All I can say is the longer I do this job, the less I seem to know. I used to think I was a pretty good judge of people. In fact I used to pride myself on being able to see through the flannel most villains give you. But now . . . I don't know . . . I suppose I've come to realise that some people can be so plausible, so manipulative. It's like a twisted gift, the sort of thing that could make a straight guy into an award-winning actor.'

'But from what you've told me about Rob Donalsen, and from what I've seen, he's given himself away at almost every turn. He's hardly a Ted Bundy when it comes to pulling the wool over people's eyes, is he?'

'You don't think he's the killer?'

'I didn't say that. What I mean is that Donalsen doesn't appear to be the kind of charming sociopath who fools people into thinking he's a harmless, boy-next-door type. If you want me to give you an opinion on whether he's a likely candidate for these murders, I'll need a lot more information about him and I'll have to talk to this prostitute about exactly what she saw. Presumably he doesn't have an alibi for Monday night?'

'No. He was on duty. Says he was out on the beat, driving around alone. He's not supposed to do that – there are always supposed to be two officers present when they make an arrest – I had a word with Costello about it, but he's very cagey about saying anything against his boss. It was Costello who brought Eileen Bunce, the prostitute, in. He drove round for a couple of hours after she'd told him about seeing Donalsen with Maria – couldn't decide what to do for the best.'

'What about relationships?' Megan asked. 'Is Donalsen married?'

'Separated.'

'When did they split up?'

'Not long ago. He was off sick for a week when it happened. It was only a couple of months ago, I think.'

'We need to check that, then. It could have been a trigger for the murders. What does the wife do?'

'She used to be a secretary here but she left last year.'

'I need more details about her. Is there anyone here she was close to? I mean a colleague she might have kept in touch with?'

'I'll find out. Would you like to go and talk to Eileen Bunce while I do that?'

'Yes, okay.' Megan drained her coffee cup and stood up. 'Before I do –'

'What?'

'On the phone you said you'd received some information that cleared Tyrone Campbell of any involvement in the murders. What was it?'

'His blood group – it's B.'

Megan frowned as she looked at him. 'So you didn't bother going to Winson Green last night, then?'

'Yes I did. We didn't have any record of his blood group on our files, you see. When I got there I had a chat with the Governor. He's a new chap and he'd come across Tyrone Campbell before when he was Assistant Governor at Shrewsbury. Evidently Campbell was done for attempted rape on a woman in Telford. He was held at Shrewsbury jail and West Mercia Police had a record of his blood group on file. I contacted them as soon as I got back from Winson Green, and I got a call from them first thing this morning.'

Megan walked across to the window, trying to avoid Leverton's eyes. She didn't want her expression to be misconstrued as gloating. 'Did you actually speak to Tyrone Campbell?' She glanced at the crowds of last-minute Christmas shoppers in the street below. 'I was wondering if he might know who the killers are.'

'He wouldn't talk,' Leverton replied. 'Didn't want to know.'

'So, we still have no idea who the O man is.' She turned round to face Leverton. 'I don't want to end up arguing with you again, Martin, but have you got any further at BTV?'

'Don't worry, I'm keeping an open mind about what you said. I spoke to the head of the security firm last night – you know, the bloke who found Maria's body – and we're checking out a staff list he gave us. We're doing the same for the catering people and the cleaning staff. Nearly all of them are casuals or part-timers and I wouldn't mind betting that a few of them will have been through the doors of this place at some time or another.'

'Could I have a copy of the lists?' Megan asked. Catch him while he's in a good mood, she thought.

'Yes, I don't see why not.' Leverton smiled. 'I'll get them photocopied for you.'

Put the flags out, Megan thought. 'Right,' she said, picking up her bag. 'I'd better go and speak to Miss Bunce. What's she like, by the way?'

Leverton screwed up his face.

'That bad, eh?'

Eileen Bunce had just lit up a cigarette when Megan was shown into the room. PC Costello introduced them and Megan sat down, trying not to stare at the crooked ginger wig.

'I'd like you to try to remember exactly what you saw when you walked past the squad car.' Megan was looking straight into the woman's eyes, noticing the thin, veined skin and the crows' feet filled with last night's blue eye-shadow.

'He's already had a statement off me,' the woman replied, jerking a thumb at Costello. 'What more do you want?'

'What you told my colleagues was that you saw Maria Fellowes and Sergeant Donalsen having sex in his car. I want you to describe exactly what you saw them doing.'

The woman turned to Costello. 'She kinky or summat?'

Megan ignored the remark and carried on. 'Were they in the front of the car or the back?'

'The front.' She looked askance at Megan.

'Could you see both of them quite clearly?'

'I could see his head and his shoulders – I was only walking past, you know. I didn't have a ringside seat!'

'How can you be sure they were having sex?'

'Well, for a start I could hear him grunting and groaning – right bloody racket he was making – and I could see her boots on the dashboard.'

'Had she taken them off?'

'No, course not!' The woman raised her eyes to the ceiling. 'Her feet was up there 'cos he was shagging her on the passenger seat and there wasn't nowhere else they could have fitted.'

'How did you know it was Maria he was with?'

'I saw her getting into the car. I stand just up the road from her and I saw him pick her up. I got a punter a few minutes later, but he changed his mind and dropped me off in Prole Street. That's when I saw them at it.'

'How do you know Sergeant Donalsen hadn't let Maria out of the car and picked up someone else?'

'Her boots,' the woman replied. 'They're the same as mine. I had them specially made by a bloke down the market who makes cowboy gear. She asked me where I got them from and went and had a pair made exactly the same. I never spoke to her again after that.'

Megan was staring intently at the woman now. 'This might seem a strange question to ask, but I can assure you it's vital to this inquiry: I need to know what position Maria Fellowes was in when Sergeant Donalsen was having sex with her. You say you saw her boots on the dashboard – did the position of her feet indicate that she was lying on her front or her back?'

'Oh, her back, definitely her back,' the woman replied, looking at Megan with a curious expression. 'Was the bugger who killed her kinky, then?'

Megan and Costello exchanged glances at this unfortunate choice of words. 'I'm afraid I can't comment on that,' Megan said. 'But thank you for your information. It's extremely important.'

Leverton was on the phone when Megan went back up to his office. He waved her to a seat and she immediately noticed how flushed his face looked.

'And she still works there now, does she?' he said to the person on the other end of the line. 'Right, that's great – many thanks.' He put the phone down and turned to Megan. 'You'll never believe this: Donalsen's wife works at BTV!'

'Really? Who told you?'

'A woman she used to work with, WPC Anderton. They both worked in the Control Room. Anyway, according to her Rob Donalsen often went to BTV to pick his wife up because she didn't have a car.'

'How long ago did they split up?'

'Two months. I checked the sick leave book.'

'And when did she start working at BTV?'

'Eighteen months ago.'

'So Donalsen was going in and out of the place for over a year,' Megan mused. 'He could have got to know some of the other staff reasonably well in that time.'

Leverton nodded. 'I asked WPC Anderton if she knew about the split and she said she'd heard the gossip about Rob being separated, but didn't know the details. She thinks his wife might have had an affair with someone at BTV.'

Neil's face flashed into Megan's mind. 'What's her first name?'

'Helen. Why?'

'Oh, just curious.' Megan felt a surge of relief. *Although he's still not off the hook*, she thought grimly.

The phone rang again and Leverton picked it up. After a moment he grabbed a notepad and began scribbling something down.

'That was the pathologist,' he said, replacing the receiver. 'They've just had the blood-group results on the swabs they took from Maria Fellowes.'

'And?'

'It's strange,' Leverton said, reading what he had just written. 'Semen was found to be present in the vaginal and anal orifices. Anal semen was blood group AB. Vaginal semen also type AB.'

'AB in the vagina?'

'That's what he said.'

'Well, I never.'

Leverton frowned at her. 'What?'

'When I was talking to Eileen Bunce I asked her to describe exactly what she saw Donalsen and Maria doing in the car. She said Maria was lying on her back in the passenger seat with Donalsen on top of her.'

'So?'

'Don't you see? Maria was the wrong way round.'

The puzzled frown lifted as Leverton realised what she was implying. 'Of course! Natalie and Tina were raped from behind. So what the hell was Donalsen doing, then?'

'Well,' Megan said, 'there are two possibilities. Either the killer has changed his modus operandi or Donalsen's innocent.'

'Innocent?'

'Of Maria's death. I'm not trying to say he's innocent of the other things you think he's been up to, but the presence of AB semen in the vagina could mean that he had sex with Maria before the real killer got hold of her.'

'But that would mean that two different men with the same rare blood group had sex with the same woman within hours or even minutes of each other. Isn't that a bit far-fetched?'

'Type AB isn't *that* rare. It's present in about three percent of the population.'

'That's still only three men in every hundred,' Leverton said, rubbing his chin.

'That first pathologist we saw, you know, Horrobin? He said the anal semen from Tina Jackson was an AB subtype present in about two percent of the population. If forensics run an enzyme test on the samples they might be able to tell us if they came from two different men.'

'Yes, I suppose I could get that done.' Leverton frowned. 'But an enzyme test might not be conclusive.'

'I know. But apart from that all we can do is sit tight and wait for the DNA results. Unless . . .' Megan paused, her eyes narrowing.

'Unless what?'

'Unless Donalsen's wife feels like helping us out.'

Chapter 13

There was a knock at Leverton's door. A freckle-faced giant of a man with hair the colour of Eileen Bunce's wig strode into the room. The tight auburn curls looked so incongruous on a man of his size that Megan had to try very hard not to smile.

'I'm just taking the SOCOs round to Rob Donalsen's place, sir.' The man shifted uncomfortably, looking at the floor. Megan sensed his embarrassment at having to search the home of a fellow officer. 'Is there anything in particular you'd like the lads to look for, sir?'

Leverton looked at Megan.

'A Polaroid camera,' she said, 'and that shamrock pendant. Look for any jewellery, clothes or personal possessions that might have been taken from the victims.'

'What about pornographic material? Magazines, videos, that sort of thing?' Leverton asked.

'Yes. Especially anything to do with bondage or sadism. Whoever killed those women is into cruelty and humiliation, so anything you see that reflects that kind of behaviour would be extremely useful.'

The detective finished scribbling notes and hurried off to join the scene-of-crime officers waiting to scour Donalsen's flat.

Half an hour later, Leverton pulled up outside a pebble-dashed house in a quiet road where Christmas lights flashed behind net curtains. Snow had been shoveled into untidy grey heaps on the pavements and a snowman with a lop-sided head stood guard on one of the mean strips of turf that masqueraded as a front garden.

Helen Donalsen stared at Leverton when she answered the door. Then her gaze shifted to Megan. A look of recognition was swiftly followed by one of total bewilderment.

'I'm sorry to spring this on you, Helen,' Leverton said, 'but I need to talk to you about something very serious.' He paused for a moment, trying to gauge her reaction. 'It's about Rob. Can we come in?'

'What is it? What's happened? He's not dead? He can't be dead. I saw his Mum this morning in Sainsbury's.' She leaned against the door for support and Megan noticed how thin she was.

Leverton put an arm on her shoulder, ushering her inside. 'No, no, of course he's not dead, love. That's not why we're here. We need to ask you a few questions about Rob.'

The woman frowned as Leverton introduced Megan. 'This is Doctor Rhys –'

'I know.' She cut him short before he could explain. She stared at Megan with a mixture of fear and suspicion. 'I've seen your face on the trailer for that documentary BTV's made about you.'

'Oh.' Megan shouldn't have been surprised, but she still found it slightly unnerving to be recognised by a complete stranger.

'Doctor Rhys is helping us with the investigation into the death of the woman found outside the BTV building yesterday,' Leverton said as he sat down on a very new-looking cream sofa.

'What's Rob got to do with it? And why have you come to me? You know we split up, don't you?'

'Yes,' Leverton replied. 'I'm sorry to have to involve you in this, Helen, but we're holding Rob on suspicion of murder. We have reason to believe he may have killed her.'

Helen Donalsen stared at Leverton, shaking her head. Her lips moved but no sound emerged.

'I can understand what a shock this must be for you, Helen, but we need to ask you some very important questions about Rob. You see, he has no alibi for the night of the murder and we have a witness who claims to have seen him with the victim on the night she disappeared.'

'She was a tart, wasn't she?' Cold rage transformed the woman's features. 'What were they doing? Blow job on the front seat of the squad car?' She turned to Megan. 'Do you know, he had the bloody nerve to blame me for it? Said I drove him to it when I walked out on him. He couldn't leave them alone, dirty bastard.'

The woman was shaking. Megan wondered why Donalsen had told his wife about his illicit liaisons with prostitutes. If he was the murderer, such an admission would be extremely dangerous. It certainly wasn't the behaviour of a calculating serial killer.

'Mrs Donalsen, we don't want to pry into the reasons why you and your husband split up,' Megan said gently. 'But we need to know if Rob ever threatened you physically in any way.' Megan paused, hoping her words wouldn't provoke an outburst.

Helen Donalsen snorted. 'Rob? Violent? You must be joking – he's a complete wimp!'

'So he never tried to hit you – even when you split up?'

'No chance. He's pathetic, a real coward. I think he joined the police 'cos he thought the uniform would make him look hard. *I* hit *him* once – it was the only way I could make him realise how bad things were between us. He wouldn't talk, you see; didn't want to know. With him working shifts and me working nine-to-five, I didn't see that much of him anyway. Then I got the job at BTV and started going out with a new bunch of people. I tried to get Rob to come but when he wasn't working all he seemed to want to do was slump in front of the telly. In the end I met someone else.'

She was staring at the lights on the tiny silver Christmas tree. Megan wondered where this new lover was now. She certainly didn't have the look of a woman in the first flush of a relationship.

'When Rob told you he'd been seeing prostitutes, what exactly did he say?' Megan asked.

'He told me some of them were really fit and were only too willing to give him sex instead of being arrested. He took great delight in telling me how good they were, how they'd do anything he wanted.'

'Did you feel hurt when he said that?'

'No, not really.' There was a half-smile on Helen Donalsen's lips. 'I almost laughed when he said it. I mean, he'd always been so straight and boring. If anything I was the one who tried to spice up the marriage by being, you know, more adventurous. I couldn't believe it when he came out with all this stuff about flavoured condoms.'

By the time Megan and Leverton left, curtains had been drawn on the twinkling fairy lights across the road and the snowman loomed from the shadows like a monstrous hunchback.

'What do you think?' Leverton glanced at Megan before pulling away from the house.

'Do you want an honest answer?'

'You don't think he did it?'

'From a behavioural point of view it just doesn't add up. I can't reconcile what Donalsen's wife has just told us with the picture we've been building up since Natalie Bailey's body was found.'

Leverton sighed. 'I admit that Donalsen doesn't sound like the kind of vicious sadist we've been looking for, but how do you know he hasn't changed? What if the break-up of the marriage turned him into a completely different person?'

'He's just not devious enough, Martin. Donalsen is incapable of concealing his emotions. He *told* his wife he was seeing prostitutes. Why? For revenge, pure and simple. The man we're looking for takes his revenge in a much more calculating, distanced way. Because he *can't* express his feelings to the person who upset him, he vents his rage on innocent victims.'

She paused for a moment but Leverton said nothing. 'Look Martin, I think we should be taking a closer look at BTV.'

Leverton grunted.

'What about that list of pimps Donalsen gave you?' Megan persisted. 'Has anyone cross-matched it with the employee lists from BTV?'

Leverton didn't answer. He was silent for the remainder of the journey back to the police station. As he drove into the car park he pulled out his mobile phone.

'Gerry? Anything interesting? Hmmm, what about his car? Okay. Ring me if you find anything, will you?'

He turned to Megan. 'Look, thanks for coming in today. There's not a lot we can do now until the SOCOs have finished going over Donalsen's flat. Forensics have got his car and that'll take a while too. Can I call you tomorrow morning?'

'Of course,' Megan replied stiffly. Pig-headed idiot, she thought. 'I'm at my sister's for the next few days. You've got the number.'

Leverton nodded and Megan got out of the car. Her own was parked a few spaces away and she drove off with a curt wave to Leverton. The half-hearted wave back spoke volumes. He was tired and frustrated and she had made things worse. Just when he thought he was getting somewhere she had told him he was barking up the wrong tree. Phoning the SOCOs had been his last-ditch attempt to show her he was right. Presumably nothing of any interest had been found so far.

If only he would stop being such an arrogant shit, Megan thought as she crunched her way noisily through a handful of Maltesers. While Leverton was wasting his time with Donalsen other, more important detective work was being ignored.

Four women were dead. How many more were going to be sacrificed on the altar of Leverton's ego? She thought of the list of BTV workers Leverton had had photocopied for her. Pretty useless without that list of pimps to compare them to, she thought. But wait a minute . . .

She snapped on the indicator, pulling off the Expressway and heading in a completely different direction. There was another way to check out that list, and she wasn't going home until she'd tried it.

Megan wasn't sure if she'd be able find Eileen Bunce. She kerb-crawled the dimly-lit streets where factories loomed like sleeping giants, passing bus stops where clumps of women clutched misshapen carrier bags. Megan caught sight of frozen legs of turkey, tufts of tinsel and the glassy eyes of a doll protruding from their plastic bundles.

Where was the woman? Where would she stand? Megan cursed herself for not asking her in the interview.

She was tempted to ask one of the many other prostitutes she passed as she drove round the red light area. But Eileen was the one she really wanted. Eileen was, as Costello had whispered on the way to the interview room, the oldest tart on the beat; the one most likely to have the knowledge Megan needed.

Suddenly she caught sight of something that made her

pull into the kerb and execute a speedy three-point turn. A flash of ginger under a street lamp – was it her?

Megan drew level with the woman walking down the road. At the sound of the slowing car Eileen Bunce instinctively turned her head. Megan wound down the passenger window.

'You want business, love?' Eileen called as she walked towards the car. Before Megan could say anything she saw the expression on the woman's face change to one of disgust. 'Oh! It's you! What the bloody hell do you want this time?'

'I need to talk to you, that's all.' Megan paused, fishing her purse from her bag. 'I'll pay for your time, of course.'

Eileen stared at her with a look of utter disdain, then, with a quick glance up and down the street, opened the passenger door and climbed in.

'Thirty quid and you can buy me a burger while you're at it,' she said, when Megan explained what it was she wanted.

It turned out to be the worst thirty pounds Megan had ever spent. They sat in the car park of a MacDonalds and while Eileen stuffed her face, Megan recited the list of forty-three names of male caterers, cleaners and security guards who worked at BTV.

'Sorry, love,' Eileen said, smearing lipstick on a paper serviette as she wiped her mouth.

Megan sighed. 'Are you absolutely sure? I mean, I hope you're not taking the piss. Someone's life could be at stake here.' She looked Eileen straight in the eye. 'Yours, maybe.'

Eileen Bunce raised her eyebrows insouciantly. 'Don't come that one. They charged whatshisface yet, have they? Don't s'pose they'd let him loose even if they haven't.'

'If you're talking about Sergeant Donalsen, he's being held for questioning but no one's been charged with anything yet,' Megan replied. 'Were you on your way to your patch when I stopped you?'

'Yeah. Why'd you ask?'

'I'll drop you off there.' Megan started up the engine. 'I want you to show me exactly where Maria Fellowes used to stand.'

Eileen Bunce's patch was literally round the corner from Inkerman Place, the dump site for Donna Fieldhouse's body. Eileen said she had seen Donna on the beat many times but had never seen any sign of a pimp.

'That's where Maria used to stand, poor cow.' She jerked her thumb towards a tyre-fitting workshop a few hundred yards along the road. 'Did the bastard really cut her feet off?'

Megan nodded. She caught the flash of headlights in the rearview mirror. A car was pulling in behind them. Eileen craned her neck round the headrest. 'Christ – bloody Vice car!' She grunted a laugh. 'Like to see the bleeders try charging me for this!'

Megan wound down the window. The face of PC Costello was inches from hers, a look of astonishment on his face. 'I'm sorry, ma'am. Didn't recognise your car.' He glanced at Eileen before straightening up. From the corner of her eye, Megan saw her wink at him.

'Lovely lad,' Eileen leered at him as he walked back to his car. 'If I was twenty years younger . . .'

'Listen,' Megan snapped as Eileen reached for the door handle, 'I'll give you another tenner if you'll go through what you told me this morning one more time.' The woman gave Megan the sort of pitying look she might have given a half-wit. Megan took another note from her purse and held it out.

'Go on then.' Eileen snatched it out of her hand and tucked it in her money belt.

'Right,' Megan said. 'I want you to tell me exactly where you went after you saw Sergeant Donalsen and Maria having sex in the squad car.'

'Back to the beat, where'd you think?' Eileen was giving

her that pitying look again. 'Like I told you, this punter picked me up just after I seen Donalsen go off with Maria. We pulled into Prole Street but when the silly bugger caught sight of the Vice car he changed his mind and made me get out. So then I had to walk back to the beat. Why you asking me all this, anyway?'

'I have to know exactly when Maria Fellowes disappeared. Are you sure you went straight back after you saw Sergeant Donalsen with Maria?'

'Course I'm sure! I wasn't going to hang around after that stupid bastard kicked me out – cost me at least thirty quid in lost business, that did.'

'What happened when you got back to the beat?'

'I was lucky. I got a punter really quick. Only had to wait about five minutes.'

'And how long were you with him?'

'Longer than normal. He wanted the lot so I took him back to my place. I suppose it lasted about three quarters of an hour. Fifty quid I got for that.'

'What happened after that? Did you go back to the beat?'

'Yeah. I did one last punter then I called it a night.'

Megan thought for a moment. 'So in theory, Maria Fellowes could have gone back to the beat after having sex with Sergeant Donalsen and you wouldn't necessarily have seen her?'

Eileen Bunce pursed her lips. 'I s'pose so, yeah.'

'What time did she usually go home?'

'It varied. Depended on how much business she'd done.'

'And presumably she'd have been losing business while she was with the sergeant?'

'Too right. It wasn't the first time, you know. I've seen him pick her up before. And it's not as if she was the only one.'

'And what about you, Eileen?' Megan asked. 'Did he ever ask you for sex?'

The woman gave a throaty cackle. 'Not me, love, thank God. He only liked the young ones.'

'And why didn't you report him before? I mean, if it was common knowledge that he was abusing his position, why didn't you or one of the other women make an official complaint?'

'Who to?' Eileen stared at Megan defiantly. 'Who the hell's going to listen to the likes of me? That's why he did it – 'cos he knew he could get away with it.'

'But when you heard Maria was dead, you decided to do it anyway?'

Eileen nodded.

Megan studied the woman's face, wondering if she could be believed. There had obviously been no love lost between Eileen Bunce and Maria Fellowes. What was it that had led Eileen to approach PC Costello? Sympathy? Self-preservation? Or something else?

At the moment Megan had no choice but to take her at face value. 'Listen,' she said. 'Just one more thing before you go. Is there anyone else around here that might have seen Maria if she returned to the beat that night?'

Eileen Bunce shook her head. 'No.' She gestured at the dark buildings and barbed wire fences lining the street. 'Look around you. This place is dead at night.'

'What about the people on the soup run?'

'No. Thursdays and Saturdays – that's when they come.'

Megan thought about what Eileen Bunce had told her as she drove back through the city centre. He'd killed two women within a very short space of time. And in such an organised way. No sign of frenzy. She shivered. This man was not going to stop unless they caught him. And if her instincts were right, they were no bloody closer than they'd ever been.

She had to go home and pack a bag before going to Ceri's.

The street was full of cars and she had to park some way from the house. Her bag had fallen off the passenger seat and half its contents were strewn across the floor. With a sigh of frustration she switched on the interior light and began scooping things into the bag. As she shifted it back onto the seat she noticed the two Christmas cards, still unopened, that she had taken from her pigeonhole the previous night.

The first one was from the police chief she had worked with in Scotland at the end of the summer. The second one was in a red envelope and she noticed it had no stamp. No address either, just 'Dr Megan Rhys' handwritten on the front. It was a picture of the BTV building inside a border of holly. Inside, in gold embossed script, were the words 'Season's Greetings from everyone at BTV'. When Megan saw what was scrawled underneath she went cold.

Hope you liked the chicken – can't wait to give you your real present.

Megan felt sick. Her first instinct was to rip the card into tiny pieces and fling them in the gutter. Instead she slid it carefully back into the envelope. She grabbed her mobile phone and rummaged in her bag for her filofax.

'Hello, Eric?' She took a breath, her heart pounding.

'Doctor Rhys?' He sounded as if he was eating something and she could hear the television in the background.

'Sorry to ring you at home but I've had a rather odd Christmas card.' She paused, trying to keep the panic out of her voice. 'I want to find out who sent it. It must have been hand-delivered yesterday because it didn't have a stamp.'

'Do you mean the one in the red envelope?'

'Yes. Do you know who brought it in?'

'One of the cleaners found it in the gents' toilets yesterday afternoon.'

'Oh . . . That's odd.' Her mind was racing. The *toilets*? Why put it there? 'Did you see anyone who could have left it? I mean was there anyone other than students or staff in the building yesterday?'

'Not that I know of; mind you I was out for most of the afternoon at the doctor's. Alf was on duty, not me.'

'Do you have his home number?'

'Yes, but you won't get him. He's gone to Sheffield for Christmas. He won't be back until after New Year.'

Megan bit her lip. 'Okay, thanks anyway, Eric. Have a good Christmas. Bye.'

Shivering, she climbed out of the car. She had told no one about the putrid chicken. Whoever sent that card had been inside her house. She stood on the pavement, fear making her stomach churn. She didn't want to go in. This is mad, she told herself. Someone's trying to scare you. You can't let them win.

She walked purposefully along the street, taking deep breaths of the chilly night air. Then she saw something that made her stop in her tracks.

The hall light was on.

Surely she hadn't left it on this morning? Perhaps Patrick had switched it on and forgotten to turn it off again when he left.

Swallowing hard, she crept up to the door. She could hear the television. Patrick would never have left that on. Someone was in the living room. As she peered through the pane of glass, a face appeared. She clutched the door handle, faint with shock.

'Megan!'

It was Tony. Striding towards the door with a cigarette in his hand, looking for all the world as if he'd never left. He opened the door and she pushed past. 'What on earth are you doing here? You scared me to death!'

'Come on, Meg, where's your festive spirit? I only called in to wish you a merry Christmas.'

'Well, you needn't have bothered,' Megan replied, wishing she'd had the locks changed. 'Shouldn't you be with Clare? I gather she's about to drop.'

Tony paused for a moment, dragging on his cigarette. Megan wondered if she'd stolen his thunder. Perhaps that had been the purpose of his visit; to inform her of his imminent fatherhood. If it was, his timing was appalling.

'You know about the baby then?' He looked like a schoolboy caught snogging behind the bike sheds.

'Yes – I've known for ages.' Megan kept her voice as cold and calm as she could make it. 'You didn't really think you could keep something like that a secret, did you?'

'I suppose Neil told you. Thought he might.'

'No, he didn't, actually.'

'Oh?'

Megan wasn't going to give him the satisfaction of hearing how she had found out. 'Is that all you came for?' She took off her coat and walked towards the stairs. 'Only I've got a suitcase to pack – I'm going away for Christmas.'

'Oh,' he said again, reminding Megan of a goldfish. 'Who with?'

'None of your damn business, really, is it?' She picked his coat from the peg on the wall and thrust it into his free hand.

'Meg, wait. Can't we sit down and talk for a minute?'

'What about? Shouldn't you be at home doing breathing exercises or something?'

'That's just the trouble. I don't want to be there right now.'

She hesitated. 'What on earth are you talking about?'

'That's why I came round to see you. I need to talk to you, Megan. It's all too much – Clare's changed – I'm not even sure I can handle being a father . . .' He walked back into the living room and slumped onto the sofa. He stubbed out his cigarette and immediately lit another.

Megan stood stock still in the hall, wondering if she had heard right.

'Meg!' It was almost a wail. 'Come and talk to me, Meg – please!'

Shaking her head, Megan stormed in. 'You selfish bastard! You complete bloody coward, you! Coming here, two days before Christmas, with your girlfriend about to give birth, whining on about not being able to handle your responsibilities. What the hell were you expecting me to do? Welcome you back with open arms crying, "Come back, Tony, all is forgiven"?'

'Look, Meg, I can understand you being upset about the baby . . .'

'Upset? I'll tell you what – I feel sorry for the poor little bastard having you for a father!' She grabbed his arm, pulling him off the sofa, and pushed him towards the door. 'Go on, get out! Get back to your girlfriend and start facing up to your responsibilities!'

'But Meg, it's you I want. I can see that now. The problems we had – I should have been more understanding.'

He turned towards her but she pushed him away. Flinging the front door open she stood with her arm outstretched, pointing to the street. 'Go on, get out! And don't you dare come back here – ever – you pathetic wimp!'

She slammed the door behind him and ran upstairs. Throwing herself on the bed she buried her head in the pillow and wept.

'What the bloody hell are you crying for?' she said aloud between sobs. 'Not for that stupid bastard. He's not worth it!'

Still shaking, she stumbled across to the bathroom and splashed cold water onto her face. 'It's the baby, isn't it?' she said to her reflection in the mirror. 'Not his baby – *your* baby.' She crumpled up and collapsed onto the bathroom floor, hugging a towel. The tears came flooding out; tears held back from years and years ago.

She didn't know how long she'd been there when the phone rang.

'Megan, is everything okay? We were expecting you hours ago.' It was Ceri.

'I'm so sorry,' Megan said, trying to make her voice sound normal. 'I got back and found Tony here.'

'No! What on earth did he want?'

'Oh, nothing, really.' Megan couldn't stop her voice faltering and cracking.

'Oh Meg! Has that bastard said something to upset you? Listen – don't try and drive. I'll come straight round and pick you up.'

'No, it's okay, I'm fine now, really. I'll be right with you. I've just got to throw a few things into a bag.'

'Are you sure?'

'Yes. This is ridiculous, you know,' she said, laughing through her tears. 'I'm the one that's supposed to be looking after you. Bet you've hardly slept the past few nights.'

'Don't worry about me. Just get yourself round here as fast as you can. Emily wants you to read her a bedtime story – she says you do it better than me.'

The girl was a pathetic sight. Skinny, with greasy blonde hair that looked as if it hadn't been washed for weeks. And she twitched. Standing in the police station she couldn't keep still. It was something the desk sergeant had seen many times before. The nervous, hyperactive rhythm of a crack addict.

She didn't look old enough to be driving a car. No wonder the drink-drive boys had flagged her down.

'You're not going to charge me, are you? I didn't know he was in there – honest! I just took the car. I didn't know he was in there!' Her voice rose to a high-pitched shriek as she paced up and down in front of the desk.

'I'd sit down if I was you,' the sergeant replied in a level tone. 'I think you're in for a long night.'

Chapter 14

Megan was glad to be at her sister's. She felt safe. Safe from whoever had sent that dreadful Christmas card. Could it have been Tony? Part of her wanted to believe it. But the chicken in the fridge – why would he pull a sick stunt like that? Did he really think he could *scare* her into having him back? Deep down she knew she was clutching at straws. Tony might be a coward but he wasn't spiteful. This was the work of someone nasty. *Can't wait to give you your real present.* What the hell had he meant by that? She thought for a moment. What if it wasn't a he? What if it was Clare? What if she knew about Tony's change of heart and was out for revenge? Easy enough for her to take his key. Megan frowned. In a way, she hoped it *was* Clare. The idea of Tony's girlfriend prowling around the flat was far less terrifying than the other possibility. The one she was trying not to think about.

She gazed at her nephew, who was sleeping peacefully in his cot. Whatever the sender of that card had in mind, they were in for a disappointment. She wasn't going to be there for Christmas and no one – other than Leverton – knew where she was.

'Are you sure you don't want to go to bed?' Ceri asked. 'I can take over now if you like.'

Megan stretched. 'I might as well stay up. It's only a couple of hours until Emily's due to wake up. Anyway, I don't think I'd be able to get to sleep. While I was sitting up with Joe I kept thinking about this case I've been working on;

it's been going round and round in my head.' She wasn't going to tell her sister about the other thing she'd had on her mind. No point worrying her.

'Neil told me about the woman they found in the car park. Sounded horrible. I think it really shook him up because he didn't know anything about it until he switched the telly on when we got back from the hospital. He phoned the newsroom and they told him all the gory details. Are the police linking it to those other deaths?'

'Yes. They're being very cagey about what they say to the press because they're worried about copycat murders. You know – some bloke who's fed up with his wife bumps her off using the same modus operandi as a serial killer and gets away with it.'

'Any idea who the killer is?'

'Sore point,' Megan replied. 'Let's just say that the bloke leading the inquiry isn't being as helpful as he could be.'

'What's his name?'

'Martin Leverton.'

'I interviewed him years ago.' Ceri frowned. 'Must have been before the Metro Rapist case. Bit of a smoothie.'

'Hmmm. Well, up to now, he's been very charming with me. He's even asked me out for a drink. I haven't been, of course, but it's very unsettling. It's as if he's watching me all the time, weighing me up. When I'm giving him what he wants to hear he can't get enough of me, but if I say something that doesn't fit in with his view of things he just blanks me out.'

'Is he married?'

'As far as I know, yes. But he never mentions his wife or any kids.'

'I'd steer well clear of him if I was you, Meg. Sounds very dodgy to me.'

'That's not the point.' Megan picked up one of Joe's teddies and retied the bow round its neck. 'He's wasting valuable time. Some other woman could be killed while he's pissing about out there.' She felt angry. Powerless. What could she do short of staking out the red light district single-handed? 'Anyway –' she turned to look at her sister – 'how are things between you and Neil? I've been wanting to ask you about it ever since I got here.'

Ceri bit her lip and looked away. Megan heard her take a breath.

'What's happened, Ceri?'

'Everything and nothing, really.' Megan could see her lower lip trembling. 'We had a lot of time to talk at the hospital and it . . . well . . . it all kind of came to a head.'

'What do you mean?'

'I asked him outright if he was having an affair. I reeled off all the things that had got me suspicious and said I couldn't think of an innocent explanation for them.'

'And?'

'He was totally gobsmacked. He's always been a hopeless liar. He admitted that he fancied this woman at work and said he'd always flirted with her, but up until recently there was nothing in it.

'He said that last summer when I was pregnant with Joe he felt claustrophobic. He used to go out to lunch with this woman and found her very easy to talk to.' Ceri's knuckles were white as she hugged her knees. 'Evidently, he tried to talk her into having an affair with him but she told him to fuck off because he was married.'

'Oh Ceri!' Megan put her arms around her sister's heaving shoulders.

'Why couldn't he have talked to me?' Ceri sobbed. 'Am I such a boring old has-been that I'm not worth making conversation with any more?'

'Of course you're not!' Megan tried to keep her voice

down in case they woke Joe. 'It's not your fault that this has happened. I'm surprised you haven't kicked him out.'

'How can I, Meg? I can't cope with Joe and Emily on my own. It's hard enough when there's two of us. And anyway, he's been making a huge effort over the past couple of days.'

'What did he say, then? After he admitted it all?'

'He said that Joe going into hospital had made him sort his priorities out. He realised how important the kids were to him and he promised to try harder with them, and with me.

'We started talking about how good things used to be, and I said he only really loved me when I was doing something glamorous and exciting.' She looked up at Megan, her eyes brimming with tears. 'He said he felt guilty about me losing my career and he couldn't stand the responsibility of it. Every time he came home and heard me moaning about the kids, it rubbed it in a little bit more. I can understand that, in a way. I was constantly laying into him about the kids and the housework, but it was my choice to give up work. I can't really blame him for not wanting to be with me.'

Megan frowned, wondering whether she should tell Ceri what had happened on Thursday night. If she and Neil really were going to make a fresh start, she reasoned, there must be no more secrets.

'Ceri, there's something I have to tell you. It's probably nothing at all, but it's about Neil.'

'What?' Megan heard the fear return to her sister's voice.

'Well, he asked me to babysit on Thursday night because you had to stay at the hospital . . .'

'Oh yes.' Ceri's face relaxed. 'The BTV party at Elizabeth's. He said it was really boring.'

'Oh,' Megan said, confused. 'Was it at someone's house? I . . . er . . . got the impression it was a restaurant he was going to.'

'Elizabeth's *is* a restaurant – haven't you been? We go there quite a lot. It's all organic. Lots of nice veggie dishes.'

'No – I've never even heard of it.' An immense wave of relief swept over her. 'Is it new?'

'Yes. It only opened a couple of months ago. Neil got an invitation to the press launch.'

'You're going to think I'm really stupid, but when Emily said Neil had gone to Elizabeth's, I thought Elizabeth was a woman he was seeing.'

'Oh Meg! You poor thing!' It was a relief to see Ceri laughing for a change.

'I switched on the telly while he was out and the bloke reading the BTV news bulletin said some woman called Elizabeth would be on the next morning.'

'Elizabeth Dawson! And you thought it was her!' Ceri's chuckles got louder and Joe stirred in his cot.

'Shhhhh!' Megan hissed, clapping her hand over her own mouth.

They sat, shaking with silent laughter, until the sound of feet padding along the landing made them both look round. Emily appeared in her pyjamas at the door.

'Auntie Megan, will you read me another story?'

Megan rose stiffly from the floor. 'Come on,' she said, yawning, 'I think you might have to read me one!'

Ceri had to shake her sister to make her wake up. 'Megan there's a phone call for you: It's Martin Leverton – says it's urgent.'

Megan groaned. 'What time is it?'

'Half past ten. I wanted you to have a lie-in after last night, but he says he needs to speak to you right away.'

Megan jumped out of bed and stumbled through the door.

'Take it in our bedroom,' Ceri called after her. Megan picked up the phone and perched on the side of Ceri and Neil's unmade bed. 'Hello?'

'Megan? Sorry to get you out of bed – your sister told me you'd been up half the night with the baby – but I thought you'd like to hear the good news. We've got the pimp!'

'What? How?'

'Warwickshire police picked up some young girl on suspicion of drink-driving last night. They thought she might be on drugs so they searched the car, and guess what they found in the boot: a man's body!'

'A *man's* body? You mean the pimp's dead?'

'Yes. Warwickshire police traced the registration of the car to an address in Birmingham. They called us to see if we had anything on him. Costello was on duty and he picked it up straight away. His name's Gianfranco Rossi and he's on that list of pimps Donalsen gave us.'

'Have you found anything at his house to link him with the murders?'

'It's an absolute goldmine. Pornographic magazines, pictures of Delva Lobelo, we even found Maria Fellowes' money belt with a photo of that little kid of hers still inside.'

'So how the hell did he end up dead in the boot of his own car? And who was the girl driving him round?'

'We think she's a prostitute. Evidently she's denying any knowledge of the body being there. She says she went to his house yesterday afternoon to score some crack and found the house empty and his car keys lying on the kitchen table. She says she decided to nick the car, drive it down to London and sell it. She was picked up driving along the hard shoulder of the M42.'

'So was she another one of his young runaways?'

'Sounds like it, yes. She's only sixteen. It's a wonder she didn't crash the car.'

'Do you think she'll know who the other killer is?'

'I hope so. That's what I wanted to ask you, actually. I'm taking Costello down to Leamington to identify the body. Will you come with us and interview the girl?'

'Yes. Shall I meet you there? I can go down the M54 from here. It'll be quicker than trying to get into the centre of Birmingham.'

'Okay. What time do you think you'll get there?'

Megan glanced at the clock on the bedside table. 'About midday, I should think.'

'Right – I'll see you then. Call me on the mobile if you get held up.'

The mortuary was a short distance from the police station and Leverton decided they should take a look at the body before interviewing the girl. The pathologist met them at the door. 'How long has he been dead?' Leverton asked.

'At least twenty-four hours – can't be more precise than that at the moment.'

'How did he die?'

'Can't be certain until we've done the post-mortem. There are stab wounds but they look fairly superficial. There wasn't much blood in the boot of the car. Do you want to take a look?'

Megan couldn't believe her eyes. 'My God!' She shook her head.

'You know him?' It was Leverton's turn to look surprised.

'He's one of the security guards at BTV.' She stared pointedly at Leverton. 'He was on reception when I was there last Monday.' Megan thought about the list of names she had recited to Eileen Bunce. She was sure this man's name hadn't been on it and she wondered why.

She stared at the bloodless face, its lips curled into a mirthless grin. The teeth were a greyish-yellow. From where she was standing she could see the wear on the tops of the lower incisors. She looked at his hair. It was quite thick, black and wavy but greying at the temples. Her eyes travelled down the length of the pallid body, past the shrivelled genitals, to the feet. The toenails were long and dirty. The thought of this man having sex with girls barely out of childhood made her want to throw up.

Leverton turned to Costello. 'Is this the man we've got on our files?'

'Yes sir.' Costello pulled a photograph from his pocket and held it next to the dead man's face.

Leverton whistled. 'Well, Megan, you've come up trumps on your profile of this one; right age, right address, right job – right car too!'

'The old Ford Sierra?'

'Yep. Forensics are taking it apart even as we speak.'

So why didn't you listen to me in the first place, you patronising git? Megan thought. She couldn't believe Leverton was being so cavalier about it all. He appeared unperturbed by the fact that this man's identity had been discovered by a lucky coincidence and that a team of detectives searching BTV had missed him completely.

'It's funny,' Leverton said on cue. 'It's such a distinctive name, isn't it? You'd think I'd remember a name like that. I saw a list of security guards the night Maria Fellowes' body was found but I don't remember a Gianfranco Rossi. Let's go and find out what this Samantha's got to say about him.'

To Megan the interview room seemed overpoweringly hot and stuffy, but the girl sat huddled in a corner, hugging herself as if she was freezing cold. She looked much younger than sixteen.

She had laughed when Leverton had asked her if she knew who Sergeant Donalsen was, calling him 'that dope-head'. When asked to explain what she meant, she clammed up.

Megan tried another tack. 'Samantha, what was the name of the man the police found in the car you were driving?'

The girl sniffed loudly. She stared at Megan with hollow

eyes. 'Shouldn't you have worked that one out for yourself?' she snarled. 'You've got his registration number, for fuck's sake.'

'We have the name of the man who owns the car,' Megan went on. 'But at the moment we have no clear evidence that the body the police found is that man.' From the corner of her eye Megan saw Leverton frown.

'Course it was Franco!' the girl retorted. 'I had the shock of my life when they opened that boot.'

Megan paused for a moment. 'You say you had a shock. Did you feel anything else?'

'What do you mean?'

'Did you feel upset that he was dead?'

'You must be bloody joking!' The girl checked herself, realising how the words would sound. 'I don't mean that really.' She twisted a stringy lock of hair around her finger. 'I didn't like the bloke, but I wouldn't have wished that on him.'

'Why didn't you like him?'

The girl stared at the ceiling, sucking on the hair between her fingers. Eventually she spoke. 'He used me, didn't he?'

'Used you?'

'Yeah. When I was in care he used to wait for me outside the children's home. He was great at first – took me out clubbing and stuff and bought me clothes.' She paused, looking Megan in the eye for the first time since the interview had begun. Her expression was desolate. 'He told me he loved me and I fell for it, stupid cow. I moved in with him the day before my sixteenth birthday and a week later he put me on the streets. I hated him for that.'

Megan could see tears in the corners of the girl's eyes. She was staring past Megan now at some spot on the wall. 'It's like someone giving you a great big birthday cake,' she said in a whisper, 'and then they smash it in your face.'

'Did he ever hurt you, Samantha?' Megan said gently. 'I mean, did he hit you or did any of his friends threaten you in any way?'

The girl's eyes snapped back into focus. 'Friends? Franco didn't have no friends. People only came round if they wanted to score. I never even saw them 'cos I was either asleep or working when they came.'

'What about Franco, then?' Megan went on. 'Did he ever hit you?'

'He didn't need to, did he?' The girl loosed her grip on the sodden strand of hair, letting it hang limply across her face.

'What do you mean?'

'He had this great big knife. When I told him I wasn't going on the streets no more, he held it against my throat and said he'd kill me if I didn't do what he wanted.'

'But you got away from him?'

'Yeah. This woman who used to come round the beat dishing out free condoms said she could get me into a refuge.'

'When was that?'

'Oh, ages ago.'

'Can you remember what month?'

'Yeah. October.' Her mouth twisted into a half-smile. 'Halloween night; you know, trick or treat.'

'How long had you been with Franco when you left?'

'Not long; only about a month, I think.' She shivered and started rocking slightly in her chair.

'What happened when you went to the refuge? Did he try to get you back?'

'He came round a couple of times, yeah. Banged on the door and shouted his mouth off. But he soon found someone else. Didn't need me no more, so he stopped making a fuss. Trouble was I needed him.' She sniffed loudly and shivered again.

Megan wondered what she meant. 'Were you still in love with him, Samantha?'

'Christ, no! It was the rocks, man! I needed the rocks, like I need one now!' The girl jumped from her seat and started to pace up and down. Her eyes were frantic. The police surgeon was called and the interview was suspended. As she walked back along the corridor Megan could hear Samantha wailing like a child.

'Well?' Leverton leaned back against one of the desks in the incident room. He and Costello were both staring at Megan. They reminded her of children watching a magician. And yes, she did have a rabbit to pull out of the hat, but it would not be done with a desire to please them.

'Franco,' she said simply. 'She called him Franco.'

'Ring any bells?' Leverton frowned.

'Yes,' she said, frustrated and angry. If they'd given her the two lists together, maybe she'd have seen it sooner. 'I think it does. I don't suppose you've got a copy of that list of BTV employees to hand, have you?'

'Has it come yet?' Leverton barked at Costello.

'No sir. I did ask them to fax it urgently.'

'I've got one.' She pulled the list of names from her bag, scanning the pages. 'That's him.' She pointed to a name near the bottom of one of the sheets. 'I'd put money on it. Frank Ross: Gianfranco Rossi!'

She held out the list and Leverton peered at it, nodding wordlessly as she took it back.

'Why has the name got an 'L' next to it?' Megan asked.

'He was on leave when Maria Fellowes' body was dumped.' Costello chimed in. 'We couldn't get hold of him on the phone so we assumed he'd gone away for Christmas.'

'Obviously he was killed before he got the chance.' Leverton added, 'I wonder how long he'd been in that boot? More than twenty-four hours, the pathologist said; so he could have been killed straight after he dumped Maria's body. The last thing he should have done was to draw attention to the place where he worked by dumping a body in the car park. Donalsen must have panicked when he found out and decided Frank was too much of a liability. The fact that his wife works there too would have made him panic even more.' He looked at Megan. 'You were there when we told him about Maria Fellowes, weren't you?'

Megan nodded, irritation pursing her lips.

'After that he went home. He could easily have gone round to Franco's and killed him. I suppose he stuffed the body in the boot of the car meaning to go back later and get rid of it, but Samantha beat him to it.'

He waited for Megan to comment, but she stayed silent.

'You still don't buy Donalsen as the killer,' he said, exasperated. 'But you heard what Samantha said about him being a dope-head. It all fits in. Donalsen saw Franco working at BTV when he went to pick his wife up. He had him over a barrel because he knew he'd been inside. Maybe Franco offered him drugs to stop him squealing to the security boss about his criminal record. Then, when Donalsen's wife left him, Franco offered him girls and they ended up killing one of them. That Samantha had a lucky escape. Natalie Bailey must have been the girl he replaced her with when she went to the refuge.'

'But why would Donalsen bother going to someone like Franco for girls?' Megan demanded. 'In his job he could have had any prostitute he wanted.'

'I know that.' Leverton was going slightly red in the face. 'Maybe Donalsen wanted something kinky and Franco offered to arrange it.'

Megan frowned. 'There's still something that doesn't fit in with all this.' Leverton looked at her. 'It's that list of pimps. If Donalsen was involved with Franco, why on earth would he include his name on that list he gave you? I mean, he could so easily have left it out.'

'Not really,' Leverton said. 'I might have checked on the computer and noticed he'd missed it out. I mean, if he's got form for living off immoral earnings, he's going to be on file anyway.'

'But he hasn't, sir,' Costello ventured.

'What?'

'He hasn't got form for pimping. If you look at the list, his name's below the line. It's the ones above the line that have got previous. The ones below are only suspected of it.'

'Are you telling me that this guy's got no criminal record?'

'No, he has got form, but it's for drug dealing, not pimping. You know when I got that printout from Drug Squad when we were after Tyrone Campbell? Well, Gianfranco Rossi's on that list, too.'

Leverton stared at Costello. The warble of his mobile phone saved him from an embarrassing silence.

Megan watched him as he listened. She saw his eyes widen and noticed the characteristic rub of the chin. When he put his hand over the mouthpiece, she noticed he was looking at Costello, not her.

'The fibres from Franco's carpet match the ones they found on the backs of Donna and Natalie's legs.'

Before Costello could say anything Leverton put up his free hand. 'Hang on! There's something else. They've just found something in the shed. A pair of human feet. They've found Maria Fellowes' feet!'

Megan shuddered.

He spoke into the mouthpiece again, 'What about Donalsen? Is he saying anything yet? Right, we're coming straight back.'

Leverton shoved the phone in his pocket. This time his words were addressed to Megan. 'Donalsen has admitted having sex with Maria Fellowes in his car on the night she disappeared. He's also admitted buying cannabis from a number of known drug-dealers in Birmingham.'

The look on his face seemed to dare Megan to say anything that would shake his conviction of Donalsen's guilt.

'Did he mention Franco?' She returned his unwavering gaze.

'He denies ever having met him, but he would, wouldn't he?' He pulled his coat from the back of the chair. 'If he thinks he's going to get off the hook that way he's very much mistaken. Thanks for all your help, Megan – that profile of Franco really was spot on. I'll keep you posted, okay?' He paused as he reached the door. 'Hey, have a good Christmas, you hear? And make sure you have a good rest. You've certainly earned it!'

That was it – dismissed. Donalsen would be banged up over Christmas until a DNA test cleared him. God alone knew how long that would take, and in the meantime . . .

'Just do me one favour, will you?' Megan hated having to ask. She steeled herself as Leverton turned, frowning. 'Humour me for as long as it takes for those DNA results to come through. Put a news blackout on the discovery of Franco's body. I know you think I'm barking up the wrong tree, but just to cover yourselves, don't let this out yet. If the killer *is* still out there he'll go underground if he knows you know about Franco.'

Leverton gave a curt nod. 'Okay. We'll embargo it until Wednesday, all right?' He pulled his car keys from his pocket.

'And one more thing.' Megan could see that he was impatient to leave but she didn't care. 'I'd like to call in at Franco's house on my way back. For research purposes,' she added in a defiant voice.

'Why not?' Leverton scribbled down the address and handed it to her. 'I'll call the SOCOs and tell them to expect you.'

Megan took the proffered scrap of paper, her lips set in a tight smile. Yes, she thought, go away like a good girl.

She watched the two men as they walked across the car park. Leverton's whole mood had lightened again. He was talking animatedly to Costello, no doubt planning what he was going to say to Donalsen in a bid to trip him up.

She thought about the Christmas card in her bag. She had been on the brink of handing it over to Leverton to ask him to check it for fingerprints. But she had held back, not wanting to expose herself to the pitying look Leverton would undoubtedly give her when he read it.

What if it's AB? That voice inside her head again. What if Leverton had not been the only one to notice her resemblance to Tina Jackson? How many times had that trailer about the documentary been shown over the past few days?

As she walked across the car park her heart was thumping. She'd be okay at Ceri's. He couldn't possibly know Ceri's address. And on Boxing Day she would be off to Borth.

But knowing that she was safe did little to dispel her fears about him striking someone else while Leverton wasted his time with Donalsen.

Reaching into the glove compartment, she pulled out a street map of Birmingham. She gasped when she realised where Franco Rossi's house was. Right in the heart of the red light district. She must have driven past it at least twice last night. And it was only round the block from Inkerman Place. How convenient for dumping poor Donna Fieldhouse's body.

As she pulled out of the car park the faces of Donna, Natalie, Tina and Maria filled her mind. There had to be *something* at Franco's house. Some clue, however small or obscure, to the identity of the other killer.

She pictured that faceless man sitting somewhere cosy, wrapping presents. Alongside, someone who had not the slightest idea what kind of monster he really was.

Chapter 15

When Megan arrived at the house she was unnerved to see that architecturally, it was very much like her own. But this once-graceful Victorian terrace had been boxed in by ugly factories. Paint was flaking from the window frames and filthy net curtains obscured the interior from prying eyes.

The houses on either side were boarded up. How easy it must have been to commit murder in such a god-forsaken dump, Megan thought. At night you could scream yourself hoarse and no one was likely to hear. Neither was anyone likely to be watching if someone emerged from the narrow alley at the side of the house with a large, bulky parcel to load into the boot of a car.

There was a twisted kind of justice in the fact that Franco Rossi had ended up in the same car boot that he had stuffed Donna, Natalie and Maria into. Megan shuddered when she thought about Maria Fellowes' feet lying in a garden shed at the other end of that dingy alley. Maria wasn't all that tall, so it must have been the stiffness of her body, from a combination of rigor mortis and the freezing weather, that made Franco mutilate her legs.

Whoever killed Franco must have put his body in the boot almost immediately after death, bending the legs and spine into a foetal position. The killer would have to have done it under cover of darkness. So, Megan estimated, the earliest Franco could have been murdered was about four o'clock on Friday afternoon.

She fished in her bag for her mobile. Had anyone bothered telling Delva that her tormentor was dead? She was certain it wouldn't have crossed Leverton's mind.

'Delva – it's Megan.' She could hear music in the background and the sound of people talking and laughing.

'Hello?' She sounded as if she was struggling to hear.

'We've found him, Delva. The guy who was sending you the letters.'

'What? Oh my God, that's fantastic! Who is he?'

'He's – was – one of the security guards at BTV. He was called Frank. Frank Ross.'

'Bloody hell! He was on duty the night I got that photo! He was one of the pair I caught slobbering over that newspaper. Have they arrested him?'

'Didn't have to. He's dead.'

'Dead?' Delva repeated the word as if she didn't think she'd heard right.

'We think he was killed by the man who murdered the woman they found in the skip.'

'But – why?' Delva stammered, 'What for?'

'We think he was linked to the killer in some way. He was a local pimp.'

'A pimp?' Delva snapped. 'What the hell was a pimp doing working as a security guard?'

'Good question. The police have arrested one of their own people – a sergeant in the Vice Squad. But I think they've got the wrong man.'

'Why?'

'It's complicated. Anyway, I just wanted you to know the good news. I'll catch up with you when you get back, okay? Have a good Christmas.'

'I will,' Delva said with feeling. 'You too. Thanks, Megan.'

Megan got out of the car and rang the bell.

Franco's killer had obviously gone to a lot of trouble to

erase any physical traces of what had gone on in the house. As she picked her way across the duckboards to the kitchen she noticed that the floor and the yellow formica table looked newly-scrubbed. The cutlery, too, was gleaming, probably leaving little clue as to whether any of the selection of sharp knifes in the drawer had been used on Franco.

Most of Franco's scant possessions had already been bagged up by the SOCOs. Megan sifted through the bags with gloved hands, pausing to inspect Maria Fellowes' moneybelt and the BTV publicity shot of Delva Lobelo.

She wondered if Franco Rossi had developed his obsession with Delva before or after getting the job at BTV. Possibly before, she reasoned, because there didn't seem to be any other good reason for him working there. It didn't make sense in financial terms; the money he made from pimping and drug-dealing would have far outstripped the wages of a security guard.

Megan thought about the letters and cuttings Delva had shown her. Teenage girls like Donna, Natalie and Samantha had been nothing more than commodities to Franco, picked up to provide the ready cash to finance his drug deals. In sexual terms they were almost the exact opposite of what he was into.

Megan studied Delva's face. The high cheekbones, the strong jaw, the overwhelming sense of confidence exuded by her eyes.

Franco had wanted domination. Domination by a strong, sexually experienced woman. But it was unlikely that any woman of that type would want someone like him. Hence his fixation with Delva, the authoritative voice of BTV news, who smiled at him every night from his TV screen.

Megan replaced Delva's photograph and picked up a plastic bag containing a plain gold chain and a pair of gold hoop earrings. She asked one of the SOCOs if the shamrock pendant belonging to Tina Jackson had come to light.

'Not yet, no,' the woman replied, 'but we've got a couple of cupboards to go through yet.'

'What about the security video that went missing from BTV?'

The woman shook her head.

Megan moved to a low coffee table to inspect another collection of bags. It was curious, she thought. Franco's killer seemed to have obliterated bloodstains and fingerprints but he had left several really obvious pieces of evidence lying around. Megan had the distinct impression that he was playing games again.

She glanced at the covers of the various pornographic magazines arrayed in plastic bags on the coffee table. Some of the more hard-core publications looked like foreign language imports. She peered at the lettering. Dutch, she thought, and some German too.

At the bottom of the pile was something slightly different. Italian, she guessed, looking at the name of the magazine. There was no picture on the cover, just chunks of text.

Megan had only the barest grasp of the language – a legacy of the brief visits from Granny Pezzotti, her mother's mother – but there was one word that leapt out at her: *CARABINIERI*. The Italian police.

She asked the SOCO if she could remove the magazine from its bag. It was clear from the pictures inside that this was some sort of internal publication for members of the Italian police force. What was Franco Rossi doing with a copy of it? She looked at the date on the cover. It was published last year.

'Any idea how long he'd been living here?' Megan asked the SOCO.

The woman looked up from the cardboard box of CDs she was carrying across the room. 'At least five years – maybe longer. We found a pile of old council tax statements in the kitchen drawer.'

Megan replaced the magazine in its bag. 'Have you found an address book, diary, passport, anything like that?'

'No. Whoever killed him made sure he didn't leave anything like that around.'

'And no-one's reported him missing?'

The woman shook her head.

Megan stepped out of the room and made her way up the stairs. Crossing the landing she glanced into one of the bedrooms. She tensed when she saw the bed. It was the one in the Polaroid photograph. She realised she was probably in the exact spot the killer had stood when he took it.

The SOCOs had not yet started on this room and Megan crossed from one duckboard to another, her eyes darting this way and that. The wallpaper looked as if it hadn't been changed in thirty years. It was a brash, abstract design in orange, brown and yellow. She turned to the window and shuddered. There, at the end of the snow-covered garden, was the shed.

The slanting rays of the setting sun lit up the door as she walked towards it. Amongst the jumble of tools on the workbench inside she could see an axe in a scenes-of-crime bag.

How long had Maria Fellowes lain in that shed before Franco dumped her in the skip at BTV? If she was murdered on the night she disappeared, it would have been three days. Why had the body been hidden away like that? It certainly wasn't consistent with the other murders.

She began asking herself if there had been some ulterior motive. What would the killer have gained by telling Franco to wait three whole days before disposing of the body?

'Doctor Rhys!'

Megan turned to see the woman SOCO she had spoken to earlier leaning out of the back door of the house.

'Something here you might be interested in.'

Megan hurried back towards the house. 'What is it?' she said, following her into the kitchen.

'This.' The SOCO picked something bright and shiny from the table and put it into Megan's gloved hand. It was a large, gold wedding ring. A man's wedding ring.

'We found it in one of the cupboards. Look inside.'

Megan held it between her finger and thumb, angling it so that the inside of the gold band caught the light. Alongside the hallmark was an inscription. *Robert and Helen, married 2.7.94, St. Stephen's.* As Megan stared at the graceful italic engraving her stomach began to churn.

'It's Rob Donalsen's wedding ring,' the SOCO said matter-of-factly.

'Are you sure?' Megan was unable to take her eyes off the names on the ring.

'As sure as I can be,' the woman replied. 'I was at the wedding.'

It was getting dark as Megan drove away. She sped through the deserted streets of the red light district, feeling a sense of relief when she hit the wide road of post-war semis that led to less dangerous territory. Only superficially less dangerous, though, she thought grimly, as she turned a corner and pulled sharply to a halt outside Tina Jackson's house.

She needed time to think things out. The evidence against Rob Donalsen seemed overwhelming. From a dark corner of her mind, she could hear Leverton's sneering voice. How could Rob Donalsen's wedding ring have got into Franco Rossi's house if he was not the killer? There had to be some explanation.

Megan thought about the conversation she and Leverton had had with Samantha at Leamington police station. The girl had referred to Donalsen as 'that dope head'. Had she seen him at Franco's house buying cannabis? Could the ring have slipped off his finger then?

No, Megan thought with a sinking feeling, it didn't make

sense. If Franco was supplying Donalsen with drugs, it would be ridiculous to believe he had any fear of being arrested for pimping. There would be no reason for him to have ferried girls like Natalie to different areas of the West Midlands to do their soliciting, as she knew he had done.

So how had Samantha known Donalsen took dope then? Perhaps it was common knowledge to the women on the beat. After all, she reasoned, Eileen Bunce seemed to have known all about his liaisons with prostitutes. Word probably travelled fast.

Megan started up the engine, a look of determination on her face. What if someone had planted that ring in Franco's house? What if the real killer had decided to set Rob Donalsen up? He was separated, so there was a good chance he'd discarded the wedding ring. She had to find out who could have got hold of it.

Megan pulled over a couple of times to look at her street map. Leverton had been driving when they went to Helen Donalsen's house and it wasn't in an area of Birmingham she knew.

In the end, it was the snowman that told her she was in the right road. The woolly cap on its head had shifted to a jaunty angle and someone had stuffed a beer can in its pebble mouth.

The dappled light of Helen Donalsen's Christmas tree shone through the curtained window of her front room, but there was no reply when Megan rang the bell. She waited on the doorstep for a couple of minutes and then got back into the car, wondering what to do.

It was pointless hanging around. Helen had probably gone to spend Christmas Eve somewhere else, leaving the lights on to deter burglars. Megan wished she had the woman's telephone number. She tried directory enquiries but it was unlisted. Bloody typical, she thought. Reaching into her bag, she fished out a pen and notebook.

She worded the note carefully, saying simply that she needed to speak to Helen urgently and giving the telephone number of Ceri's house and the cottage at Borth as well as her mobile number.

She pushed it through the letter box, ringing the bell one last time as she did so. No reply. She sighed, watching her breath swirl smokily in the cold night air. There was nothing more she could do. Not tonight anyway. She shivered. Not from the cold, but from the thought of *him*. Nameless, faceless and deadly. He could be cruising the streets at this moment, looking for another victim.

As she drove away, she grated the gearbox and swore loudly. She flicked on the radio in a half-hearted attempt to ease her frustration. Slade were belting out the chorus of *Merry Christmas Everybody*. 'Merry Christmas,' Megan muttered under her breath. 'Merry bloody Christmas!'

'Auntie Megan! Look what Father Christmas brought me!' Emily's little body landed on the bed with a thump. Through bleary eyes, Megan could see a Barbie doll with improbably long red hair waving about a few inches from her face. It made her think of Eileen Bunce and in the few seconds it took to wake up properly, she found herself speculating what the woman might have looked like when she was young.

'Come on! Wake up!' Emily was tugging her arm. 'I want you to open your presents.'

Megan had never felt less like a celebration. She went through the motions, willing the phone to ring. Ceri and Neil both had hangovers and Gareth, her brother, arrived for lunch looking as if he'd also had one too many the night before. They all slumped in front of the TV when the meal was over. Emily had fallen asleep over her Christmas pudding and Joe was in his cot upstairs.

Megan stared at the screen, not watching. Unable to concentrate on anything other than the identity of AB. She thought about Rob Donalsen and wondered what kind of Christmas he was having. There had been nothing on the news, so presumably he hadn't been charged yet. Perhaps Leverton had decided to wait until the DNA results came through. With the weight of evidence against the man, Leverton would have no trouble persuading a magistrate to extend the length of the time Donalsen could be held in custody.

Megan thought about the forensic evidence. If Donalsen was innocent, that DNA test would clear him of any involvement with the murders of Natalie and Tina; the real killer must know that. And if he was simply out to frame Donalsen for the murder of Maria Fellowes, he would have to have known that Donalsen's blood group was the same as his own, wouldn't he?

Was that *really* likely, Megan asked herself?

She stared at the twisting tinsel on Ceri's Christmas tree. No, she thought, he didn't need to know Donalsen's blood group. That was why Maria's body had been kept in the shed for all that time. The killer didn't want the police to get hold of it until all the semen traces had decayed. That would muddy the waters enough to make Maria's death look like a copycat killing. All AB needed was to know that Donalsen was seen having sex with Maria the night she disappeared. The sergeant would get a life sentence for Maria's murder, even if the other deaths couldn't be pinned on him. It was the ultimate fantasy for a man with a vehement hatred of the police; making a cop take the rap for a murder he didn't commit.

But the weather had screwed things up, Megan reflected. The sub-zero temperatures had preserved Donalsen's semen *and* the killer's. What was Leverton going to do if the DNA analysis proved that only one of those AB samples came from Donalsen?

Gareth was first up on Boxing Day. He'd had so much to drink that Ceri and Megan had refused to let him drive home, so he'd had to get up at seven to get to Manchester for nine.

'He must be the only person I know who's got to go to work on Boxing Day.' Megan sat down at the kitchen table.

'Serves him right,' said Ceri as they started a brunch of turkey sandwiches. 'He told me he was meeting up with you at the cottage for New Year – don't let him drag you off to the pub for any of his marathon sessions, will you?'

'I probably won't be there.'

'Oh. Been invited to a party in Birmingham or something?'

'No. It's the case. I'm still going to go to the cottage – I promised myself and there's bugger all I can do now that Leverton's stopped talking to me – but I'll probably come back tomorrow afternoon.'

'What time are you off?'

'About one o'clock, I think,' Megan said. 'I want to be there before it gets dark.'

'What about food? There won't be anything open. I'll pack a few things for you to take with you – there's enough in the fridge to feed an army.'

'Thank you.' Megan looked at her sister. She seemed happier than she had for ages, but Megan wasn't totally convinced by the bright smile. 'Look, are you sure you're going to be all right?'

'What do you mean?' Ceri's eyes were still smiling as she returned Megan's gaze.

'It's just that I was wondering if things are working out okay with Neil.'

'We're fine, honestly. He's really trying to give me a good Christmas. Look what he gave me this morning.'

She delved under the polo neck of her sweater, pulling out a fine gold choker chain with something dangling from it. Megan's heart missed a beat.

'Oh, that's pretty,' she faltered. 'What is it?'

'I think it's a Tudor Rose. Neil said he got it from a gift shop at the art gallery. He left it on the pillow and I found it when I woke up. He said it was an extra surprise present to make up for the way he'd been acting over the past few months.'

'Very romantic!' Megan said, relaxing again. For one awful moment she had thought the pendant dangling from her sister's neck was a shamrock.

As soon as Megan stepped into the cottage she remembered the logs. She had meant to buy some at a petrol station in Wolverhampton but it had slipped her mind. She looked at the clock. There might be somewhere open in Aberystwyth if she was quick.

There was hardly any traffic about as she drove back through the country lanes. She passed a few cars when she hit the trunk road leading into Aberystwyth, but the town itself was deserted. By comparison the petrol station was a hive of activity. Families on their way home after the festivities were queuing to fill up.

Megan bought a sack of logs and loaded them into the boot. Then, on a whim, she drove to Saint Michael's church. It was a fine, clear evening and the sun was just sinking into the sea. She stood in the car park gazing out towards the horizon. The water was turning blood red where the sun touched it. In half an hour it would be dark. She turned towards the church door. Strange to think that she hadn't been inside since her wedding day.

Going in was like exorcising a ghost. It was as if the intervening years had never existed; everything was exactly as it had been the last time she saw it.

Walking up to one of the side chapels she noticed an inscription on its ornately carved door. It was slightly ajar, splitting the sentence in half, and she stood for a moment working out what it said: '*So he bringeth them unto the haven where they would be.*'

She realised almost immediately that it referred to the war dead, whose names adorned a stone tablet in the chapel. But it made her think of the dead women she had left behind in Birmingham: Donna and Natalie, Tina and Maria. She whispered their names into the thick, silent air.

She wandered across to the Lady Chapel on the other side of the altar. A bible rested on a wooden lectern. It was open at Psalm 139, and as she scanned the copperplate script she felt the hairs on the back of her neck stand on end: '*You knew my soul and my bones were not hidden from you when I was formed in secret and woven in the depths of the earth . . . look well lest there be any wickedness in me.*'

It made her think of babies, psychologically damaged babies: Ted Bundy left in a nursing home for months while his teenage mother decided what to do with him; Ian Brady left alone in a Glasgow tenement while his mother went to work. Embryonic souls starved of love, stunted forever.

Is that what had happened to AB? For the umpteenth time she tried to picture him. She took the Christmas card out of her bag. Was he the one who'd sent it? She stared at the scribbled message, shuddering at the thought of this monster creeping around her house. First the shells, then the window, the maggots and then the card. Each one more unnerving, less explicable than the last. Was this an extension of his game with the police? Playing her like a cat with a mouse, trying to scare her to death before moving in for the kill?

She hurried back to the car. It was getting dark. At the cottage she lit a fire and sat on the hearthrug eating turkey in curry sauce. Outside she could hear the waves thudding against the sea wall. It was a comforting sound. She had always felt very secure in her grandmother's house.

The sound of the waves drowned out the car engine in the street outside. The driver paused for a moment, peering at Megan's front door before pulling out and driving to the place where the houses ran out.

He drove onto a windswept caravan site. There were no lights. No people. He began walking along the narrow road that led back to the village.

Chapter 16

Megan couldn't sleep. Running through endless possibilities in her mind, she tried to work out how AB could have known about Rob Donalsen having sex with Maria.

She felt very uneasy about Eileen Bunce's role in Donalsen's arrest. It was hard to believe that the woman's decision to go to the police was motivated by concern for the fate of a fellow prostitute. In Megan's experience the camaraderie between sex workers was an invention of the media. Real life on the streets was simply not like that. It was every woman for herself.

So had the killer paid Eileen to spill the beans?

She sat bolt upright in bed. What about Eileen's punter? The one that made her get out of the car when they got to Prole Street. Had AB seen Eileen soliciting a few yards along the road from Maria, picked her up and used her as his witness?

Megan shivered and pulled the duvet up round her shoulders. She tried to focus on the killer's behaviour, imagining what would have gone through his mind if he had indeed seen Donalsen picking up Maria. Donalsen had been in an unmarked squad car. He was a plain clothes officer. How had the killer known who he was? And what had made him so sure that Donalsen was not simply arresting Maria?

She had a feeling that the killer must know rather a lot about Donalsen. Enough to make a snap decision to use the man to his own advantage. He would have to have known that Donalsen's liaison with Maria was not just a one-off, but the latest in a string of misdemeanours with women he was supposed to be policing.

Who would have that kind of knowledge? Prostitutes and their pimps? Other police officers? Someone close to a member of the force?

Megan thought of Helen Donalsen. It had been two days since she pushed that note through the woman's door. The more Megan thought about it, the more convinced she became that Helen held the key to the killer's identity. She would surely know who could have got hold of Rob's wedding ring. And who hated him enough to want to set him up for murder.

By 7.30 Megan was on the beach. It wasn't really light, but there was a faint yellow tinge over the sea. She walked along the shore, listening to the gulls screeching as they swooped over the waves.

Swirls of mist drifted in from the sea, giving the weathered backs of the houses an other-worldly air. Some were shut up for the winter, but here and there a light twinkled. Megan gazed out to sea, watching a shoal of tiny clouds turn pink with the coming of the sun. She turned and hurried home. She had made up her mind to phone BTV. There was just a chance that Helen Donalsen would be at work today. And if not, Megan would find out from her colleagues where she had gone for Christmas.

As she hung up her coat in the hall she noticed a copy of the *Birmingham Post* lying on the table. It looked slightly yellow and Megan picked it up, noticing the date on the front page. It was six weeks old. She caught sight of a small photo of her own face smiling from beneath the masthead. 'Profile of a Profiler' the text beside it read. It was an article that had appeared while she was away at a conference. Gareth must have left it for her last time he was at the cottage. Funny that she hadn't noticed it last night.

She made coffee and took it over to the phone. It had occurred to her that Helen Donalsen might be in on the plot to set her ex-husband up. If she did manage to get hold of the woman she was going to have to play things very carefully.

The woman on reception put Megan on hold. She sipped her coffee impatiently, her eyes wandering over the medley of family photographs on the wall in front of her.

'Hello?'

The sound of Helen Donalsen's voice took Megan by surprise.

'Oh, hello,' she said brightly. 'It's Megan Rhys – we met last week. Did you get my note?'

'Er, what note?'

'I pushed a note through your door.' Megan paused, trying to lead Helen in the direction she wanted her to take.

'Oh. My boyfriend might have picked it up when he went to feed the cat. I've been away over Christmas.'

Boyfriend? Megan felt a surge of adrenalin. 'I did say it was urgent.' She kept her voice light and chatty. 'But Christmas is a busy time. Does he work?'

'Well, he works at BTV, yes.'

'Oh, is he involved in the documentary?' Megan's pulse was racing.

'No, he's in charge of security – his name's David. David Simon.'

Oh God, Megan thought. The one that found the body. He'd been so shocked, Leverton had said. It had never occurred to her that *both* killers could be security guards. 'Really?' She tried to sound unconcerned. 'He didn't say anything about me trying to get hold of you?'

'No,' Helen said. 'But I haven't spoken to him since Christmas Day. I only got back this morning. What was it you wanted to ask me?'

Megan took a second to remember. 'It's about Rob, actually.' She heard a heavy sigh at the other end of the phone. This was going to be very tricky. 'Do you happen to know if he still wears his wedding ring?'

'His wedding ring?' There was a note of incredulity in Helen's voice. Was it genuine? Megan wished she could see the woman's face.

'Yes. I know it's a strange question, and I can't really go into details at this stage but it could be extremely important. Do you know if he stopped wearing it after you split up?'

'Yes, he did. I know exactly when as well. He threw it at me when I told him I'd met someone else.'

Megan's hand felt clammy against the receiver. 'Do you know where it is now?'

'Yes. After he left I picked it up and put it in a drawer in the spare bedroom. Why?'

'It's been found at the scene of another murder,' Megan said in a deadpan voice. 'Have you any idea how it could have got there?

'No. I – er – I can't think . . .' Helen sounded as if this news had knocked her sideways. She was telling the truth. Megan was sure of it. Now she had to get hold of this David Simon without arousing Helen's suspicions.

'Have you had any break-ins since you and Rob split up?'

'Er, no. Nothing like that.'

'What about over Christmas?'

'Well, I haven't actually been home yet.' Helen sounded alarmed. 'But I'm sure David would have phoned me if anything like that had happened.'

'Would you mind if I phoned him anyway and asked if he'd noticed anything peculiar when he went to feed the cat?' Megan crossed her fingers as she spoke. 'Have you got a number I could contact him on?'

'Yes. I'm not sure where he's working today but I can give

you his mobile.' Helen recited the number robotically. She sounded as if she was in shock.

'Look, if he does mention anything, I'll phone you straight back.' Megan had to make sure Helen didn't phone him before she did.

Her hands were trembling as she replaced the receiver. She stared at the number she had scribbled on the back of an envelope. Could he be the killer? He was Franco's boss and Helen Donalsen's boyfriend. Helen had probably told him all about Donalsen's penchant for prostitutes. Enough to frame him for Maria's murder. One thing puzzled her. Why was Helen Donalsen still alive? If Megan was right the woman had been dating a serial killer for at least two months, during which time he had murdered four people. Why spare her?

Helen had told her and Leverton about Donalsen's liaisons with prostitutes. And she would tell others. In a courtroom. That was why the killer had left her alone. She would be the star witness at Donalsen's trial; far more credible than poor Eileen Bunce.

Megan wondered why he had gone to so much trouble for someone as pathetic as Donalsen. Was he settling some old score? Or was he an ex-cop out for revenge on the police, with Donalsen a convenient vehicle?

She picked up the phone and punched out the number Helen had given her. As she heard the double purr of the ringing tone she held her breath.

'Hi, you're through to Dave Simon.'

'Oh God!' she said aloud. 'An answerphone!' She listened to the message and put the phone down. There had been something very strange about his voice. Something familiar.

Megan picked up the phone and rang again. As she listened to the message she felt her stomach tighten and she had an overwhelming urge to throw up. She didn't know

why. She put the phone down again and sank into an arm-
chair. Where had she heard that voice before?

She grabbed the phone again and dialled her sister's
number. Neil picked it up.

'Oh Neil,' she said. 'Listen, I need your help. It's something
really serious.'

'What's the matter, Meg? Have you had an accident? Are
you okay?'

'I'm fine. Look, it's this murder case I've been involved
with. I can't explain it all – it'll take too long – but the police
have got the wrong man. I think I know who the real killer
is. It's someone who works at BTV.'

'What? Are you sure?'

'Yes,' Megan insisted. 'It's the head of security. He's called
David Simon. Do you know him?'

There was a silence at the end of the phone.

'Neil?'

'I'm sorry, Meg – there's something I should have told
you.' His voice was so quiet it was almost a whisper.

'Told me what? What are you talking about?'

'It's him, Meg. The one you said . . .' He tailed off.

'Who?'

'I didn't tell you because I knew you'd be upset.'

Megan went cold. 'Do you mean who I think you mean?'

'He changed his name.' Neil sounded as if he was apolo-
gising for him. How typical, Megan thought. Her whole
body trembled.

'Obviously,' she hissed. 'How long have you known? How
long has that bastard been back?'

'I don't know,' Neil faltered. 'A year or so, I think. He was
in a bad state, Meg. He'd been working abroad and lost his
job. He was trying to set up in business and he asked me to
help him get a foot in the door at BTV.'

'And you never thought to tell me? To warn me?' The

thought of him getting into her house turned her insides to ice.

'Warn you?' Neil sounded incredulous. 'It was fourteen years ago, Meg. I can't believe you think he's . . .'

'Rapists don't stop being rapists.' She cut across him. 'If they get away with it they go on doing it. And some of them turn into killers.' There was silence at the end of the phone. 'Did he ever tell you why he'd lost his job?'

There was a pause before he answered. 'He just said he'd been working in Italy and got fed up with it.'

'Italy?' Megan's heart began to race. 'Why Italy?'

'His mother's Italian. He's got relatives there.'

Oh God, she thought. It all made sense. Those Italian police magazines at Franco's house. Is that what he'd become? A policeman? She shuddered at the thought of it.

'I need you to find out where he is,' she said. 'I know he's not at home and he's not answering his mobile. I want you to phone BTV and pretend you need to get hold of him urgently. Ask if he's got a bleep or something.'

'Well, I suppose I could . . .' He sounded flustered.

'Listen, Neil.' She fought to stop herself from shouting down the phone. 'You wouldn't believe me last time. Don't take a chance on being wrong again. Someone's life could be at stake. Do you really want that on your conscience?'

'Okay, okay. Give me a couple of minutes to cook up an excuse, though.'

'Phone me back on my mobile if you get anything. And tell Ceri I'm on my way back.'

Megan raced upstairs. The images of that long-ago night flashed in front of her eyes. Her hands shaking, she threw the few things she had brought with her into a holdall. She grabbed the bag and made for the stairs. She would phone Leverton from the car and if he refused to listen she would drive straight to police headquarters and barge into his office if she had to.

Halfway down the stairs, she heard the click of the latch on the back door. Instinctively she froze. The door had been locked.

'Megan! Where are you?' The voice had broken free from her nightmares. Clear in the silence of the cottage she recognised it instantly. Fourteen years on, that voice was still unmistakeable. She heard heavy footsteps crossing the flagstones in the kitchen. Her mobile was on the kitchen table. The footsteps came nearer. If she ran for the door he would see her.

Grasping the banister for support, she turned and inched back up the stairs, her legs like jelly. She crept along the landing to the bathroom, sliding the bolt across as silently as she could. Then she turned on the shower. He would hear it, of course, and come upstairs, but she could pretend not to hear him and it would give her time to think.

She sank to the floor and sat there, hugging her knees. She'd have to try to keep him talking. How could she get out of here? Whatever she did, she must not show her fear.

'Megan? You in there?' She jumped. Despite the noise of the shower she could hear him quite clearly. He must be standing right outside the door.

'Is that you, Gareth?' she called out. 'You're back early! Were they out?' It was a long shot, but if she could get him to believe her brother was staying at the cottage it might put him off.

'Nice try, Megan. Always were a smart bitch, weren't you?' His voice sent a chill up her spine. 'You're all alone, aren't you? All alone.'

There was a thud as he pushed his body against the door, trying to force it open. She glanced at the bathroom window. As a child she had been able to slither out of it onto the flat roof beneath.

'Who is it?' she shouted, trying to stall him while she

fiddled with the catch at the side of the window. 'I'm not dressed. Hang on a minute and I'll open the door.'

The window was stiff, but she managed to force it open. Jumping onto the sill, she thrust her right leg through, her foot searching for the flat roof. As soon as she felt it against the sole of her shoe she realised there was no hope. Her hips were wedged in the window.

The door rattled. The screws holding the bolt shuddered with the impact. She was going to have to face him out. Pulling the clasp from her hair, she soaked it quickly under the shower, then wrapped a towel turban-style around her head. Before turning off the water, she opened the airing cupboard, searching frantically for anything that might serve as a weapon.

She spotted a packet of razor blades and ripped it open. She tucked one into the pocket of her jeans, another inside the turban. Then she took a deep breath and slid back the bolt.

That face. She wanted to cry, scream, lash out. 'Dave!' She struggled to control her voice. 'How did you get in?'

He was taller than she remembered, and thinner in the face. Standing inches away from her, he stared at her through half-closed eyes, weighing her up. She wondered if he could hear her heart thumping.

'I was just about to make some tea. Would you like a cup?' She felt like a character in some absurd farce. He could have no idea that she knew he was the killer, but he would be expecting her to be as shocked, angry and frightened as she'd been all those years ago. Acting relaxed might confuse him enough to allow her downstairs.

She made for the landing. He let her take a few steps before reaching out and grabbing her by the arm. 'Oh, I can't let a Doctor of Psychology make tea for *me*,' he mocked. 'You're not half as clever as everyone thinks, are you, Megan? Never mind, I've brought you something.'

He put his free hand into his pocket. 'Think of it as a belated Christmas present,' he said, dangling the gold chain with its shamrock pendant in front of her eyes. 'Go on, put it on!'

Megan took the necklace, trying to stop her fingers from trembling as she undid the catch. Tina Jackson's necklace. As the gold chain touched her throat a surge of nausea made her chest heave.

In a sudden movement he jerked her chin up. His eyes boring into hers. 'I've waited a long time for this.'

'What are you talking about?' She tried to keep her terror from her voice. She strained her ears for the sound of her mobile. Why hadn't Neil rung back? Had Dave seen the phone and switched it off? What would Neil do if he couldn't get hold of her?

'Do you know what I'm going to do with you? Do you?' His fingers dug into her jaw. 'What we did before, that was kid's stuff.' He slid something from his pocket. Handcuffs. Her mouth went dry. He dangled them in front of her, waiting for some kind of reaction. She stared straight back at him.

'I know you framed Donalsen.' She blurted the words out, desperate to stall him.

'Poor old Rob.' He swung the handcuffs back and forth like a hypnotist. 'Still, serves him right, really. What can you expect if you go round screwing tarts?'

'I thought that's what you did?' Her eyes narrowed. 'Was Natalie Bailey the first or did you do that sort of thing when you were in the Italian police? Was that why they got rid of you?'

A tensing of the muscles in his face betrayed his surprise, but he quickly struck back. 'You're all tarts. That Tina was gagging for it. Bet you are too. How long since you had a good shag? That husband of yours has knocked up a nice little piece, hasn't he? I've seen her waddling round BTV. What happened? Weren't you giving it to him often enough? Too busy chasing murderers and rapists?'

'I've got to hand it to you.' She nodded. 'Donalsen fitted that profile perfectly. You fooled me and the police, the way you set him up to take the rap. How much did you have to pay that tart Eileen? Bet she'd have done it for nothing, you know – they all hate Donalsen's guts anyway.'

She paused for a second. A deep line had appeared between his eyebrows. 'Thing is though,' she said, 'it's no fun when nobody knows it's you, is it? You couldn't even have a good laugh about it with Franco because you'd already killed him. Well, if you've come here to kill me too, you're wasting valuable time.'

The flash of confusion on his face was enough to tell Megan what she needed to know. 'Oh! Don't tell me you've slipped up? Were you really so cocky that you left his body in that boot all over Christmas? How long were you going to wait before you got rid of it? New Year's resolution, was it? "Must ditch Franco before the weather turns and he starts to stink"?'

He grabbed her wrists with one hand and pinioned her against the wall of the landing. 'Has that bitch been talking to you?'

'If you mean Helen Donalsen, yes, she has.' Megan tried to keep her voice steady, confident. He needed to know what she knew, and until she told him he could not kill her. 'I'm surprised at you. Why didn't you kill her the first time you screwed her? Wanted to prolong the agony, did you, because she was a copper's wife?'

The sky beyond the landing window was heavy with storm clouds. In the dwindling light his eyes were like holes in the snow. 'You're bluffing. That bitch knows nothing. Nothing!' He screamed out the word and it rang in her ears.

'Oh, but she does. You should have stuck to the stupid ones. She told me about Rob Donalsen's wedding ring. Was Franco supposed to leave it near Maria's body? Really dropped you in it, there, didn't he?' She watched his face. 'Thought you'd fooled them, coming back to the UK and changing your name. Cops aren't known for their communication skills, especially across international boundaries – and if they've got no record of your DNA, well, you're laughing, aren't you? Unless, of course, someone starts cramping your style.'

Megan could feel the sweat from his hand running down her arm. 'Did you know Franco took a photo of Maria Fellowes after you'd killed her? He sent it to that black newsreader at BTV.'

She watched his face. A red flush was spreading from his neck to his cheeks. 'No. I don't suppose you did. I reckon he saw you playing games with the cops and thought he'd go in for a spot of it himself. If you'd known, you'd never have left him to dump the body, because you might have guessed he'd leave it somewhere stupid like the car park at work. Did you know they found her feet in his garden shed?'

Now was the time. She could see that his anger was about to erupt. She must use it. 'You see, Dave, that's why I said you're wasting valuable time, coming here to kill me. They're already on to you. But I'll make you a deal. If you let me live, I'll give you my car. You can drive it down the coast to Fishguard – if you hurry you'll catch the ferry to Ireland. You can lose yourself there. And there's no need to worry about me telling the police – you can handcuff me to the towel rail in the bathroom. As long as I can reach the tap I'll survive until Gareth gets here on Saturday.'

Megan hoped that in his confusion Dave wouldn't see through the naiveté of this plan. 'The keys are in the pocket of my jeans,' she pressed on, 'on the left hand side.'

With his free hand he made as if to reach into her pocket. But he stopped as his fingers touched the fabric.

'You must think I'm fucking brain-dead, woman!'

Megan tensed as his hand swung up towards her throat, but the silence was suddenly broken by a tinny warbling. Instinctively he loosed his grip, his right hand dropping to his back pocket.

Neil! She seized her chance. Reaching one hand into her pocket, the other inside the towel, she plucked out both razor blades and slashed at his neck. He roared in pain and staggered back against the banisters. She sped across the landing to the stairs, leaping down them two at a time until she reached the hall. She could hear the thud of footsteps behind.

She fumbled with the front door knob. It wouldn't budge. *God, he's locked me in!* She made a dash for the kitchen. Reaching for the back door, she felt him grab her wrist. She screamed and kicked out. Twisting round, she saw he was on his knees, blood pumping from his neck, dripping onto the flagstones. For a second she was paralysed, staring at the blood in horrified fascination. Then his hand tightened on her wrist and she lashed out, kicking his head, his arm. He let out a gasp of pain and collapsed, his fingers slithering down her hand and twitching before falling to the floor.

'My God,' she said aloud. 'I've killed him. I've killed him!'

She slumped beside him, not knowing what to do. 'Call an ambulance,' she ordered herself. Her voice sounded like someone else's. 'Call for help. You can't let him die.' Her mobile was still on the table where she'd left it. She walked unsteadily across the room. She picked up the phone and punched out the number nine once, twice. She never made the third. She screamed and the phone fell from her hand.

His hand was round her ankle, the nails digging into her flesh. She tried to break away and lost her balance. As she fell she heard the sound of glass being smashed. Her head struck the edge of the table. The impact sent a flash of white across her eyes before the room turned black.

When she came round the room was full of people. Paramedics stretchering a body through the kitchen door. And there was someone holding her hand. Moving her head slowly, painfully, she saw Patrick's face. She opened her mouth but all that came out was a croak.

'Don't try to talk,' he whispered.

Chapter 17

The rain was lashing down on New Year's Eve. The fairy lights in Harborne High Street swayed in the wind and people ran from their cars to the pubs with coats and umbrellas shielding their party clothes. Megan was curled up on the sofa, her hair pulled back from the black-stitched wound on her forehead.

'I still can't believe you found it.' She leaned across to pour whisky into Patrick's glass.

'Well, I didn't exactly have to be Sherlock Holmes,' he said. 'You pointed it out in that photo – remember? And you said it was opposite the bakery.'

'I wonder what would have happened if you hadn't turned up when you did?' She shuddered.

'He'd be dead.' His tone was matter-of-fact. 'He passed out at the same time you banged your head. You'd have come round to find him lying in a pool of blood.'

She looked at him. 'I wanted to kill him. But now . . .' She bit her lip. 'I'm glad I haven't got him on my conscience. Does that sound terrible?'

The phone rang out before he could reply. 'Leverton,' she mouthed. By the time she put the phone down her face was flushed. She tugged distractedly at a strand of hair that had fallen across her forehead.

'What's the matter? What did he say?'

Megan took a deep breath. 'His condition's stable and he's been talking,' she said. 'He *was* in the Italian police. Leverton's had him checked out. He was sacked just over a year ago.'

216

'What for?'

'He'd been stopping women drivers for minor traffic offences. He used to note down the car registrations of the ones he fancied and get their addresses through the police computer. Then he would go round to their houses and con his way inside. One of the women he did it to reported him.' Her hand went involuntarily to the inch-long cut on her forehead, her fingers touching the stitches. 'He was never charged with anything. Sounds like they got rid of him to hush it up.'

'Well, that explains his downer on the police.'

'Not exactly,' Megan replied, staring into the fire. 'It goes back further than that, evidently. He told Leverton that the reason he went to Italy was because he'd tried to join the West Midlands force but was turned down.' She frowned. 'That was my fault.'

'*Your* fault? How?'

She pressed her lips together so hard they turned white. 'Leverton checked the records. It was fourteen years ago. He wasn't called Simon then. His surname was Garvey.' She paused, staring at the table. 'Fourteen years ago I reported Dave Garvey to West Midlands police for raping me.'

Patrick's face tensed and he drew in his breath. 'That nightmare you had when I stayed at your place. It was him, wasn't it?'

She nodded and he slid his arm around her, pulling her close.

'I'd been to a party.' Her voice dropped. 'Friends of my sister.' She blinked. It was hard to talk about it after bottling it up for so long. 'I got really drunk and didn't even notice him following me home. I can't remember what time it was when he knocked the door but I must have been asleep. I opened the door in my dressing gown . . .' Megan closed her eyes, screwing her face into a tight frown. 'He came out with some story about needing somewhere to spend the night. I let him in and told him he could crash on the sofa. I went back upstairs and I must have gone straight to sleep. Next thing I knew he was on top of me. I woke up with him . . .' Her voice trailed off as she buried her face in her hands.

'What did you do?'

'I just lay there, sort of paralysed. He didn't say a word. Just got up and walked out of the room. A few minutes later I heard the front door close and I ran down and bolted it. It was still dark and I didn't know what to do. I was too terrified to go back to bed. I had visions of him breaking into the house and doing it again. I just sat wrapped up in a blanket on the sofa until it got light.'

'And then you went to the police . . .'

'Yes. It was awful. They didn't have rape suites and sympathetic female officers in those days. When I got to the bit about opening the door in my dressing gown, they just looked at one another and I could tell what they were thinking.' Megan sighed, fiddling with the wedding ring on her right hand. 'They actually got as far as arresting him but by that time I'd decided to drop the charges.'

'Why?'

She turned to look at him, slowly shaking her head. 'I don't know. Looking back, I can't believe I was such a wimp. It wasn't just the police. My solicitor said the defence would demolish me if it went to court. And I was in a pretty bad state emotionally at the time.' She paused, staring at her hands. 'He'd made me pregnant.' Her words came out in a whisper. 'I had an abortion, but it went wrong. They told me I'd probably never be able to have children.'

She blinked, wondering if she should really be telling him all this. He stroked her hair, saying nothing.

'I had no idea he'd applied to join the police. I never saw him again. He was my brother-in-law's friend – that was the only connection. Neil knew but he never really believed me. I made him promise not to tell anyone else in my family. Not even my sister. I just sort of blanked it out, I suppose. And all those years he was harbouring this terrible grudge.' She got up and walked into the hall, bringing the newspaper she had found at the cottage. 'Look at this.' She handed it to Patrick.

He stared at the photo and frowned, looking back at her.

'That's how he found out,' she said. 'He came back to the UK, set up his security firm and one day he opened the *Birmingham Post* and saw that feature on me. He couldn't have had any idea what had become of me – Neil knew how much I hated him so he wouldn't have said anything. To see me being hailed as a success and working with the very people who'd rejected him must have made him really mad.'

Patrick peered at the date on the newspaper. 'This came out the week they found Natalie Bailey.' His eyes narrowed. 'Could it have been the trigger?'

'Possibly,' Megan said. 'But I can't believe that would be enough of a reason to turn him from a rapist into a killer.' She took the newspaper from him. 'I think he'd already killed Natalie when he saw this. I think he'd come back from Italy hating the police and was just looking for an opportunity for revenge. He met Helen Donalsen and found out her husband was a cop. He started dating her, pumping her for information, looking for something he could use. She told him all about Donalsen knocking off prostitutes, which would have been just what he was after.' She reached for the whisky bottle and topped up both glasses. 'He started stalking Donalsen. Watching who he picked up. Franco, the pimp, would have helped because he owed Dave a favour. Leverton said Franco asked Dave to give him a job after he killed Donna Fieldhouse. He was worried the police would come sniffing round and needed to appear respectable.'

'So Natalie was one of the prostitutes Donalsen was screwing?'

'I don't think so, no, because she was soliciting in Wolverhampton. I think Dave used her to confuse the police.'

'How?'

'Well, think about what he was doing.' She ran her finger
round the rim of her glass, staring at the clear brown liquid.
'He had to find a way of framing Donalsen without DNA
evidence playing a part. So he gave them a victim who'd
obviously had sex with more than one man on the day she
was killed. That confused them.'

Patrick rubbed his chin. 'Go on.'

'When he killed Maria Fellowes he planned to keep the
body hidden for long enough for the DNA to deteriorate,
but it didn't work because the body froze. If that hadn't
happened the police would have discovered a body that bore
all the hallmarks of Natalie's killer but no DNA trace. Franco
was supposed to leave Donalsen's wedding ring nearby but
he cocked up. Not only did he forget the ring but he dumped
the body in the BTV car park.'

'So Dave had to kill him?'

Megan nodded. 'I think he knew about Franco's obsession
with Delva Lobelo. But in the end it got to be a liability so
Franco had to go.'

'But what about Tina Jackson? What was the point of
killing her?'

Megan stared into the fire, her eyes clouding. 'I think that
happened because of me.' Patrick gave her a puzzled frown.
'I didn't tell you at the time, but I think he broke into this
house.'

'When?'

'I don't know – it could have been more than once. I kept
noticing odd things but I thought I was just being paranoid.'
She told him about the maggots and the Christmas card.

'God, Megan! He could have . . .'

'I know,' she cut in. 'But I think at that point he was trying to frighten me. My guess is that when he saw that newspaper article and realised I worked with the police it became part of his game. And when I think about Tina Jackson's death it seems like a sort of ghastly dress-rehearsal for killing me.'

'Why? Because she looked like you?'

'Yes. It's bizarre. Leverton even commented on the resemblance himself. God!' Megan buried her face in her hands. 'If I hadn't been such a bloody wimp when he raped me, Tina and Maria and Natalie would all be alive now.'

Patrick pulled her hands away, stroking them with his own. 'What about all the other women he victimised while he was in Italy? They probably felt the same as you. Rape is such a difficult thing to prove, especially when the victim already knows the rapist. Even if you'd taken him to court the chances are he would have got away with it.'

She looked at him, knowing that he was right but not feeling any less guilty. She was aware of his fingers on her skin, comforting and tempting. She drew away, reaching for the whisky bottle so it wouldn't seem like a snub. 'You never did tell me,' she said. 'Why did you come to the cottage?'

He laughed. 'Do I have to spell it out?'

'But your girlfriend – fiancée – whatever she is –?'

'Let's just say she wasn't very impressed with what I had to say. I was there all of half an hour. I took what little stuff I'd left in the flat and jumped on the next plane.'

'Patrick, I hope you don't think . . .'

Before she could complete the sentence he slid off the sofa, pulling her with him until they were both lying on the rug in front of the fire.

'Patrick . . .'

He laid a finger gently on her lips. 'I've got a confession to make,' he said. 'I'm putting in an application to change supervisors.'

'You what?' She raised herself on her elbows.

'Don't worry – I can still study at Heartland,' he smiled, 'but I can be assessed by someone else. I phoned Liverpool University before Christmas and they said it would be okay.' He tried to kiss her but she broke away. All she could see was that face. The dark eyes like holes in the snow, the handcuffs dangling like a noose.

'I'm sorry, I can't do this,' she whispered, swallowing hard to stop the tears she wouldn't allow him to see. 'Maybe sometime.'

She stroked his cheek with her finger, wanting to believe herself. 'Sometime. But not yet.'

Lindsay Jayne Ashford studied criminology at Cambridge University, where she became the first woman to graduate from Queens' College in its eight-hundred-year history.

She went on to train as a journalist with the BBC. The idea for *Frozen* came while she was researching the vice trade in the Birmingham area of the UK, where she was born and raised.

Lindsay has written two more novels featuring forensic psychologist Megan Rhys, *Strange Blood* and *Death Studies*. She now lives in West Wales with her husband and four children.

OCT - - 2011

FEB - 2008

DEC - 2009